*Acclaim for JER*____ __

"Will remind readers what chattering teeth sound like."
—*Kirkus Reviews*

"Voracious readers of horror will delightfully consume the contents of Bates's World's Scariest Places books."
—*Publishers Weekly*

"Creatively creepy and sure to scare." —*The Japan Times*

"Jeremy Bates writes like a deviant angel I'm glad doesn't live on my shoulder."
—Christian Galacar, author of GILCHRIST

"Thriller fans and readers of Stephen King, Joe Lansdale, and other masters of the art will find much to love."
—*Midwest Book Review*

"An ice-cold thriller full of mystery, suspense, fear."
—David Moody, author of HATER and AUTUMN

"A page-turner in the true sense of the word."
—*HorrorAddicts*

"Will make your skin crawl." —*Scream Magazine*

"Told with an authoritative voice full of heart and insight."
—Richard Thomas, Bram Stoker nominated author

"Grabs and doesn't let go until the end." —*Writer's Digest*

# THE TASTE OF FEAR

### Jeremy Bates

Ghillinnein Books

*For Alison*

*"I have almost forgot the taste of fears. The time has been my senses would have cool'd to hear a night shriek, and my fell of hair would at a dismal treatise rouse and stir as life were in't. I have supp'd full with horrors; direness, familiar to my slaughterous thoughts, cannot once start me."*

—WILL, MACBETH

# THE TASTE OF FEAR

# PROLOGUE

*Thursday, December 26, 5:53 p.m., 2008*

*Dar es Salaam, Tanzania*

T HE ASSASSIN STARED at the TV set in the hotel room, his face impassive.

"At least twenty-three people have been killed in the dual attacks on the American embassies in Nairobi and Dar es Salaam," the suit-and-tie anchorman said.

He stood before a video image of the United States Embassy emblem. The ticker read: "Breaking News."

"Our African correspondent, Sebastian Briers, has the latest from Dar es Salaam. Sebastian, good evening to you."

The camera jumped to a somber-looking field reporter dressed in khaki pants and a white linen shirt. "Good evening, Cary. The attacks, which seem to have involved car or truck bombs, both occurred inside the periphery gates of the embassy compounds. There were, as I believe you said, twenty-three casualties so far counted. Eleven of those were here in Dar. Four are believed to have been the Marine Security Guards stationed at the front gate. Witnesses reported hearing a short burst of gunfire, followed by a loud blast, what was likely a grenade attack on the gatehouse. Then came a much louder explosion which could be heard miles away." The camera jumped again to shaky, low-resolution video footage of the embassy complex. It was crowded with emergency response teams. Billowing clouds of black smoke trailed into the air. The anchorman said in voice-over: "The images you're seeing were captured on a cell phone immediately after the attack and played on a Gulf news channel. But this was not the first time attacks have been carried out on the American embassies in these two countries. Exactly ten years ago truck bombs exploded out front—"

The assassin flicked the channel.

"—various claims of responsibility have already begun to surface on jihadist websites from groups with Al Qaeda connections. One has threatened more attacks against American and British interests overseas. Despite recent efforts to suppress militant groups, today's events are a grim reminder that cells are—"

Click.

"—though it hasn't been confirmed by official sources yet, we have just gotten word that American actress Scarlett Cox and her husband, American billionaire hotel tycoon Salvador Brazza, were among those kidnapped today in what appears to be a fresh Al Qaeda tactic. Sasha, what do you make of this new approach?"

"We can only speculate, Nicole. But if you remember the 1998 bombings, of the more than two hundred casualties, only twelve were American. Embassies nowadays—especially these two, which have just been recently rebuilt—are constructed to withstand bomb blasts. Consequently, the majority of those injured are people passing by on the street or workers in the adjacent buildings. So what we're seeing here seems, as you said, like an entirely new plan of attack. An initial bomb to create as much destruction and confusion as possible before terrorists pour in to take hostages."

"A one-two punch."

"You got it. And you also have to remember there are literally hundreds of terrorist attacks around the globe every year.

The media only covers the biggest ones intensively, and even those get old after a day or two. I mean, does anyone remember much about the attack on the American Embassy in Islamabad back in July? On the other hand, when there are hostages involved, the story is often covered until the situation is resolved, like we saw in Mumbai in September. So I think that, yes, it is definitely a new strategy we're seeing here. And whoever turns out to be responsible seems to have hit the jackpot. You couldn't have asked for two more high-profile Americans short of the president and the first lady themselves."

"Unfortunately, I would have to agree. Thanks, Sasha. Coming up next, we'll go live to our freelance correspondent, Kim Berkoff, who has information on what exactly Scarlett Cox and Salvador Brazza were doing in the Dar es Salaam embassy in the first place—"

The assassin snapped off the TV and remained sitting on the bed for a long while, thinking. His job, it seemed, had just become a hell of a lot more difficult.

# CHAPTER 1

*Sunday, December 22, 1:44 p.m.*

*Los Angeles, California, Four Days Earlier*

I F SCARLETT COX knew she would be careening down a forty-foot ravine in the next sixty seconds or so, she probably would have put on her seatbelt. As it was, she wasn't clairvoyant, and she pushed the white Aston Martin Vantage up to fifty, fifteen over the limit. She knew she shouldn't be speeding. She'd just passed the intersection with Mulholland Drive, and there were a lot of hairpin turns and potholes coming up. But she felt comfortable behind the wheel of the Vantage. The salesman had told her it was a front-mid-engine sports car, which meant the engine was positioned low behind the front axle, just before the cabin, dropping the car's center of gravity and boosting the handling and traction. Besides, she'd just finished production on her latest film. She was feeling good, liberated. She eked the needle up to fifty-five.

Keeping one hand on the wheel, she used the other to turn down "Magic Carpet Ride" by Steppenwolf, which was playing on the radio, loud. Was there any other way to listen to music when the top was down? She scrounged around for her cell phone inside her handbag on the passenger seat. The salesman had also told her the Vantage had a Bluetooth thing that could sync her phone's signal with the car's voice recognition technology and speakers. That was all too Knight Rider for her, so she checked her voicemail the old-fashioned and illegal way: punching numbers in to the phone's keypad. Three new messages. The first was from her hairstylist, confirming her appointment at two thirty. *Goodbye blonde, hello red,* she thought. The other two were from Gloria, her publicist, wanting to clarify details about the birthday party this evening. Number thirty. Christ. It seemed as though she'd just celebrated twenty-nine. She pressed End and tossed the phone back in the bag.

Scarlett swooped around a sharp bend and found herself closing quickly on a black pickup truck. She'd known her luck wasn't going to last forever. Traffic on the stretch of Laurel Canyon Boulevard between San Fernando Valley and West Hollywood was sparse in the middle of the afternoon, but going fifty-five in a thirty-five zone, you were bound to run up someone's tail sooner or later. She thought about passing the pickup, but only for a second. The road was divided by solid double yellow lines. She might speed when she could get away with it, but there were some things she didn't mess with: pit bulls, blondes with chips on their shoulders—real blondes, which she was not —and double yellow lines.

The pickup was an old Chevy with a tall CB antenna poking up from the roof and white silhouettes of women in provocative poses on the mud flaps. The two stickers on the chrome bumper read: "My Other Car is a Hybrid" and "If You Can See My Mirrors Show Me Ya Tits!"

Classy.

Scarlett slowed to forty, keeping one car length between them. Any closer and she'd likely catch an STD. Her thoughts turned to her husband, Sal, and she realized with apprehension that tonight would be the first time in over a month they would see each other. The time apart had been their marriage counselor's idea. She'd said it would do them good. Give them perspective on their relationship. Admittedly, it had been good for them—at least it had been good for Scarlett. She still hadn't forgiven Sal for what he'd done. But she'd believed him when he said he was committed to saving the marriage, and during their time apart she'd come to the conclusion she wanted to save it as well. They weren't back to how it had been before, and they likely never would be, but they had gotten out of the mucky waters and were now schlepping their way up onto dry ground.

The Chevy's brake lights flashed, tugging Scarlett's wandering mind back to the road. She tapped her brakes and kept pace. Another flash. She frowned but didn't slow. They were on a relatively straight stretch of road. Then a man's stringy, tattooed arm extended from the driver's window. His middle finger uncurled from the fist. Scarlett rolled her eyes. Nevertheless, she eased back to give the good ole boy his room.

The Chevy swerved.

Scarlett thought Bubba was playing another game when a large pothole appeared directly in front of her. The Vantage thumped up and down, jolting her in the seat and reawakening the migraine which for the past hour or so had settled to a low, dull throb she could almost ignore. She grimaced. Sometimes the migraines were mild and bearable. Sometimes they made her grind her teeth and rub her head while watching the minute hand on the clock do its rounds, as if that would somehow pass the time more quickly. And sometimes they made her feel as though a little gnome were riding a jackhammer through her skull and into her brain, grinning sadistically the entire time. Today had been one of those gnome-on-the-jackhammer days.

She reached into the handbag again and fiddled around until she found the aspirin bottle she'd brought from the trailer on the CBS lot in Studio City. She tried to thumb the cap off, but couldn't budge it. Then she remembered it had one of those safety lids meant to prevent four year olds from developing aspirin habits. She lined the arrow on the cap up with the arrow on the bottle and tried again. This time the cap popped like a firecracker. Pills went everywhere. She cursed. When it was one of those days, it was one of those days. She glanced down at the triangular wedge of red leather between her inner thighs. Two white tablets were sliding toward the depression her rear was making in the seat. She scooped them up and returned her attention to the road—

Her eyes bugged out. Her mouth dropped open. A loud, hollow sound filled the air as the Vantage exploded through the cable-and-post guardrail. She stamped the brake, but that did nothing. There was no longer any road beneath her.

Scarlett had the sickening, unnatural sensation of going airborne, and for a split second she thought she must be dreaming, because the reality was too frightening to immediately comprehend. Then the hood of the sports car nosed forward. The gray sky disappeared. She opened her mouth to scream, but nothing came out. Not a single breath. Fear had stolen her voice.

This was how she was going to die, a car accident, a statistic.

The Vantage crashed back to earth with jarring force and plunged wildly down the ravine through a blur of crackling vegetation. Then, abruptly, the greenery parted to reveal the black trunk of a massive tree.

Impact.

## Sunday, December 22, 9:30 a.m.

### Dubai, United Arab Emirates

"THERE ARE TWO police officers here to see you, sir," Salvador Brazza's secretary, Lucy, informed him over the intercom.

"Did they say what it concerned?"

"No, sir, only that it's urgent."

"Send them in."

Sal swiveled his high-backed chair to face Edward Lumpkin, a tall, pale American lawyer who'd been in Dubai for the last six years and Oman for four before that. They'd been discussing the merits of a legal system, free of charge, for future guests of the hotel who were bound to cross cultural taboos while visiting the Emirates. "Why don't you stick around for a few minutes,

Ed," he told the lawyer. "I might need your advice."

The door to the office opened, and Lucy showed the two police officers inside. Sal and Lumpkin stood. The taller man introduced himself as Brigadier Khaled Al Zafein, the Deputy Director of the General Department of Criminal Security. He was dressed formally in a peaked cap and a light brown uniform with rank badges on the shirt collar and a red band looping under the left arm and through the left epaulette. The short fat one said he was Inspector Abu Al Marri. His beret was cocked rakishly, and he had a smug smile on his ugly moon face. Sal disliked him on sight. "To what do I owe the honor, gentleman?" he said without offering them a seat.

"I'm afraid we have some rather disconcerting news, Mr. Brazza," Al Zafein said in fluent British English. "It concerns the fire at the Prince Hotel earlier this month."

Sal frowned. "I've already spoken with the fire investigators."

"Yes, of course. However, circumstances have changed. New evidence has surfaced that leads us to believe the fire might not be a result of faulty wiring, as initially believed." He paused. "It's now thought to have been set deliberately."

"Arson?" Sal said, unable to conceal his surprise. "What are you talking about?"

Al Marri spoke in English as fluent as his superior's: "Let me begin, Mr. Brazza, by saying that arson is one of the easiest crimes to perpetrate, but one of the most difficult to identify and verify."

"Forgive my bluntness, Inspector," Sal said, "but I don't need a lesson on arson."

"Please, sir, if you would allow me to explain?" He smiled apologetically. "Generally speaking, investigators begin their investigation of a fire in a V-like pattern, from the area of least damage to that of the most damage, which is usually equated with the point of origin—and which, in the case of Room 6906 of your hotel, was the wall surrounding the electrical socket with the purportedly faulty wiring."

"I'm aware of all this. As I've said, I've already spoken to the fire investigators."

"Please, sir?" Al Marri offered up his practiced smile once more. It squashed his thick mustache between his upper lip and nose, giving the mustache the appearance of a fat, black slug.

"I said the area of the most damage is *usually* the point of origin. But that is not always the case. There are any number of circumstances that can change the dynamics of the fire. Ventilation, for example. Or fuel load. Or the unique characteristics of the environment in question. Even the water and foam used by the firefighters can confuse typical burn pattern interpretation. In many cases—as was the case with Room 6906—the fire can reach the post-flashover stage, whereby it gets hot enough to destroy vital evidence and mimic the effects that can be caused by ignitable liquids, such as charred patterns on the subfloors, and concrete spalling. What is my point in all this?" He opened his small, neat hands, as if in prayer. "It has recently come to our attention that one of the first firefighters through the door claims to have seen black smoke near the electrical socket in question. Now, wood and most other combustible items in Room 6906 burn brown-gray smoke. Accelerants—including chemicals with low ignition temperatures such as gasoline, kerosene, and alcohol—burn black. In light of this new information, the investigators were forced to take a second look at the evidence. They reassessed their original conclusion of faulty wiring in favor of the theory that someone had been trying to make it *look* like an electrical fire."

Sal gave himself a few seconds to let this information sink in, a kind of delayed bewilderment washing over him. "I don't get it," he said. "Why would someone want to set a fire? The hotel was—still is—unoccupied. Why would someone want to burn it down?"

"According to your statement," Al Marri said, "not all the rooms were unoccupied."

"Of course they were—" Sal clamped his mouth shut. The hotel hadn't been completely unoccupied. He had been staying in it for most of December, in the Royal Suite, which was on the seventieth floor, directly above 6906. The night of the fire the alarm had woken him at 4:12 a.m. By the time he'd gotten dressed, the stairwell had been full of smoke. He couldn't go down, so he went up, to the roof. Fifteen minutes later his ex-Mossad security chief, Danny Zamir, picked him up in a helicopter and got him the hell out of there. From the air he had a clear view of the blaze, which by then had consumed the top two floors and the one-hundred-foot script sign. If Danny had been even a few minutes later, he knew he likely wouldn't have made it.

"So you're telling me someone was trying to murder me, Inspector?" Sal shook his head. "Forgive my skepticism, gentlemen. I find that extremely difficult to believe."

"We have already ruled out the motive of financial gain," Al Marri said. "That leaves either random violence or pyro-terrorism or revenge."

"Do you know of anyone who might have some sort of vendetta against you, Mr. Brazza?" Al Zafein asked.

"I'm not in the business of speculation, Mr. Zafein."

"You should know, sir," Al Marri added gravely, "that this has become an attempted murder investigation. It would be in everyone's best interest to get it solved."

"I'm not a crook, Inspector. Nor do I associate myself with criminals."

Al Marri glanced briefly at the deputy general, then returned his attention to Sal. "I am sure you are a very busy man, sir." He handed Sal a business card. "If you should think of anything, anything at all, please do not hesitate to contact me."

The two police officers left.

Edward Lumpkin folded his gangly arms across his chest, his face pulled down in thought. "Christ, Sal. I don't know what to say."

"Will this have any impact on the hotel's opening?"

"Hard to say, but I'd keep an eye on the reservations during the first few weeks of operation. An attempted murder in the hotel could potentially turn off a lot of families. Thankfully, that's not our core demographic."

"This is going to be a bloody circus."

"I heard what you told the cops, Sal. But be straight with me. Can you think of anyone who might have a bone to pick with you?"

"Everybody has enemies, Ed."

"But someone serious enough to, you know, want you dead?"

Sal didn't reply.

"Could it be a union thing?" Lumpkin asked suddenly.

When Sal went non-union with the Prince last summer, labor picketed and sent death threats. One had threatened to blow up *After Taxes*, his $60-million, 155-foot yacht docked over at the Marine Club, while another had promised to gouge out his eyes while he slept.

"These union guys, they talk the talk," Sal said simply. "But they're neither inclined nor capable of pulling off something like this." He shook his head. "If you'll excuse me, Ed, I have some calls I need to make. Write up what we discussed, and we'll get together again next week."

When Lumpkin left, Sal called his security chief, Danny Zamir, and summarized the last twenty minutes. "I want you to find out everything you can," he concluded. "Understood?"

"Yeah, capo," Danny said. "Understood."

Sal hung up and gazed out the bank of windows overlooking Dubai's Business Bay, the city state's latest multibillion dollar project. As he watched a crane atop an ambitious skyscraper swivel to the east, he thought about everything the two cops had told him.

*Someone wanted him dead.*

The intercom on his desk buzzed. He punched the talk button. "What is it, Lucy?"

"The car's waiting to take you to the airport."

"Fine."

He shrugged on his blazer, grabbed his briefcase, and left the office. He suddenly couldn't wait to get out of Dubai.

# CHAPTER 2

S CARLETT OPENED HER eyes. Brightness. God, it was so bright it hurt. She tried to piece together where she was, but her thoughts were groggy and uncooperative. She could smell traces of disinfectant and iodine, and then she could make out shapes. She was lying on her back in a bed—a mechanized bed with those side railings so you didn't fall out. Beside her stood a blood-pressure monitor and an IV pole. A tube led from the bag hanging on the pole to a needle that disappeared into a vein in her right forearm.

Okay, so she was in a hospital. And it appeared to be a very nice hospital, evident by the polished laminate flooring, high-gloss maple walls, and large-screen TV. Even the linen on the bed was of high quality. The door to the bathroom was ajar, and she could see gleaming blue-and-gray tile work, more maple, and faux-granite countertops. There were no flowers or cards on the side table. She took that to mean either one of two things. She'd only just arrived, and no one had gotten wind of whatever had happened to her. Or she'd been in a coma for a hell of a long time, and everyone had given up on her long ago.

Scarlett wiggled her toes. They moved. She raised a hand to her head and felt a bandage, which her fingers probed. A spot in the center of her forehead was sore and tender. What had happened? Had she been mugged? Shot? Stabbed? In a car accident —?

It all came back to her in a rush of images: Laurel Canyon Boulevard, bursting through the guardrail, her stomach in her throat as she plummeted to the ground. She remembered the crushing landing, bouncing wildly out of control down the ravine, the tree...

*But I'm alive.*

The door to the room opened and Sal strolled in with his head down, his eyes glued to a story below the fold of the *Wall Street Journal*. Seeing him, Scarlett felt a burst of gratitude and affection. He was here, back from Dubai. If she had the strength, she would have jumped up and hugged him.

He wore a crisp white shirt and navy merino wool suit, one of his made-to-measures from appointment-only William Fioravanti in Manhattan. It was something Al Capone might have fancied had he been around today. In fact, she often kidded Sal that he resembled an Italian gangster. He had short-cropped black hair, hazel eyes, and a generous Roman nose. And he was Sicilian, which sort of sealed the deal.

"Scarlett!" he said, tossing the paper onto one of the leather chairs and rushing over. He knelt beside the bed and took her hand. "*La mia bella donna.*"

After so long apart, the feel of his touch and the sound of his voice and the smell of his cologne all hit her like a truck, smashing through the cobwebs in her head, and she realized suddenly just how close she'd come to never experiencing any of those sensations ever again. The reality of her situation sank in with numbing force. She'd been in a car accident, one bad enough to knock her unconscious and land her in the hospital. She felt very fragile. Life felt very fragile.

"Is that all I am to you?" she said, teasing him, happy to find she could speak. "Beautiful?" Her throat was dry. The words were a papery whisper.

"What else is an actress but a pretty face to look at?"

She wanted to laugh, but a sob escaped instead. A tear tripped down her cheek. "Sal..." She swallowed, tried to work up saliva. "I'm sorry."

"For what?"

She didn't know. For speeding? For not paying attention to the road? For all the terrible things she'd said to him after discovering the affair? She shook her head.

"How do you feel?" he asked.

"Groggy. But okay, I think. Am I okay?"

"You're fine."

Relief swamped her, and something inside her chest that had been very tight loosened. "What about this?" She touched the bandages around her head.

"It's just a bump."

"How long have I been here? What time is it?" She glanced toward the window. The blinds were drawn. No sunlight slipped in between the cracks.

"You came in this afternoon. It's about midnight now."

Less than twelve hours. Not as bad as she'd feared. "How long have you been here?"

"A couple hours. I would have gotten here sooner, but we ran into some bad weather over the Atlantic and had to detour."

Scarlett frowned. There was something she was missing here. Something about Sal coming back to LA, coming for—

"My birthday!" she said. "The party!"

"Don't worry about that. Gloria's taking care of it."

Scarlett groaned. Her actual birthday was on December 13, nine days earlier. But because of filming she'd postponed the celebration to today. She usually didn't make a fuss over birthdays, but this one, number thirty, was big, up there in importance with sixteen and twenty-one, the last big fun one until you seriously began dreading them. Over two hundred invitations had gone out. Every actor who had made the headlines within the past six months would have been there—not to mention executives from HBO, Castle Rock, Warner, and all the other big studios. Sal had invited the mayor of LA and the former Vice President, both of whom were his close friends. On top of the Who's Who guest list, a tabloid paper had paid her $2.5 million to photograph the event, the money of which was supposed to go to one of her charities.

"I'm such an idiot," she said, shaking her head and instantly regretting doing so as pain flamed beneath the bandage. She put a hand to the sore spot. "I've ruined everything."

The door to the room opened again. This time a fiftyish doctor with a graying beard and a ponytail entered. Scarlett had seen plenty of men sporting ponytails before, of course. Just never a doctor. She wasn't sure what to make of it. It was like your doctor having tattoos—or worse, a bowtie.

"Hello, Bill," Sal said, standing and shaking the doctor's hand. "Scarlett, this is Dr. Blair, the neurologist who looked you over when you came in."

"Welcome to Cedars-Sinai, Miss Cox," he said, coming to stand before the bed.

"Cedars? I thought I was in the Beverly Hilton."

"Not everyone gets a private room, Miss Cox. You can thank your husband for arranging that." He shifted the clipboard from his left hand to the right one. "I'm sure you've noticed the bandage around your head. You hit it pretty hard in the accident—hard enough to have lost consciousness for several hours at any rate. Your forehead will likely be sore for a few days. But, as I've told your husband, the X-rays and CT scan came back clean. No fractures or hematoma, which is a good thing. How do you feel?"

"A little groggy," she said.

"Any dizziness or nausea?"

"Not now."

"As opposed to?"

"Earlier this morning. I get migraines."

He scratched some notes down on the clipboard. "How often do you get them?"

"A couple times a week."

"How long have you been having them?"

"A few months."

More notes. "Any change in diet? Change in sleeping habits?"

"No."

"Are you drinking any more coffee or alcohol than usual?"

"No, no. It's none of that. It's just stress. From work—and other things. My life's been a little hectic recently."

Dr. Blair nodded, but didn't say anything right away. Scarlett found herself wondering whether he knew about her and Sal's marital problems. God knows the affair had been played to death on all the television entertainment channels, including several respectable news outfits. Not that she cared if he did know. She'd long ago become desensitized to what the general public thought of her personal life. "Welcome to the jungle," her agent had told her six years back when she was still starry-eyed after her first big feature film success.

Dr. Blair said, "Are you feeling any nausea now?"

"No."

"Can you touch your nose?"

She did what he asked.

He held a finger in front of her face. "Follow my finger, please." He moved his index finger left, then right. "Any blurred vision?"

She shook her head.

He straightened. "It doesn't seem you have any post-concussion symptoms. But I'd like to keep you overnight for observation. I believe the police would also like to get a statement from you. After that, in the morning, you should be good to leave. However," he added, "I want you to take it easy. That means nothing stressful for the next seven to ten days. Understood?"

"Impossible," she said. "I have too much to do." Her mind was already fast-forwarding to the weekend. The calls and apologies she'd have to make. Rebooking the venue for the party, sending out fresh invitations, the appearance Monday on *Good Morning America*...

"Miss Cox," Dr. Blair said. "You said so yourself. You believe stress has been triggering your recent spate of migraines. That sounds reasonable to me. On top of that, you've just been in a serious car accident. You've suffered a mild to moderate traumatic brain injury. True, you seem to be doing fine. But any sort of TBI should be taken seriously. Just because you're not currently exhibiting certain symptoms doesn't mean they won't emerge tomorrow, or the day after that. And the best prevention against that is to take a break, relax, slow down."

"I really don't think—"

"I'll keep an eye on her," Sal cut in.

"Make sure you do. Now, I have to continue my rounds. A nurse will be in shortly."

They thanked Dr. Blair, and he left the room.

Scarlett looked skeptically at Sal. "You don't really think I need to sit around the house for a week, do you?"

"You heard the man, cara mia. You need to relax. Whatever you have to do can wait." He took her hand in his again and rubbed the top of it with his thumb. "It's good to see you."

She wanted to tell him the same, but she bit back the words. She didn't want to confuse her gratitude at surviving the car accident with her still uncertain feelings for him.

Unable to meet his eyes, she looked down at the hand holding hers. It was tanned, strong, manicured nails, platinum wedding band on the ring finger.

"Listen," Sal said, clearing his throat. "What about we take a trip somewhere?"

Scarlett raised her eyebrows in surprise. "You mean, just you and me?"

"Sure," he said, pushing up his bottom lip. If lips could shrug, that's how they'd do it.

"I don't think that's such a good idea right now, Sal."

"I meant what I said about getting through this. I want this marriage to work."

"I want it to work too, I really do, but I don't think the next step is us vacationing together."

"But it is," he insisted. "It's exactly what we need."

She searched his eyes. "What about the hotel?" she said cautiously. "The opening?"

"I'll have my phone. I'll keep in touch with the office."

"I don't know—"

"It'll be good for you."

"Humor me then. What do you have in mind?"

He shrugged. "Something private, away from the crowd."

"The Caribbean?"

"And lie around on a beach?"

"Well?"

"What about a safari?" he suggested.

She was surprised. "As in Africa?"

"Dubai's on the same clock as Kenya, or Tanzania. If there's an emergency, and I have to get back for whatever reason, it's only a couple hours flight. You could come. Check out the hotel. The movers and decorators are finishing up this week."

Scarlett considered it. In her head she saw an acacia tree silhouetted against a sapphire sunset. Giraffes and zebras and elephants gathered at a watering hole. Antelope grazing on the savanna. Elegant game resorts and tented camps. It sounded nice. She could almost hear Elton John singing "Circle of Life."

"All right," she said, warming to the idea. "I'm game."

## Monday, December 23, 11:11 p.m.

*London, England*

LIKE THE DEVIL, the *fugu* was known by many names —blowfish, puffer fish, globefish, balloon fish, toadfish, more. The second most poisonous vertebrate in the world, it was a nasty piece of work, its neurotoxin ten thousand times more deadly than cyanide. If ingested, the poison numbed the lips and tongue, induced vomiting and muscle paralysis, and eventually caused death from suffocation. If you somehow survived, chances were good you'd end up in a prolonged coma, cruelly conscious of everything happening around you, a kind of hell on earth.

The Irishman Damien Fitzgerald had one such *fugu* on the cutting board in the kitchen, cold and dead. He picked up what the Japanese called a *fugu hiki*—a thin, single-edged carbon blade—and removed the eyes. He sliced a circle around the mouth, stuck his fingers into the incision, and peeled back the skin. It came off cleanly, like the shell off a hardboiled egg. A jelly-like substance coated the denuded meat. He scrubbed it away with water and salt. Gutting the sucker was the tricky part. Most of the neurotoxin was contained in the liver and ovaries. If you ruptured either, the poison would seep through your skin and into your flesh. So very slowly, with the precision and dexterity of a surgeon, he removed the internal organs and filleted what remained of the meat into thin strips, cutting upward against the bone. Afterward he placed the sashimi onto a plate and poured himself a glass of a '96 Domaine Laroche Chablis. Before he could sit down and enjoy his dinner, however, his computer beeped.

Fitzgerald popped a piece of the fish into his mouth—it was gelatinous but not fishy tasting—and entered the study, where the floor-to-ceiling bookcases were filled with thousands of books on the history of warfare. He was going through the centuries in chronological order, a hobby he'd begun shortly after his wife and eight-year-old daughter were brutally murdered nine years ago. He'd started with the Battle of Megiddo in 1469 BC—or BCE, if you cared to be politically correct—and was currently up to the Battle of Talasa in 751 AD, a conflict between the Arabs and the Chinese for control of a major river in Central Asia. The Chinese lost, which was a shame for them. Had they won, Central Asia today might have been Chinese, not Muslim.

The computer, a MacBook, was on the desk in the corner. He sat down in front of it and logged into specially encrypted software. He had one new email message:

How's my favorite assassin, Redstone? If you're not keeping up, the FBI is still holding its collective dick over the last job. All they've got is the killer wears size 12 loafers. Next time don't step in the fucking blood, yes? See the attachment, per usual. There's good news and bad news. Bad news—the first guy we used fucked up, so you're cleanup on this one. The good news— the mark's going to Africa for a few days, which, if you're quick, should make things a little easier than usual. Shit happens in Africa, right?

Good luck, God bless. M.

Fitzgerald spent the next several hours going over the information he'd been sent. Then he booked the first flight leaving for Tanzania the following morning.

# CHAPTER 3

*Tuesday, December 24, 10:01 a.m.*

*Arusha, Tanzania*

"**W**HEN WOULD YOU like me to pick you up?" asked the guide, a native of Zanzibar. He was small, bald, quick to smile, and dressed exactly how Scarlett thought a safari guide should dress. Khaki shorts, an olive vest with about twenty pockets on it, and a cotton twill bush hat. He'd met Scarlett and Sal at Kilimanjaro International Airport forty minutes ago before driving them to Arusha, the first and last stop of any size before they reached the lodge atop the volcanic caldera.

"Come back in an hour," Sal told him.

Once the guide wheeled the big Land Rover away into traffic, Sal and Scarlett were immediately swarmed by a dozen men, each toting the cheapest safari package in town. They explained repeatedly that they were not interested. The street hawks were by degrees obstinate, indignant, but finally resigned.

"Good God," Sal said, straightening his blazer.

"It's what they do," Scarlett said.

"It's barbaric." He shaded his eyes with his hand against the morning sun. "There should be a supermarket somewhere nearby. I'll get the supplies. Why don't you browse around and meet back here in, say, thirty minutes?"

Scarlett agreed and Sal left, waving off a new group of vultures that had descended upon him. Scarlett took a moment to get her bearings. She was standing at the base of a white-trimmed clock tower, surrounded by belching trucks, taxis, and an eclectic mix of locals and khaki-clad tourists. On the drive into the city the buildings had been rickety wooden things with tin roofs. Here, in the government district of the CBD, most were concrete, painted various shades of washed-out white, blue, yellow, and red. Almost all of them were plastered with gaudy, dated advertising.

She started down what a street sign announced was Sokoine Road, storing the name away in case she got lost. She passed tailor shops filled with row after row of sewing machines and kiosks selling candies and phone cards. Women with perfect postures balanced fruit or baskets on their heads while men led their cattle and other livestock. Children played in the alleyways with toys fashioned out of string and empty bottles. She even spotted a couple native Masai warriors dressed in their checkered regalia and holding long spears. From somewhere in the distance came the toxic smell of burning garbage.

All in all, Scarlett's first impression of Arusha was that of a tourist-hungry frontier town—Africa's twenty-first century equivalent of the Wild West. It was fascinating and exotic and a little intimidating all at the same time.

On the next block she came to what appeared to be the central marketplace. A few hundred cages containing squawking chickens and roosters surrounded the entranceway. Beyond them, inside the tented structure, the maze of stalls was filled with everything imaginable. Sandals soled with tire tread grips, colorful cotton kangas, traditional medicines, vividly colored vegetables, you name it. Some people were sucking baobab seeds and tamarind-like sweets. Others offered to guide her around for a private tour, probably looking for a tip. She politely declined. If she started doling out money, she'd never leave the place in one piece.

While she wandered up and down the aisles, merchants tried to lure her to their stalls with shouts of *"Karibu!"* and "Hello friend!"

Scarlett waved, flashed the smile she usually reserved for the paparazzi, and felt irrationally guilty for not stopping at each.

Once she did a big loop and was returning to the main entrance, she paused at a display selling beads, woodcarvings, and jewelry on which the outline of the African continent had been painted. She pantomimed a ring around her finger. "Rings?" she said, to clarify.

The old woman behind the counter—she must have been sixty-five or seventy, well above the life expectancy in the country—nodded eagerly. She plucked from her wares not a ring but an ugly steel pendant with a black string attached to it. She cracked the thing in half and dropped it in Scarlett's cupped hands. Scarlett was surprised to find it housed a tiny compass. She turned left, then right. The needle spun accordingly. The woman punched 3000 into a calculator, obviously Tanzanian shillings.

"Do you take American money?" She pulled a ten from her wallet.

The woman snatched the bill and tucked it away inside her clothing. She smiled at Scarlett, revealing a mouthful of crooked and broken teeth. Scarlett smiled back. Several seconds passed before it became apparent that no change was forthcoming. She had never been very good at bartering, but that exchange felt more like highway robbery. Still, the old woman was happy—which she should be. Ten dollars was likely ten days of wages for her.

Scarlett left the market and found Sal back at the clock tower. A zippered sports bag was at his feet. "What's that?" she asked, pointing to the bag.

"The supplies," he said.

"They don't use plastic bags here?"

"Guess not. I had to buy the damn thing." He nodded toward a small café across the street. "Why don't we eat there? Then we'll be able to see the guide when he returns."

They got a table on the patio in the shade of the awning and ordered eggs, coffee, and a platter of fruit. The coffees came first. While Scarlett was sipping hers—milk, no sugar—she saw a woman pass in front of the café, carrying two plastic bags stuffed with groceries. She chuckled to herself.

"You mind sharing?" Sal said, looking at her curiously. When he saw what had amused her, his face darkened and he stood.

"Where do you think you're going?"

"To get my money back."

"Please, Sal. You're going to go all the way back to the supermarket to argue over a two dollar bag you bought, or however much it cost?"

"It's the principal behind it."

"If you do, I'll mention it during my next interview. They'll love it—billionaire scrooge."

Sal hesitated, but sat back down. Scarlett studied him. What was on his mind? He'd been gung-ho about this safari, this stage for reconciliation, when they had discussed it at Cedars-Sinai Hospital. But ever since—back home, where he'd slept in one of the guest bedrooms, in the car, on the plane—he'd been quiet, detached even. Was he second-guessing coming on this getaway with her? Having doubts about the whole process of working things out? Or did his surly mood have more to do with his work? Perhaps he was more concerned with the Prince Tower opening than he was letting on. After all, the biggest economic downturn since the Great Depression wasn't the best time to be launching a $1.5-billion hotel with rooms that ranged from $800 to $30,000 a night.

She was about to ask him this when he leaned back in his chair and said, "You know, I don't understand why Western imperialism has gotten such a bad rap." He was staring past her to the dirty street, the paint-peeled buildings. "How can advancing law and order, reforming health and education, implementing a modern economy be a bad thing?"

"Because it wasn't ours to change," she said. "How would you feel, Sal, if some hotshot came in and instigated major changes in your company?"

"That would be impossible, cara mia, since I'm both CEO and chairman."

Scarlett smiled despite herself. His playful arrogance was one of the things she'd missed most about him during their separation.

"We literally flattened Japan," Sal went on. "But look at them sixty years later. They're the world's second largest economy. Look at this place after sixty years of self-rule. They've gone backward. Barely one in ten Tanzanians has electricity or a flushing toilet. Look beyond this relatively affluent city to the wars and famine, genocide, disease, human rights abuses, and military dictatorships that plague nearly every corner of the continent. Did you see the International Criminal Tribunal for Rwanda? It's right down the street. We passed it coming in."

The waiter returned with their breakfast. Scarlett tried the eggs, which were greasy but good. She sucked on a piece of pineapple.

"What about self-determination?" she said. She knew she couldn't win this argument. One of Sal's causes was Africa, just as hers was ending the wars in Afghanistan and Iraq.

"Self-determination?" He smiled thinly. "What good is self-determination when your leaders are corrupt despots? At least when the British sent money to the Colonial Civil Service, the Englishmen in charge spent it according to design. Contrary to that, the majority of foreign aid poured into sub-Sahara Africa since the fifties has leaked back West as capital flight—mainly to the Swiss bank accounts of the ruling elite."

"It's not as simple as that—"

"No, it's not," he quipped. "What is simple is to blame all of Africa's problems on colonialism, apartheid, globalization, multi-nationalism." He finally turned his attention to his plate. He cut a slice of egg white and set it atop a piece of dry brown toast. He cut the toast, speared it with his fork, and stuck the bite-sized piece in his mouth. "All I'm saying," he concluded with uncharacteristic snappishness, "is that things have gone to hell here. The people of Africa were better off under the British and the French, the Germans and the Portuguese."

Scarlett set down her fork and knife, convinced there was something weighing heavily on his mind, something that had nothing to do with their marriage. "If you need to get back to the office, Sal, I understand. We can postpone this safari. I'll fly back to LA in the morning—"

"I'm not going back to the office, and we're not postponing anything." He dabbed his lips with a paper napkin and stood. "Take your time eating. I'm going to stretch my legs. It's a three-hour drive to Ngorongoro Crater."

Scarlett watched Sal walk down the sidewalk until he disappeared from view. She pushed her plate away from her, leaned back in her chair, and sipped her coffee thoughtfully.

DAMIEN FITZGERALD SPOTTED the sign for the travel company, a red-and-yellow thing that filled the entire second-floor window of a brick building on Mikocheni Coca Cola Road. He didn't know why someone would name a road after Coca Cola. Maybe the city's first Coke bottling shop used to be on this street. Or maybe the guy whose job it was to name streets was drinking a Coke when he got to this one. Fitzgerald didn't care one way or another. All that mattered was that he'd finally found the office for Magic Africa Safari.

After landing in Julius Nyerere International Airport, he'd browsed the Internet for all the safari companies in Dar es Salaam that serviced Tanzania's northern safari circuit. There had been several dozen. The addition of the keyword "luxury" narrowed the search significantly. He wrote down the telephone numbers and addresses of the ten most expensive companies. He didn't think Salvador Brazza would settle for anything less. It turned out he was right. He hit the money on the third outfit he called. Yes, Salvador Brazza and Scarlett Cox had booked a safari with them, the woman on the phone had said. But no, she could not provide any details. It was prohibited by management.

*Bollocks to management,* Fitzgerald thought once more. What was the big deal with giving out some information? It was just an itinerary he wanted. Was it because Brazza's wife was a celebrity? Did she receive special treatment?

Probably. Bloody actors.

So instead of getting the information he wanted neat and tidy over the phone, he'd been forced to drive around Dar for the past forty-five minutes, searching for the travel company. Dar was a big city with a lot of one-way streets and mindless pedestrians. Needless to say, he was no longer in a very good mood.

He swung the rented Toyota Land Cruiser to the curb and parked behind an idling meat truck. He got out, the heat hitting him like a blast from an open oven. It was the middle of the summer below the equator. He crossed the street and entered a brick office building. The lobby was small but well-maintained with polished floor tiles, a potted plant, and an imitation leather sofa. The number between the Up and Down buttons on the bronze elevator plate read 4. He pressed Up and waited. The stainless steel doors had a bright annealed finish in which he could see his reflection. At sixty-one, he was as tall and lean as he'd been at thirty, if slightly softer around the waist. His graying hair had receded into a well-defined widow's peak while white stubble textured his sharp jawline. Seeing himself now, he thought he looked absurdly how someone in his line of work was supposed to look. That, of course, was because he knew what his line of work was. To a stranger on the street, he could just as easily have passed as a fit university professor, or a lawyer.

A chime announced the cab's arrival. He took it up to the second floor. The doors opened directly into the travel company. A long counter lined with neat piles of magazines and flyers separated the customer area from the employee area. A WWF poster on one wall showed a sea turtle swimming in marine-blue water. The caption read: "Warning: It is ILLEGAL to kill turtles in Fiji." Fitzgerald wondered how many East Africans were flying ten thousand miles away to Fiji to kill turtles.

In the employee area two black men clicked away at their computers, while a white woman was wading through a sheaf of papers with a fluorescent yellow highlighter. The woman saw Fitzgerald, smiled, and approached the counter. She was dressed in maroon slacks and a cream blouse. A colorful silk scarf was knotted around her neck. It was just like the one around his own neck, only his was mud brown, and he didn't think she was wearing hers to conceal a six-inch-long scar.

"Can I help you?" she asked him in the same South African voice he'd heard over the phone.

He took off his sunglasses and hooked them on the V-neck of his black T-shirt. "I called earlier," he said, the words coming out raspy, like a man who smoked three packs of cigarettes a day. He'd been speaking like that for the better part of thirty years, ever since he'd been garroted and left for dead in the hills of Northern Ireland. "I asked for Salvador Brazza's itinerary."

Her smile faltered. "I told you. We cannot give out that information."

"Yes, you can."

"No, we can't."

Fitzgerald withdrew the Glock 17 from the holster beneath his jacket. The barrel was outfitted with a Gemtech threaded suppressor. He pointed the pistol at her face. "Yes, you can," he repeated.

She froze. The two men at the computers jumped to their feet.

"Stay still," Fitzgerald warned them without taking his eyes off the woman. She was young, early twenties, just a girl really, somewhat pretty. Her eyes were wide, her cheeks flushed, her heart probably racing. The funny thing about fear was that it produced the exact same symptoms as excitement, the only difference being the addition of willingness to the latter. "I would like Salvador Brazza's itinerary."

She didn't move.

He nodded to her computer. "Go on, lass. Go print it off."

Still didn't move.

He slapped the counter. "Go on!"

That broke her paralysis. She hurried to her desk and fiddled with the mouse. Her hand shook badly.

The older of the two men said, "You don't need a gun, man. Put away the gun. We'll give you whatever you want. Just take it easy, hey?"

There was always a hero. Fitzgerald pointed the Glock at the hero and squeezed the trigger. The term "silencer" was a misnomer because you could never truly silence the report of a gunshot. But you could suppress it. Now the suppressed shot made only a soft pop. A purple dot appeared in the man's forehead, leaking a line of blood. He toppled backward.

The woman screamed.

The second man bolted for the back door. Fitzgerald fired three rounds into his back. The impact threw him forward onto his chest.

"Shut up," he said to the girl.

She stopped screaming, though her mouth was quivering, as if she was keeping it closed by force of will alone.

"Did you print the itinerary?"

She hunkered down over the keyboard and hit a few keys. She made a frustrated noise, like she'd screwed something up. Her hands were shaking worse than ever. Then the freestanding laser printer in the corner clicked and hummed and spat out a sheet of paper into the tray.

"Go get it," he told her.

She went to the printer, retrieved the single piece of paper, and brought it back. The flush had drained from her cheeks, leaving her face an alabaster white. Her mouth was still quivering, and she was making small, pathetic noises. She was no longer very attractive.

Fitzgerald snatched the paper from her hand and gave it a quick scan. It was what he wanted. "If you had given me this information over the phone," he told her, "none of this would have happened."

"Please don't kill me."

"Why didn't you give me the fecking information over the phone?"

"Management prohibits it."

"Management's dead, lass."

"Please don't shoot me."

"Was it because Scarlett Cox is a celebrity? Is that the reason?"

"What?"

"Is that why you wouldn't give me the itinerary?"

"No. I don't understand. What?"

He shot her twice in the chest. She collapsed to the floor, dead.

It was her own bloody fault.

Fitzgerald slid across the counter and searched the men for their wallets, collecting a combined grand total of twenty-five thousand shillings—or about ten quid. The girl had what looked like a real half-carat diamond on her engagement finger, which he took. He didn't see her handbag, but he didn't bother searching for it. He cleared out the register to complete the robbery-gone-wrong scenario, then left through the back door, where he discovered a gray-painted stairwell. He holstered the Glock beneath his jacket, slipped on his sunglasses, and skipped down the stairs to street level, whistling an old Irish tune as he went.

# CHAPTER 4

"**I**S THAT IT, Silly?" Scarlett asked the guide as she peered out the window of the Land Rover at the volcanic caldera in the distance. It was rocky and huge and, well, permanent, like it had been there forever. According to Sal, the lodge where they were spending the night was perched right up on the rim, overlooking the crater. She couldn't wait to check out the view.

"Yes," Silly told her. "Ngorongoro Crater." His name was Sirily, pronounced "Cereal," but he said he preferred Silly. She went with it.

"How much longer until we get to the lodge?" Sal asked.

Scarlett patted his thigh reassuringly. He'd had an upset stomach for the past half hour or so, a result, he believed, of the fruit at the café in Arusha. She wished there was something she could do for him. She'd had a bad case of food poisoning while in the Bahamas last winter, and she'd spent two full days in bed, barely able to muster the strength to sit up.

"Not long," Silly told him. "I can pull over if you would like?"

"No," Sal grunted.

"Then I will stop at the next village."

"No," Sal repeated. "Just get us to the lodge."

They fell silent after that. Scarlett spent the time staring out the window, captivated by the scenery. The sky was big and blue, the grasslands flat and endless. It made her wonder what early man had thought when he came down from the trees and was confronted with this new and alien world full of opportunity and danger.

They zipped through the farming country of Karatu and Oldeani, which was dotted with farmers and their oxen, then began the ascent into the crater highlands. The dusty landscape became greener, the road steeper and steeper. Silly identified some of the local birds for them, which included Carmine bee-eaters, recognizable by their black eye masks, and brilliant malachite-colored rollers, which stayed closer to the ground, searching for grasshoppers and snails and whatever else they found good to eat. Halfway up the forested slope they arrived at Loduare Gate, the entrance to Ngorongoro Conservation Area. There were no flashing lights or music or fanfare in any way, just a little hut and a sweaty ranger with a red beret and an AK-47. Silly flashed him their permits and they carried on.

The sealed road petered to a rutted and grooved earthen track. Scarlett poked Sal when she spotted a troop of baboons lounging in a sausage tree, drinking the nectar from the blood-red flowers that hung in long panicles. The baboons watched the Land Rover pass with their sparkling black eyes, unalarmed, likely used to seeing their distant cousins come this way.

They continued onward and upward through increasingly dense vegetation until they arrived at a T-junction at the crater's rim. Silly turned west. A few miles later they reached Tree Camp of Ngorongoro Crater Lodge. The five-star resort was composed of a main building and six smaller villas. They were all constructed from local wood and thatch and resembled oversized, hairy-topped mushrooms. As soon as Silly parked alongside four other Land Rovers, Sal was off to search out a bathroom. Scarlett got out and performed a few yoga poses to stretch her cramped muscles. Two men emerged from the main building, catching her in the Warrior Pose. They welcomed her to the lodge and introduced themselves as Wilson and Onesmo. Wilson was older, pasty white, with a thin mustache, while Onesmo was tall and black. He held a silver filigree tray on which rested two long-stemmed glasses of champagne and two warm, scented towels.

Scarlett accepted a glass, then followed her two hosts inside the main building. She was impressed with the décor, a unique mishmash of Western opulence and African themes. Her first thought was of a Masai version of Versailles. She went directly to the bank of windows that offered a panoramic view of the crater. The rocky rim of the collapsed volcano curved away from the lodge to form an enormous ring, while thousands of feet below, in the vast depression, grassy plains stretched away for miles. A sprawling soda lake glittered like quicksilver beneath the midday sun.

Sal had told her Ngorongoro Crater was sometimes referred to as Africa's Eden, and now she understood why. It was a paradise of unspoiled nature.

*Maybe he had the right idea after all,* she thought. *Maybe this is exactly what we need.*

Scarlett went to the front desk and checked in. Wilson handed her an additional waiver to sign that absolved the lodge of any wrongdoing in the event that either she or Sal were injured or killed on the premises. The legalese sounded rather ominous, so she asked Wilson what he had up his sleeve.

"Zebra, water buffalo, and elephants roam freely on the property," he explained. "If you don't respect them, and keep your distance, they may charge. That's why we enforce strict precautions. After 7 p.m. every evening, if you would like to leave your villa, you must first ring the main lodge on the telephone in your suite. One of our staff will come to escort you to wherever you need to go."

"Fair enough," she said, and signed away.

Wilson led her to her villa, explaining on the way that there were in fact thirty suites in all. Twelve in South Camp, twelve in North Camp, and six here in Tree Camp, which supposedly offered the most privacy. The villa was perched on ten-foot stilts. She wondered if that was to give the guests a better view of the crater, or to keep the wildlife out.

Wilson held the door open for her. She stepped inside to teak walls, hardwood floors, and a domed banana-leaf ceiling. She eyed the king-size bed with the purple bedspread and massive carved headboard and decided it would suffice. On the plane from LA to Tanzania, Sal had told her there had been no doubles available, and he could sleep on the sofa or a cot. She'd told him sharing a bed was fine—as long as he stayed on his side. She didn't know how long she was going to enforce that invisible line, but one thing was for certain: a romantic getaway to the top of the world was not going to make it easy.

"No mosquito net?" she said.

Wilson shook his head. "Those nasty little buggers don't survive at this altitude. It's one of the perks of being located atop a volcano. Now, in an effort to conserve electricity, the generator is turned off twice daily, between three and five in the afternoon, and midnight and three in the morning. Make sure your cameras or what-have-you are not plugged in during those times as there may be a surge when the power resumes. Oh—there is one more thing, Miss Cox," he added, red patches the size of cherry tomatoes blossoming on his cheeks. "Would it be too much of an imposition to ask for an autograph? I have a teenage son. He'd be delighted."

Scarlett obliged willingly and scribbled her name on the back of a postcard of the lodge Wilson proffered her. After he left, she went to the luggage at the foot of the bed, which the Silly Express must have brought in while she'd been signing her life away down at the main lodge. She was in the process of unpacking a few things when Sal returned.

"How do you feel?" she asked him, wondering if the lodge sold antacid.

"Blah." He collapsed into one of the two high-backed leather club chairs that faced the fireplace. He considered the decanter of complimentary sherry on the low table in front of him, then poured himself a glass.

Scarlett took the chair opposite him. "What's going on, Sal?"

He gave her a questioning look.

She nodded at the sherry. "It's barely noon."

Sal rarely drank. He might have a glass of wine or a single malt Scotch on special occasions, but that was all. Drinking diluted the senses, and he despised not being in control at all times. It was one of his quirks.

Before he could answer, however, his cell phone rang. He took it from his pocket and answered it. Scarlett watched him. His jaw tightened. His eyes darkened. About two minutes later he said, "Do it."

Aside from the curt greeting, those were the only two words he spoke before putting the phone away once again.

"Who was that?" she asked.

"Danny."

The name gave Scarlett an involuntary start. Danny Zamir. She'd never liked Sal's security chief. Part of the reason was simple jealousy. Danny always had Sal's full attention, regardless of the time or place. Back when Scarlett and Sal had first begun dating, Sal would never answer his phone when he was out with her—except when it was Danny. Then he might step away from whatever they were doing for five minutes or forty, it never seemed to matter. Scarlett had first met Danny when he'd visited their Bel-Air home on some sort of business the year before. He was darkly handsome and roughly her age. And she had never forgotten how he'd walked—languid, like a large cat, or a supremely confident soldier.

She might not know much about him, but she knew one thing for certain: Danny Zamir was a very dangerous man.

"What did he want?" she asked, trying to parlay idle curiosity.

"He's just keeping me up to date with the hotel."

"Is everything all right?"

"Sure." He sipped the sherry.

"Be straight with me, Sal."

He met her gaze evenly. Clockwork ticked behind his eyes as he seemed to assess whether to open up or not. Finally he said, "There was a fire at the Prince a few weeks ago."

Scarlett blinked. Whatever she'd been expecting to hear, it hadn't been that. "What kind of fire?" she said.

"It gutted the top two floors and put us behind schedule."

"Why didn't you tell me before now?"

He shrugged. "It wasn't a big deal at first."

"What does 'at first' mean?"

"We thought it was the result of bad wiring."

"And now?"

Sal hesitated.

"Tell me," she pressed.

"It's looking more like it might be arson."

"What?" Scarlett's mind reeled. "Why would anyone want to burn down one of your hotels?"

"They didn't."

Sal took another sip of the sherry, acting as if the topic bored him, which she knew meant it concerned him very much. At her urging, he reluctantly explained how he had been the only person staying in the hotel at the time, how the fire had been set directly below his room, and how, if it hadn't been for Danny Zamir, he might very well have perished.

Scarlett felt numb. "Maybe it was accidental?" she said. "Maybe it was only a coincidence it happened right below where you were staying?"

"The police don't seem to think so."

"Do they have proof it was set deliberately?"

"Proof enough to convince me."

"Who would do something like this?"

Sal was silent.

"You don't have any idea?" she said.

He shrugged. "The police are investigating. Danny's investigating. That's why he called. To give me an update on what he's found out."

"And?"

"And nothing. He doesn't know anything yet."

Scarlett recalled the angry look on Sal's face while he'd been on the phone. Was it because Danny hadn't found anything out?

Then again, Danny had spoken for a solid two minutes, uninter-rupted. That was a long time to tell someone nothing.

*Do it,* Sal had said. Do what?

"I can't believe you've been keeping this from me," she said.

"I only learned about it the other day," he replied. "The same day you landed yourself in the hospital. You didn't need to be burdened with this."

"Someone tried to kill you, Sal! That's not a burden. That's something you need to talk to me about...regardless of what-ever else is going on." She took his hand, softened her voice. "I'm still your wife. Don't forget that, silly."

"I love you, cara mia."

"I—I love you too, Sal."

She released his hand and sat back. Wow. She felt shaky but thrilled. They'd just made more progress than they had with months of expensive therapy sessions. Death, or even the threat of death, put the most serious of secular matters into perspec-tive. "What happens now?" She realized how that might be in-terpreted and added quickly, "With the Prince."

He shrugged. "Nothing. It's over."

"What if they try something again?"

"They won't."

"How do you know?"

"The police are on it. Danny's on it."

"Isn't there anything more you can do?"

"Look," Sal said, setting his drink aside. "Even if someone wanted to hurt me, I'm in Africa. Nobody knows I'm here. Maybe a few people from the office. That's it. By the time I get back to Dubai, chances are good the police will have some news for me. If they haven't already caught whoever's responsible, they'll at least have leads. We'll take it from there." He stood and kissed her on the forehead. "Now excuse me for a moment. My stomach's acting up." He went to the bathroom.

Scarlett slumped back in her chair and shook her head, try-ing to absorb everything she'd learned.

*Who would want to kill him?*

The half-full copita of sherry on the table caught her eye. She picked it up and knocked the rest back.

Screw it being noon.

AT TWO O'CLOCK in the afternoon, Damien Fitzgerald arrived at a salvage yard located in the middle of a shitty industrial neighborhood that made all the other shitty neighborhoods he'd driven through in Arusha seem almost nice in comparison. He entered through the front gate and passed between fleets of junked cars until he came upon a rickety office with a rusted corrugated iron roof. He knocked on the door. No one answered. He tried the handle, found it unlocked, and went inside. The walls were melamine-finished particleboard, the rug green and torn, the few pieces of furniture as decrepit as the cars outside—including one bench seat that looked like it was straight out of a Volkswagen Bus.

"Hello?" he called. The word came out raspier than usual, and his hand went unconsciously to the scarf at his throat.

A back door opened and a Tanzanian man wearing a yellow-and-green football jersey entered. "Hello!" he said merrily. "Welcome!"

"I'm looking for Land Rover parts," Fitzgerald said. "Do you have any?"

"Yes. Yes, I haf many. There are more Land Rovers in this city than flies because of you *mzugus* and your safaris. What do you need?"

"A front driveshaft."

"Yes. I can help you. Yes. Come this way."

The man led Fitzgerald through the back door into a lot filled with more junked cars. He pointed to a Land Rover sitting on tireless axles. The driver's side door was smashed in, the roof crushed. "*Ile accident ilitokea alipo-lose control na aka-overturn and landed in a ditch,*" he said.

"What does that mean?"

"Ah! Why do I know English, but you do not know Swahili, or

even half Swahili? I said, 'The accident happened when he lost control and overturned and landed in a ditch.' But do not worry, my friend, it is only body damage."

"I'm looking for an old driveshaft."

"Why do you want that?"

"Do you have one or not?"

"Yes, I haf plenty. There, with the power train parts." He pointed to a pile of scrap metal.

Fitzgerald went to the pile. There were hubs, differentials, transfer boxes, gears, and driveshafts. He examined each drive-shaft closely. The front end splines—gear teeth—were maligned and worn on four. Two looked okay. One was nearly bald. He chose the bald one and asked the Tanzanian how much it cost.

"That one's no good," the man said. "Why do you want that one?"

"How much is it?"

"Fifteen thousand shillings."

Fitzgerald paid him, then turned to leave.

"Hey," the Tanzanian called. "You never told me what you need a no-good driveshaft for?"

"*Neco quispiam.*"

"What does that mean?"

"You're the language man," Fitzgerald told him over his shoulder. "You figure it out."

# CHAPTER 5

*Tuesday, December 24, 4:43 p.m.*

*London, England*

"**H**OW ABOUT THIS one?"

Jahja al-Ahmad looked at his wife, Sara, who held up a colorful scarf. "Too bright," he said. He returned his attention to the belt rack, where a number of belts were hanging from the hooks like dead snakes. He wanted a black one, so he ignored the brown and white ones. All the bands were made from leather and looked similar to one another. It was the buckles that made the decision difficult. There were sterling, enamel, pewter, square, and rectangular ones. He was holding a black belt with a simple pewter buckle in his hand; it was the best he had seen so far.

He and his wife were in Harrods in Knightsbridge, in the fashion accessories department, which was on the ground floor, along with the rest of the menswear shops. Plastic Christmas trees, mistletoe, tinsel, holly, Santa Clauses, and wreaths suffocated the place. Ironically, these decorations all had non-scriptural pagan origins, nothing to do with the Messiah's birth. But the Christian infidels out shopping likely didn't know or care about that. Christmas for them was merely an excuse for consumerism and gluttony and drunkenness.

"How about this one?" Sara held up another colorful scarf. She was dressed conservatively in heavy wool pants and a long winter jacket. A plain green hijab covered her hair.

"No," Jahja said.

"Well, there's not much left to choose from. Two days before Christmas isn't the best time to go shopping."

They weren't shopping for Christmas gifts, of course. They were Muslim. Jahja had been born in Algeria; Sara in Bosnia, to Turkish parents. But Jahja needed a new belt. He hadn't been eating much lately, and his waist size had shrunk two sizes. Sara asked him what was wrong every evening at the dinner table. He told her he was dieting. She didn't believe him. If she did, she wouldn't keep asking him what was wrong every evening. Nevertheless, she was a good wife. They had a good marriage. She would never in a thousand years suspect what was causing him to lose sleep, to lose his appetite.

"I don't need a scarf," he told her. "Just a belt."

"Try it on. Please?"

Jahja went to her. She wrapped the mint-green scarf around his neck, turning him toward the mirror. He was average height, dark-skinned, and clean shaven. The entire left portion of his face was covered in leathery scar tissue. The burn that had caused the grotesque disfigurement had not only destroyed the skin but the underlying fat, muscle, and nerve structure, so now that side of his face was frozen in a mask of dumb horror. As always, he avoided looking at the deformity. He wished other people could be so considerate. They weren't. Nearly everyone he'd passed in the department store this afternoon had stared. The women behind the fragrance counters, the other shoppers, the kids in the food court—and kids were the worst. They often stared unabashedly until their parents saw what they were staring at and tugged them away.

Jahja adjusted the scarf. He decided it looked good, sophisticated.

"I like it," he said.

"Great! Did you get a belt?"

"Yes." He held up the black one with the pewter buckle.

"It's so plain."

"I like it."

"Can't you pick a different one?"

"I like this one."

Sara rolled her eyes. "Okay." She kissed him on the cheek—on the burned cheek. She didn't care. That was one of the reasons he loved her so much. "You go pay for them and meet me up in toys. It's on the fourth floor, next to that big pet center."

Jahja frowned. "Why are you going to toys?"

"I want to get something for Hana." Hana was their five-year-old daughter.

Jahja's frown deepened. Last year Hana had begun asking why they didn't put up a Christmas tree and lights like everyone else. So this year, to get her excited about Eid ul-Fitr, they'd put up green-and-white lights around the house throughout Ramadan until the end of Eid. Apparently that wasn't good enough. Hana still wanted a tree and lights during Christmas. Sara suggested it wouldn't hurt to put up the green-and-white lights again. Jahja refused. He was worried Hana might begin to reject her Islamic faith in tawhid. Worse, she might start believing that the Prophet Isa—Jesus—peace be upon him, was something more than a mere prophet and servant of Allah.

"We've talked about this, Sara," he said.

"I know, I know. But all her friends get presents. I just want to get her something small. One gift. Please?"

Jahja shrugged. He was not going to argue about this, not now. Sara beamed, kissed him on the cheek again, and hurried off toward the escalators. Jahja went to the service counter and stepped into line. The man ahead of him was trying to get a refund on a pair of shoes. After a minute of complaining—he didn't have a receipt—he walked off, grumbling. Jahja stepped up to the counter. The saleswoman had dyed silvery-blonde hair. Her makeup was bright and offensive. Jahja would never let Hana wear her hair or makeup like that when she grew up.

"Good day," the woman said, smiling at nothing. When she glanced up from the cash register, her eyes darted to the left side of his face. The smile remained in place, but it immediately left her eyes, which had become vacant, like someone trying not to look at something.

Jahja set the belt and scarf on the counter. "Just these."

"Of course," she said cheerfully, overcompensating for her initial reaction. He hated it when people did that.

His phone vibrated in his pocket. He took it out and checked the number.

"Excuse me," he said to the woman. "I'll be right back."

He went to a secluded corner of the shop and pressed Talk.

"*Salaamu alaykum,*" a man's voice said.

"*Wa alaykum salaam,*" Jahja replied.

"The plane ticket is waiting in your mailbox," the man continued in Arabic. "The flight is for tomorrow morning. A friend will be at the airport in Dar es Salaam to meet you. He will take you where you need to go."

"I understand."

"May Allah protect you."

"Glory be to Allah."

Jahja hung up and returned to the service counter to pay for his belt and scarf. The woman smiled at him again. He smiled back. But he no longer wondered whether his burned face was making her feel uncomfortable; he was now wondering whether he would ever make it back to England.

He'd like to. He'd like to wear the scarf for his wife one day.

# CHAPTER 6

*Tuesday, December 24, 6:55 p.m.*

*Ngorongoro Conservation Area, Tanzania*

T HE DINING ROOM was redolent with the smells of saffron, vanilla, cumin, nutmeg, and the rest of the now devoured Pan-African cuisine. Everybody seated at the long table was on their third or fourth drink, speaking loudly and laughing raucously.

Scarlett was still sipping her first glass of wine. After what Sal had told her about the Prince Hotel fire/attempted murder, she wasn't in a festive mood. On top of that, ten minutes into the meal Sal's stomach had started acting up, and he'd said he needed to lie down. Her first thought had been he wanted to call Danny Zamir in private. When you've been married for four years, it becomes second nature to intuit these types of things. In fact, that's how she discovered the other woman. Not perfume on Sal's shirts. Not racy text messages on his phone. Not hearsay from a friend. Just plain old woman's intuition.

Then, acceptingly, Scarlett became ashamed of her suspicious response to his departure. He *was* sick after all, and it was perfectly conceivable he wanted to be alone.

Setting the ruminations aside, she studied the menu. There

was a brandy snap coming for dessert. It sounded good, but her diet said no. To avoid temptation, she took the Merlot she'd been nursing to the outdoor deck. The clouds to the west were a striking pinkish-orange, those closer darkening to a deep blue, broken with cracks of silver and dove white. Way down on the crater floor shadows lengthened and pooled, gobbling up the greenery. She closed her eyes and let a wave of serenity wash over her.

"Quite a view, isn't it?"

She started. A dollop of wine jumped the lip of her glass and splashed the deck, just missing her silver Christian Louboutins. She turned and discovered an older gentleman standing behind her. His graying hair had receded with age and white stubble textured his jaw, like a sprinkling of fresh snow. He seemed fit for his age, someone who might have ridden the Tour de France in his prime.

"You startled me," she said.

"Sorry, lass. That's the last thing I wanted to do." His voice was coarse yet strangely alluring, softened by a charming Irish brogue. He nodded at the crater. "Three million years."

"Is that how old it is?"

"Have you been down there yet, Miss . . . ?"

"Cox. And no, I haven't. I'm going with my husband tomorrow. We're cutting through it, to get to the Serengeti."

"And where is your husband, may I ask?"

"He went back to the room. He hasn't been feeling well today."

"Shame. But you believe he will be up and about tomorrow?"

"I certainly hope so. Have you been down there yet, Mr . . . ?"

"Hill. Benjamin Hill. And no, not yet. I'll be going down tomorrow as well."

"Perhaps we'll see each other?"

"Perhaps we will." He extended his hand. "I've taken up enough of your time."

She shook it. "Good night, Mr. Hill."

"And a good night to you too, Miss Cox."

Scarlett watched the Irishman walk away. He didn't leave through the dining room but followed the perimeter of the building until he turned a corner and was lost from sight. She frowned. He had been well-spoken and polite, but something about him had bothered her.

Back in the dining room, she asked the waiter if he could round up someone to escort her to her villa, then she went out front to wait, keeping in the heat of the twin fire bowls that flanked the lodge's entrance. Up here, at this altitude, the temperature plummeted after the sun went down. She folded her arms across her chest, her thoughts returning to the Irishman, and she realized what had nagged at her. He hadn't been at dinner. There had been twelve chairs at the long table, twelve place settings, each occupied. Until Sal left, that is. So was the Irishman from South or North Camp? If so, what was he doing here? She glanced at her watch. Ten to eight. Hadn't Wilson said guests were prohibited from moving around the property freely after seven?

Hearing a noise behind her, she whirled, only to find her escort—a Masai warrior wrapped in a checkered red cloth and carrying an AK-47. She'd had her fair share of bodyguards, but this was a first for her. She wondered if the assault rifle could take down a charging buffalo, or even a big cat. She hoped she never had to find out and stayed close to the escort's side until she was climbing the steps to the villa. In the bathroom she washed up, brushed her teeth, then slipped into a pair of silk pajamas. She got into bed, making sure she kept on her side of the line.

"You awake?" she said.

"Am now." Sal's voice was disembodied in the dark.

"Are you feeling better yet?"

"Yes, I think so."

"Will you be okay for tomorrow?"

"I should be fine."

"Good." She was quiet for a moment. The silence was absolute. "I met a man after you left."

"Should I be the one calling my lawyers this time?"

"Not funny, Sal. Anyway, his name was Benjamin Hill. I think he was walking around without an escort. We need an escort if we—"

Sal made a small rumble. Laughter?

"What?" she asked.

"Benjamin Hill?" There was definitely amusement in his voice. "Was he an old British chap?"

"Irish," she said, frowning. "You know him?"

"Sure."

"But how?"

"I've seen him on TV. He had his own show."

It clicked. "He was more Sean Connery than Benny Hill."

Never one for pillow talk, Sal didn't say anything more, and soon he was breathing the regular rhythm of sleep. She closed her eyes.

Sometime later she was shaken awake. She sat up, and it took her a moment before she remembered she wasn't in her bed in LA.

"Someone's outside," Sal said quietly.

The words cut through her sleepiness like a knife.

"What?"

"I heard a noise."

"Where?"

"Shhh."

Scarlett listened. All was perfectly quiet. "I don't hear anything," she whispered.

"Listen."

Then she heard something on the other side of the wall, right behind the headboard. It sounded like leaf litter crunching under a heavy weight. "That's an animal," she said. "What else could it be—?" She clamped her mouth shut.

The Prince Tower. The fire.

*Had someone followed Sal all the way to Africa?*

Her fear surged. Had she locked the door? God, did the door even have a lock?

"*Do something*," she hissed.

Sal shifted off the bed. He crossed the room, pulled back the curtains, opened the balcony door. A cool lavender-scented breeze swept into the room. He stepped outside. Looked left and right. Went left. Three steps later he was beyond the glass and out of sight.

The seconds slugged by. Scarlett heard nothing more. No shouts of alarm. No scuffle. Nothing. Which, she realized with dread, was the sound an assassin made. Paranoia swelled inside her as she imagined Sal lying in the bushes, his throat slit. She called out to him, not caring who heard her.

"Come here," Sal replied.

Exhaling the breath she'd been holding, Scarlett got out of bed and crossed the threshold to the wooden veranda. The cold wind played around her wrists and ankles and slipped down the throat of her pajama top, causing her nipples to harden and gooseflesh to break out on her skin. She followed the veranda left and found Sal leaning up against the railing, his elbows on the header, his arms crossed in front of him, like he was watching a Sunday afternoon baseball game in the park. She scanned the darkness below.

Two jackals were sitting on their haunches in a patch of bracken, licking their fur.

Sal barked. The jackals looked up. Their yellow eyes shone in the dark, indifferent yet somehow malevolent.

"Sal, stop it," she whispered.

"They're just dogs."

"They're dangerous dogs."

"They can't get up here."

"What if they wait around until the next time you're crossing the grounds to the main lodge?"

"They're brainless animals. And brainless animals don't hold grudges."

Inside once again, Scarlett slapped Sal on the rump, hard. *He* was a brainless animal. She slid the door closed and flicked the lock. She left the blinds open, welcoming what little light the moon and stars provided.

Back in bed she couldn't sleep. She had thought there had been somebody out there, another arsonist or a hit man or whatever you called someone who came to kill you during the night...

No—she was letting her imagination get the better of her. She and Sal had already discussed this. He was safe. Nobody knew he was here. What were the chances that somebody would fly all the way to Africa and follow him to the summit of a collapsed volcano? It was ridiculous, something out of Hollywood. The noise had just been a couple wild animals.

Sometime later, Scarlett slept.


AT TWO THIRTY that morning Fitzgerald opened his eyes. He had been sleeping but not really sleeping, a skill he'd learned long ago in the British Army. He opened the door to the Land Cruiser and stepped into the night. The moon was nearly full, the sky awash with icy stars, and he could see well enough. A nightjar made a musical churring sound that rose and fell with a ventriloquist-like quality. He heard little else, although he knew the surrounding forest was alive with life. He started down the dirt road toward the lodge where Salvador Brazza and Scarlett Cox were staying, whistling "Johnny I Hardly Knew Ye" so he wouldn't come upon any wild animals by surprise. The animals would usually run away, but sometimes they would panic and attack, especially if they were injured or with their young. He was carrying the driveshaft he'd purchased earlier, but a driveshaft wouldn't stop a Cape buffalo, or a leopard.

Five hundred meters later he arrived at the car park in the clearing behind Tree Camp where six SUVs were parked in a line, side by side. They were all Land Rovers. Three were Land Rover Discoverys. Only one was the latest model, a Series III. It was the second from the right. It was the one he wanted.

He lowered himself onto his back and stuck a penlight between his teeth. Then he inched his way beneath the high chassis and studied the underside of the vehicle. He took a small wrench from his pocket and undid the six bolts securing the coupling. The first five came off easily enough. The sixth was a bitch, taking him nearly the same time to get it off as the first five combined. He slid the driveshaft forward to disengage it from the transfer case, slid it backward to free it from the differential, gave it a jog, and tugged it loose. The lubricated O ring inside the drive tube fell onto his chest. He left it there while he examined the driveshaft. The splines were not very badly worn, nor had he thought they would be. He set the good driveshaft aside, replaced the O ring, and inserted the nearly bald driveshaft he'd brought with him. He refastened the six bolts, the sixth going back on a lot easier than it had come off. There was a metaphor about life somewhere in there, but this was not the time to consider it. He extracted himself from beneath the vehicle.

With one solid tug, Fitzgerald tore the CB antenna from where it was mounted on the Land Rover's rear tire carrier. He retraced his steps back to the Toyota Land Cruiser, reclined the seat, and closed his eyes, hoping sleep would come quickly. He would be waking with the sun in a few hours.

# CHAPTER 7

*Wednesday, December 25, 6:55 a.m.*

*Ngorongoro Conservation Area*

"SAL, YOU READY?" Scarlett called. "Silly's packed the Land Rover. He's waiting outside."

"I'm coming."

Sal emerged from the bathroom moments later. His hair, still damp from the shower, was combed back from his forehead as usual. It might just have been a play of the light, but he looked darker than he had the day before, healthier. She felt a slight stirring in her loins.

"You look good," she said, wondering if tonight would be the night the invisible line in bed was erased. She thought maybe it might be.

"I certainly feel better," he said. "Whatever bug I had is gone."

She spontaneously kissed his freshly shaven cheek, which smelled of a mix between lime and eighteenth-century medicinal balm. "Merry Christmas."

He arched an eyebrow. "You're in a good mood."

She was. Whatever dark thoughts she'd had during the night about world-hopping assassins seemed even more ludicrous on such a fine sunny morning. Moreover, she was excited about heading down into the crater, given it was one of the best places in Africa to view animals in their natural habitat.

Outside the villa, Silly was standing next to the Land Rover dressed in his neatly pressed safari uniform and bush hat. Scarlett snapped a picture of him with the Nikon camera hanging around her neck, then they were off, traveling west along the crater rim. Early morning dew coated the long grass and shrubs while a thousand birds chirped and whistled and sang in the branches overhead. At the gate to the crater, a green sign announced that the caldera was a conservation area, a world heritage site, a biosphere reserve, yadda yadda. Scarlett told Sal to go stand in front of it so she could snap a photo. He was having none of it. He might be many things, but a picture guy he was not.

Seneto Descent Road was the official name of the road that switch-backed down the interior wall of the crater. Silly, however, referred to it as the Elephant Pass, which Scarlett found to be more fitting. It wasn't so much a road but a narrow, winding, and very steep dirt track.

As they progressed, the morning mist thickened, creating a primordial, Jurassic atmosphere, as if they were not only descending into a collapsed volcano but back in time as well. At one point the track tiptoed along the edge of a sheer cliff face that plunged away hundreds of feet to the crater floor below. A signpost with the words "POLE POLE"—which Silly translated to mean "Slowly Slowly"—drifted past in the curdling fog.

Scarlett looked away from the window. The memories of Laurel Canyon were still raw. And if she went over the edge here, she wouldn't be waking up in a hospital; she wouldn't be waking up anywhere ever again.

Her anxiety, however, turned out to be for naught. Thirty minutes later bright sunlight pierced the thinning fog, and by the time they reached the bottom—thank God—the weather was postcard perfect. The view was just as spectacular as it had been from the lodge. The soda lake shimmered pink with thousands of flamingos. The savanna, which was dotted with yellow fever trees and gently undulating hills, stretched away like spun gold. And in every direction the rocky walls of the caldera towered high, a forbidding barrier to keep the outside world out.

"Look!" Silly said, slowing to a halt and pointing to a patch of tussock three hundred feet to the left of them.

Scarlett poked her head out the Land Rover's modified roof and peered through the binoculars. She zeroed in on a cheetah that was stretched out on its side, its long, thick tail curled behind it. She passed the binoculars to Sal, wiping the sweat from her brow with the back of her hand. Damn hot. And it was barely eight in the morning.

Silly snatched the CB microphone from the radio unit attached to the dash, depressed the transmit switch, and said something in Swahili. His small face melted into a frown. He fiddled with a few knobs, flicked between channels, and spoke again.

"What's wrong?" Scarlett asked him.

"The radio isn't transmitting."

"Who do you need to speak to?"

"I was going to call in the cheetah sighting, so the next group down the Elephant Pass will spot it." He shook his head in frustration. "It works both ways. Now we will not hear when any of the Big Five are spotted."

"Maybe the antenna's broken?" Sal suggested.

Silly went around to the back of the Land Rover and examined the tire carrier. He returned to the front seat and said, "It's gone, the entire antenna, gone. It must have snapped off in the bush. Or maybe an animal snagged it during the night." He looked devastated. "I'm sorry. This is my fault. I should have checked the vehicle before we left."

"Cheer up, boss," Sal told him. "We're only passing through the crater. It will be more of an adventure this way."

Scarlett squeezed his thigh, grateful for his understanding.

As they progressed west across the crater floor, they saw more gazelles and zebras and buffalo than she could count. She glassed the grasslands through the binoculars for a bottleneck of Land Rovers, hoping it would indicate a predator sighting. The strategy paid off. The first gathering led them to a chilled-out leopard lounging in the crotch of an acacia tree, the second to a pack of spotted hyenas making whooping-giggling noises while tearing apart the ribcage of an antelope with their bone-crushing jaws.

When Silly mentioned they were coming up to a picnic spot, Sal told him to pull over so he could use the restroom. They still had a long trip ahead of them, and Scarlett decided a visit to the ladies' room might be prudent. She went to the single-person cinderblock lavatory and waited outside for Sal to finish. She was watching a secretary bird wading through the tall sere grass, stomping about on its long legs, when she heard Sal talking on his cell phone. She went a little closer, but only caught one or two words before he hung up. He exited moments later and gave her a curious look.

"I need to go too," she said.

"Be my guest."

Scarlett did her business, then went to the sink to wash her hands, all the while wondering who her husband had been speaking to. And why in the restroom? Why not in front of her?

She glanced in the mirror on the wall, tracing her fingers around her eyes, as if she could magically erase the small wrinkles forming there.

"You're thirty now, Scarlett," she said to herself. "Happy birthday. These are your stripes. You've earned them—and you only get more."

Her thoughts turned to Marie Dragomiroff, the thirty-six-year-old, dark-haired, dark-skinned heir to a French shipping conglomerate. The woman could speak six languages, had her own successful clothing line, and her exotic beauty upstaged anyone in the room with her, whether it be a prince, rock star, or Scarlett herself. Their first and only meeting had been at a Washington fundraiser the year before. Scarlett remembered the day perfectly. Marie had been dressed in something elegant and of her own creation, looking ten years younger than she was, working the room effortlessly, a fluttering butterfly, a natural socialite, the faces of the lawmakers and powerful business types smiling when she approached, their eyes following when she moved on.

The way she flattered Sal, innocently touching his arm...

*How had I not known earlier?*

She closed her eyes, rubbed her forehead.

She left the restroom.

Back at the Land Rover, Silly pointed to the sky, where a swelling of dark storm clouds was gathering. "We need to be quick," he said. "If there is a storm, the rain could wash out parts of the road up the crater wall."

"What would happen then?" Scarlett asked. "Would we be stuck here overnight?" She shivered at the thought of spending the night on the floor of an enclosed crater that was home to the highest density of mammalian predators in Africa.

But Silly shook his head. "That cannot happen. The rangers would come and get us."

"Even with the road washed out?"

"There are other roads in and out of the crater that I do not know of. They would find a way."

"The radio isn't working, remember? How would we call them?"

"They would know," he said simply, though she thought she saw a flicker of doubt cross his eyes.

Silly climbed behind the wheel of the Land Rover while Sal and Scarlett got in the back. Thunder rumbled in the distance. Low, angry clouds moved in front of the sun, darkening the sky. Scarlett could smell ozone and the general grayness that accompanies a storm. Then the rain began to fall. It made a tinny plink-plink-plink on the truck's roof and patterned the dirt track with brown splotches. Within thirty seconds it had become a downpour. The windshield wipers sloshed back and forth, only just clearing the water now gushing down the windshield. A clap of thunder exploded so loudly it made her flinch, and she silently urged Silly to go faster.

They reached the western crater wall five minutes later. A sky-wide flash of lightning stung the sky white, illuminating what looked like a pencil-thin road zigzagging its way up the rocky slope. Scarlett's stomach dropped. Two thousand feet looked almost insurmountable from the bottom up. Nevertheless, Silly barely slowed as he reached the steep gradient, and she relaxed. They were fine. They were going to make it—

Scarlett heard a loud clunk, followed by a grinding noise.

"What was that?" she said, stiffening in her seat.

"I don't know," Silly said. "The message center is telling me to put it in neutral."

"Then do it, man," Sal told him. The grinding noise was getting louder.

Silly downshifted. The Land Rover came to a quick stop, then began rolling backward.

"Put it in park, for chrissake!" Sal said.

"It's not working!"

The backward momentum picked up.

"Do something!" Scarlett said. She looked out the back window, but couldn't see anything through the rain and poor light.

Silly yanked the handbrake. The Land Rover shuddered to a stop.

"Leave the brake, but put it in first and try again," Sal told him.

"It's not letting me. I can't move the gearshift anymore."

"Step on the gas."

"I am. Nothing is happening. Nothing."

"What the hell?" Sal opened the door and stepped into the storm. He circled the truck, kicked the tires, and bent twice out of sight. He tapped on Silly's window. Silly rolled it down. "Can you lock the differential?"

"Yes."

"Do it. Then try the gas again."

Silly followed the instructions but shook his head. A crackle of lightning backlit the black clouds, turning them a mossy green. More ear-splitting thunder followed. Swearing, Sal climbed back inside. He was soaked to the skin.

"Power is sapped," he told them. "It isn't reaching the wheels. That means the problem has something to do with the transmission. I thought it might have been the differential."

"What's that?" Scarlett asked.

"It transmits torque to the four wheels evenly, even if they're rotating at different speeds. If one was spinning on mud, it would deliver all the power there, effectively making us immobile. But Silly locked it, making both wheels on the axle turn at the same speed, regardless of traction. That did nothing."

"So we're stuck?" This was exactly what she'd feared. "There's no radio. We can't call for help."

"Do you think anyone's still in the crater?" Sal asked their guide.

"I don't know. Maybe. Wait! Someone's coming!"

Scarlett looked out the rear window again and saw the headlights of a vehicle approaching. Sal hopped outside and waved it over. He had a few words with the driver, then motioned for Scarlett and Silly to join him. Scarlett ducked her head and dashed through the pelting rain to the idling vehicle, some kind of big four-by-four, like the Land Rover. She tugged open the back door and climbed inside, Silly right behind her. Sal got in the front.

She was about to thank the driver for stopping, but the words died in her throat. "You!" she exclaimed.

Sal looked puzzled. "Benjamin Hill?"

The Irishman extended his hand. "Indeed I am. Your wife must have mentioned our brief encounter?"

"Yes." Sal shook. "Call me Sal. This is our guide, Silly."

"What an interesting name." He smiled. "Now, what's the problem, may I ask?"

"The truck lost all power going up the road," Sal explained. "It's not the differential. Could be a worn ring and pinion gear."

"I can't help you there, unfortunately. I'm afraid I know rather little about mechanics. What I can do, however, is give you

THE TASTE OF FEAR

all a lift to the top."

They got underway, and Scarlett was incredibly grateful to be moving again. Sal fiddled with a knob on the dash until the vents blasted out warm air. A CD played Latino music on very low volume.

"So you're here on safari by yourself?" she asked the Irishman.

"I'm in Africa on business, Miss Cox. A coworker recommended Ngorongoro Crater."

"What do you do, Ben?" Sal called everybody by their first name.

"My firm specializes in risk analysis."

"Well, if you're looking for a risky place to do business, you found it."

Sal and the Irishman talked shop for another few minutes before moving on to their golf games. When Sal started on his hole-in-one story, which involved several Japanese investors and requisite gift-giving, Scarlett tuned out. She'd heard it many times before.

Half an hour later they reached the summit of the crater.

"If I recall correctly, Miss Cox," the Irishman said as the truck bumped and slid over the muddy road, "you mentioned you were heading to the Serengeti today?"

"Yes, that's right. But it seems like we're going to be delayed, seeing as we have no vehicle."

"Would you like me to take you back to your lodge, where you can get some sort of transportation arranged?"

"That would be marvelous! But is it out of your way?"

"What else does an old man have to do with his day?"

"Hold on, Ben," Sal said, leaning forward to peer out the windshield. "Yes. Slow down. I think that's a park ranger's vehicle up ahead."

"Nonsense," the Irishman said. "I have no problem driving you back myself."

"Pull over."

"Really, Mr. Brazza—"

"Dammit, Ben, pull over."

For a crazy moment Scarlett thought the Irishman was going to continue driving straight past. But then he eased to the side of the road next to the parked vehicle. Sal got out and knocked on the ranger's window. The ranger set aside his radio and wound the window down. Sal began talking and gesturing. When he returned, he told Silly to transfer their luggage to the other vehicle.

"What's going on?" Scarlett asked.

"I offered the guy some money to drive us to the Serengeti. Now we won't have to waste time going back to the lodge and waiting around for another truck."

"What about the one down in the crater?"

"I'll have someone back at the lodge take a look at it. Silly can return today with the ranger instead of tomorrow as originally planned and pick it up."

It sounded good to Scarlett. She said, "Looks like we'll be getting out now after all, Ben. Thank you so much for the lift. I hope you have a fabulous time here."

"Thank you, Miss Cox," the Irishman replied, giving her a strange smile. "The same to you."


AS FITZGERALD WATCHED Brazza and Cox get into the ranger's Land Rover and drive away, he continued to smile to himself, both pissed off and amused at how one unknown variable could throw a wrench in the most simple of plans.

Originally he'd planned to take the two of them plus the guide down the road toward their lodge, beat them all senseless, and leave their bodies in the forest for the wildlife to feast upon. By the time morning came and a search party was organized, there would be little left of their remains to be found, certainly not enough to determine their true cause of death. Investigators would be forced to conclude that when their vehicle broke down, they'd attempted to leave the crater on foot, got lost on the way back to their lodge, and were attacked by an animal and eaten. It happened more than most people thought.

What bad luck running into the bloody ranger. For a moment he had considered driving on, but if the ranger spotted Brazza or Cox in the cab, and reported this fact when their bodies were found, the circumstances surrounding their death would be much more closely scrutinized. That was unacceptable. The reason he was getting paid so handsomely for this job was because Brazza's death had to look like an accident. More than that, Fitzgerald's reputation was at stake. There weren't many assassins of his caliber for hire in the world, and news of a sloppy hit spread quickly.

He lit a Kent, shoved the gearstick into drive, and started after his quarry.

They would not get so lucky a second time.

# CHAPTER 8

A S THE LAND Rover wound down through the western crater highlands, leaving Ngorongoro Crater behind, it continued to rain lightly, though the worst of the storm had passed.

"So you and Ben seemed to have hit it off," Scarlett said to Sal. They were in the backseat, Silly up in the front with the ranger.

Sal had changed into a dry set of clothes and was now puffing thoughtfully on one of his cigars, blowing the pungent smoke out the window. "Did he say what lodge he was staying at?"

"I don't think so. Why?"

"If I remember correctly, there are only four or five lodges up there on the rim. I don't recall any as far west as ours. Why would he be leaving via the western wall?"

"Who knows? Maybe because he was closest to it when the storm broke?" She paused, wondering how to broach the next subject. Blunt was best, she decided. "I heard you speaking on your phone earlier."

"When?"

"At the picnic stop—you were in the restroom."

Sal appeared momentarily annoyed. Then his face smoothed over and he took another puff of the cigar. "It was Danny again."

That's who she'd expected. "You can speak with Danny in front of me, you know."

"He called. I was in the restroom. I answered the phone.

What's the big deal?"

"I didn't hear your phone ring."

"It was on vibrate. What is this? I feel like I'm getting the third degree. I feel like..." He trailed off.

She knew what he was going to say. "I wasn't implying—"

He waved the matter aside. "It was Danny," he said firmly.

"I know. I believe you."

"Then what's with the interrogation?"

"I just don't think I'm getting the entire story here."

"What story? I told you about the fire."

"But what else is going on? Have the police found something out? Has Danny? I'm worried about you."

"I told you it's under control."

"I want to know, dammit!" she said. "No more secrets between us, Sal. I don't care how big or small, just no more secrets."

He stared at her, hard, like he wanted to make this into a fight. In the end he shook his head and sighed. "I think you have more Italian in you than I do, cara mia." He took a final puff on the cigar, then tossed it out the window. "Do you want me to tell you what Danny told me?"

"Please."

"He thinks he knows who set the fire."

Scarlett's heart skipped a beat. "Who?"

"A man named Don Xi. In fact, you may remember him. You met him once."

"Don Xi?" she repeated slowly. The name, pronounced Zee, sounded vaguely familiar. Then it hit her. Last spring she'd been in Macau with Sal while he looked at potential sites for a future casino along the Cotai Strip. They'd had lunch with this man, this Don Xi. He was one of Sal's partners. "Yes, I do remember him now. But he's just a frail old man."

"He's also part of the Chinese syndicate that held a de jure monopoly on gambling in Macau for the past forty years. Consequently, he's made a lot of powerful friends—which include half of Asia's organized crime ring."

"And he's your partner?"

"Was."

"What happened?"

"After the Macau government ended the monopoly system there in '02, a number of casino operating concessions were put up for tender. I didn't win one. So as a last resort, yes, I partnered with Don Xi, because he had a license."

"Knowing he was a criminal?"

"He has criminal connections, sure. But you check his Rolodex, you'll also find the private numbers for the Clintons, Thatcher, half the world leaders. The world's not so black and white at the top. You know that."

She shook her head. They were getting distracted. How Sal knew Don Xi wasn't what was important. "Why would he want to kill you?"

"The man was impossible to work with. We clashed over everything, from the number of VIP suites to who was supplying us with the fucking steel. Being in Dubai finishing up the hotel, I couldn't oversee every decision. But I was to be informed of the major ones. I wasn't. Xi had started calling all the shots. I had enough. I had a talk with the directors and we got Xi to walk—and we kept his license."

"How'd you manage that?"

"Our lawyers were better than his." Sal shrugged. "Anyway, it seems old Don didn't take it all very well."

Scarlett felt numb. It was a lot of information to take in. So Sal knew who had set the blaze at the Prince. Okay. That was good news. That was fantastic news. Better someone he knew than someone who could disappear, maybe to come back and pick up where he left off another day. However, the fact this guy was some sort of Asian crime lord meant he had a lot of cash and a lot of connections, which meant he could do pretty much anything he wanted.

Like try another hit.

"Have you told the police?" she asked.

"Not yet," he said.

"Why not?"

"Danny doesn't have enough proof."

"So what? Let the police get the proof themselves."

"We tip the police off now, Don Xi gets tipped off. By the time the police mount any sort of investigation, Don will be so clean his balls will squeak."

"At least if he knows that you know, and that others know, he won't try anything else."

"He won't try anything else, regardless."

"How do you know that?"

"I know what I'm doing, cara mia. Let me handle this."

She started to protest, but he held up his hand. "I don't want to talk about it anymore."

"Listen to me, Sal," she said, gripping his forearm. "Danny isn't MacGyver. This isn't a game. Don Xi tried to kill you. He might try again. You have to go to the police."

"You heard what I said." He turned away from her and looked out the window.

Scarlett clenched her jaw tight. He was impossible sometimes. Maddeningly impossible. If they'd been in LA or Dubai or Paris—or anywhere that had a goddamn infrastructure in place —this would be the time she'd hop out of the car and do some shopping to cool off.

A faint thrumming had started behind her left eye, matching the beat of her pulse, and she knew another migraine was coming on.

# CHAPTER 9

*Wednesday, December 25, 7:03 a.m.*

*Macau, China*

A S XI DONG stood in the doorway of his son's bedroom, watching the boy sleep, he smiled to himself. His life had turned out well. He was a very lucky man. But his good fortunes had not come easy. It had taken perseverance and hard work and passion to transform his thirty-five thousand dollar inheritance into the multibillion dollar empire he helmed today.

The inheritance had come after his parents had died in a plane crash somewhere over the Rocky Mountains in August of 1955. He had been twenty-three. Instead of blowing the money, however, he invested the entire lot in a logging company after he learned the provincial government of British Columbia granted logging companies large concessions on land at discount prices. With his considerable profits, he built a chopstick factory and exported the chopsticks to Japan and China, eventually expanding throughout Southeast Asia. In 1960 he moved his head office from Canada to his ancestral country of Hong Kong, to a large building on Nathan Road, which was still referred to as the Golden Mile in those days. Three years later he joined a group of wealthy businessmen who won the bid for all forms of gambling in Macau. And since then everything he touched had turned to gold, from shipping to banking to a newly opened theme park.

Nevertheless, more than any of this, the reason Xi Dong thought he was the luckiest man in the world was his son, Ka-chun. Xi's first two wives had failed to provide him with a child. By the time he married his third wife, Zhang, he was seventy-one, what he thought would be too old to produce an heir to his vast empire. But within months of their wedding day Zhang became pregnant. It was the happiest day of his life, and ever since his heart had been full of pride and joy.

Xi closed the door to his son's bedroom, then went down the hall to Zhang's office. She was sitting in front of the computer. Shopping, he thought. "I'm going to walk the dog," he told her.

She had been born in Guangxi and spoke Zhuang and Mandarin, not Cantonese, so they communicated in English.

"Okay" was all she said. She didn't look at him.

They were in the middle of a prolonged fight that had begun after she discovered various rooms in his various casinos were permanently occupied with a close circle of mistresses who called him "master." He was trying to make it up to her with expensive gifts. He didn't have the energy for another divorce, and Ka-chun needed a mother.

In the kitchen, he found the white-and-brown shih tzu asleep on the slate floor. "Leash," he said in Cantonese.

Sun immediately leapt to his feet, spun in a circle, then disappeared from the room, returning moments later carrying his leash between his jaws and wagging his tail furiously. Xi hooked the clasp to the dog's nylon collar and went outside.

October to December was his favorite time of year in Macau because it was neither too hot nor too humid. Tonight it was overcast, and he could not see the ocean, but the sulfuric smell of decomposed plankton and seaweed told him it was low tide.

As he crossed the villa's landscaped yard to the high stone fence, Sun scurried ahead of him, tugging at the leash. At the gate he started yapping loudly.

"Hush," Xi ordered, punching a code into the alarm box.

It buzzed. He shoved the gate open and stepped through the Roman archway. As he was pulling the gate closed behind him, something hard was pressed into his back.

"Walk," a man's voice commanded in English.

"What is this?"

"Walk. Or I carry you. Limp."

Xi walked while Sun barked away at his side. Unfortunately, he was no guard dog. Nobody else was on the street, which wasn't surprising. It was late, and it was a very private neighborhood.

The stranger directed him to a black minivan parked alongside the curb. "Open the side door."

Xi refused. "Do you know who I am?"

"I know exactly who you are, *koos*. That's why I'm here."

Xi felt a sharp whack on the back of his head, then consciousness fled.


WHEN XI DONG came around he was in a dark room. The air was musty and smelled of concrete and sawdust. He tried to move, but his hands and ankles were fastened to the chair in which he was seated. A gag was in his mouth. Where was he? In a basement somewhere? A construction site? How long had he been out for? He didn't have answers to any of those questions, but his throat and eyes were dry, which meant he was dehydrated, a consequence of being unconscious for a substantial amount of time.

He turned to see what was behind him, and a smoldering pain awoke in the back of his skull. He grunted. Moments later he heard footsteps approach. A gas lantern in a far corner of the room cast enough light to reveal the man who appeared on his right. He was young, muscular, dressed entirely in black, and moved with a confident swagger. Xi recognized him immediately. He'd seen him enough times over the past year. His name was Danny Zamir, and he was Salvador Brazza's muscle—the same muscle who'd rescued Brazza from the Prince Tower fire. But he was more than a mere bodyguard. At least, that's how Xi read it. Zamir showed deference to his boss, of course, but Xi didn't think Danny Zamir believed he was beneath any man, regardless of their wealth or power.

It was an extremely cocky paradigm. It was also an extremely naïve one.

"I'm going to ask you a few questions, old man," Zamir said. "I want you to nod your head if the answer is yes, and shake it if the answer is no. Do you understand me?"

Xi only glared at him. Despite his predicament, he did not jump through hoops for anyone, especially this snake.

Zamir went behind the chair, and Xi heard the light grating noise of metal being dragged on concrete. A pipe? He tried to turn his head again, but couldn't see anything. He gave up and stared forward. His heart pounded inside his chest.

*What was coming?*

From the corner of his eye, Xi caught a flash of movement—something silver—moments before pain exploded in his right kneecap. The gag muffled his scream. He writhed in misery and fury until the chair toppled over. His head smacked the ground, like a bowling ball hitting the hardwood on the lane. Dazed, he remained on his side. Cold concrete pressed against his cheek. His breathing came in rough, animalistic snorts through flaring nostrils.

Danny Zamir's black boots appeared a few feet from his face. The steel club face of a putter appeared in front of the boots. "Was the Prince Tower fire set deliberately?" His voice seemed to be coming from somewhere far away.

Knowing he was already a dead man—you didn't kidnap and torture the most powerful man in Macau, then let him go, not if you wanted to live past the next sunrise—Xi remained silent. To forget the pain, he concentrated on what he'd be doing to Zamir right then if their positions were reversed.

Suddenly he was being swung through the air as the chair

was righted.

"Was the fire set deliberately?"

"Go to hell." He could barely muster the words.

With a curt laugh Zamir ruffled Xi's hair, like you do to little children. Somehow that gesture was worse than the putter to the knee. It was humiliating.

Zamir went behind the chair again. Xi's muscles tensed involuntarily in preparation for the inevitable assault.

Nothing happened.

Five seconds became ten. Thirty stretched into a minute. Two minutes passed, three. And against every instinct Xi found himself relaxing. Zamir wasn't going to do it. He didn't have the balls—

Xi Dong's other knee, his good knee, dissolved into a sea of white-hot needles. The gag stifled his scream once more.

"Was the fire set deliberately?"

"Go to hell."

Zamir slapped him across the face. "I can do this all day."

"You're dead . . . a dead man."

Another slap, harder. "Was the fire set deliberately?"

Xi barely heard the question. He was slipping into the numbness of unconsciousness.

At some point pain catapulted him from his stupor. His eyes slashed open. There was a table beside him now. No, not a table —an industrial drum of some sort. It was standing vertically. His left arm was strapped to the flat top with silver duct tape.

His ring finger was gone, he noticed in a hazy epiphany of horror. Completely gone. The stump where the finger had been was spurting blood. Xi turned his head, not wanting to look at the butchery, and his eyes fell on Danny Zamir, who held a knife in one hand and the dismembered appendage in the other. The gold wedding band Zhang had given him winked in the feeble light.

"I'm getting tired of this game, *ben zona*," Zamir said. "I'm also getting hungry. So I'm going to ask you one final time whether the fire was set deliberately. But"—he shook the severed finger meaningfully—"I want you to think about your answer carefully. Because if you tell me to go to hell one more time, I'm going to go back to that nice little beach house of yours, round up your nice little wife and boy, and bring them here to join the party—"

"No!" Xi hissed, though the word might only have been inside his head.

The gag was torn away. He gulped in a mouthful of air.

"What did you say?"

"Ka-chun—"

"Did you arrange the fire?"

"Yes," he breathed. He had no choice. He would die one hundred times to protect his son.

The world went black again, inky. Xi heard a series of beeps. A cell phone? He heard words being spoken. Felt the phone press against his ear.

"Don't go away just yet, old man," Zamir told him. "Your partner wants to have a word with you."

# CHAPTER 10

*Wednesday, December 25, 2:58 p.m.*

*Serengeti National Park, Tanzania*

S CARLETT'S MIGRAINE WAS just waning when they arrived at Naabi Hill Gate, the eastern entrance to Serengeti National Park. The digging behind her left eye had been maddening for the past several hours, the gnome on the drill in a particularly evil mood. But the three aspirin she had taken seemed to have helped. So, too, had the big Dior sunglasses she wore to combat the migraine-induced photophobia.

As the ranger drove them through the vast yellowish-brown grasslands, patches of blue sky began to form between the dreary clouds, lightening her mood. What buoyed her even more were all the animals they passed. Dozens of burly roan antelope with their ringed, sweptback horns hanging out beneath the branches of an umbrella tree. Ungainly looking Coke's hartebeest, which were built like horses, grazing nervously on red grass. A harem of Bambi-like dik dik hiding within a patch of whistling thorn. At one point the ranger had to swerve to avoid hitting a warthog and her piglets, which had darted out across the muddy road, each of their little tails pointing skyward, like antennae.

Along the way Scarlett snapped thirty or forty pictures, including two of Sal, which, admittedly, she did to irk him. She told him she was going to put them on her Facebook page, which irked him even more. Although he had acquiesced and said he would give Danny one last day to do whatever he was doing before he went to the police, she was still miffed with him. It didn't make sense. She should have been happy with the compromise. But she wasn't. She thought it was because Danny was still number one in Sal's eyes. Sal was choosing Danny over her, or something like that. It was petty, but she couldn't help it. She really didn't like Danny Zamir.

The ranger shouted over the noise of the engine for them to put on their seatbelts. Scarlett promptly obeyed, wondering what he knew that she didn't. Suddenly the Land Rover swung off the dirt track they'd been following west and jerked over the uneven ground through a forest of strangler figs. The trees thinned and they emerged in a clearing shaded by an immense kopje. They stopped beside a doused bonfire. Sal paid the ranger whatever they had agreed upon, and he and Scarlett got out while Silly unloaded their luggage.

Scarlett barely had time to give the ranger a tip before a bald, barrel-chested man dressed in khakis emerged from the nearby mess tent and called jovially, "Mr. Brazza? Miss Cox? Merry Christmas! And welcome to the Safari Moving Camp. Cooper's the name, and wildebeest are the game!" He pumped both their hands with equal enthusiasm. "Sorry about the rough jaunt in, but it's too dangerous to set up out in the open. You'll understand if I don't want to wake up smack-dab in the middle of a sea of wildebeest."

"We didn't see any on the way in," Scarlett said.

"That's because they haven't arrived yet."

"Do they need an invitation?" Sal remarked.

"Predicting where the herd is going to be isn't an exact science, Mr. Brazza. They follow a general migration pattern. But their speed and direction are determined just as much by the weather. Where it's raining, to be precise. They may congregate in one area for two days or five days, it's impossible to say for certain."

"So you're saying we're not in the right position?"

"Oh, we're in the right position. They'll be coming down this way, that's for sure. They just might not be getting here today, that's all."

"But we're only here for one day," Scarlett pointed out.

"Don't you worry about a thing, love. That's why we have the balloon. As soon as you're ready to go, I'll show you more of those ugly beasts than you can count. In the meantime, come with me." He led them to the mess tent. "Kitoi!" he bellowed. "Get out here and meet our guests."

A lanky black man wearing loose trousers and a plaid button-down shirt emerged through the zippered door.

"This is Kitoi," Cooper announced. "Or Kit, if you can stand being affectionate toward him. He's my tracker, and the best I've ever seen. He can follow the spoor of a chipmunk through Times Square."

Kitoi smiled at the compliment, showing very white teeth. "That is true. Without me, Mr. Cooper cannot even find his boots in the morning."

"His English is better than his humor. Now, let's head around the tent. You're late for lunch. Mind you, watch where you step."

"Snakes?" Scarlett said.

"Shit. Great piles of it, love. Giraffe, rhino, elephant—you name it."

They arrived at a small outdoor table done up with a red-and-green tablecloth, red candles, china, crystal, and silver. Scarlett appreciated the Christmas touch. Kitoi apologized for not having turkey and served them duckling sautéed in curry tomato sauce, cooked bananas, potatoes, cassava, ugali made with white cornmeal, and papaya for dessert. A couple of lilac-breasted rollers and ring-necked doves hovered nearby throughout the meal. Scarlett suspected they were either hungry themselves or trying to see if it was their buddy on the menu. After the late lunch, all four of them packed into the double cab of a Toyota Hilux and drove to an open patch of grassland about a mile from camp.

"We're lucky with the weather," Cooper told them as he unloaded the balloon equipment from the bed of the pickup. "Meteorological conditions are lovely after a storm. Visibility and wind speed, perfect. Kit will follow us on the ground so we can pack everything back up when we land."

With everyone lending a hand, the balloon assembly went quickly. They stretched the rip-stop nylon envelope on the ground, attached it to the wicker basket with special karabiners, then hooked up the burner to liquid petroleum gas cylinders with intake hoses. A petro-powered ventilator blew cold air into the envelope. Cooper fired a burner to heat the air, which expanded, becoming less dense than the ambient air. The envelope plumped up. When there was sufficient lift, Sal, Scarlett, and Cooper hopped into the basket. The tear-shaped balloon rose from the ground. Below, Kitoi untied the anchor rope that was attached to the Hilux's bull bar, and Sal reeled it in.

Up and up they went until Cooper pulled a cord to open the parachute valve at the crown of the envelope. Hot air escaped, the ascent halted, and they began to drift horizontally. Scarlett remained holding tightly to Sal's arm, half expecting to hear a loud pop, and for the balloon to zigzag wildly through the sky before crashing back to earth. That never happened, of course, and slowly her fear ebbed. To her surprise, she realized there was no wind because they were moving *with* the wind. She finally let go of Sal's arm, baby-stepped over to the high wicker rail, and peered down. She swallowed back a shot of vertigo. The savanna unfurled beneath them in every direction for as far as she could see, the scattered trees appearing in miniature.

Cooper told them the word "Serengeti" came from the Masai word "*siring*" which meant "endless plains." He pointed to a golden tawny eagle wheeling through the sky, and later, a swirl of dark specs in the distance that he said were vultures circling a potential meal.

Then a long black line materialized on the horizon. As they

sailed closer, the line became a thick column several miles long. Eventually it resolved into an army of wildebeest hundreds of thousands strong. Their bodies, tiny from so high up, coated the ground like a colossal oil spill. Scarlett had never seen anything quite like it before.

"Incredible," she breathed.

"They live in greater concentrations than any other animals on this planet—well, except for us, that is." Cooper opened the parachute valve again, causing the balloon to descend. After fifty feet or so, he released the cord and fired a silent flame. "Whisper burner," he told them. "So we won't scare the beasties."

From the lower altitude Scarlett could make out the wildebeests' long, boxy faces, curved horns, and unruly manes. Their upper bodies were well-muscled, but their hindquarters were slender, the legs spindly, giving them the appearance of being top-heavy. They were making a low, ceaseless bleating, which sounded like a football stadium full of croaking frogs. Burchells zebras were scattered throughout the herd at a count of about one to ten. Scarlett thought they were the ones making the yelping bark.

"Where do they all come from?" she asked.

Cooper gestured vaguely to the north. "From the permanent waters on Kenya's Masai Mara Game Reserve. They come down here during the rainy season because of the abundance of lush grass. In February they'll give birth to almost a half-million calves within a three-week period, right around here."

"The calves would be sitting ducks."

"It's simple mathematics. They're easy prey, yes. But there's only so much a predator can eat in such a short timeframe. It's nature's version of a buffet." He slapped his solid belly. "Stuff yourself now, but you're not allowed to take any home."

A harsh ringtone trilled.

Scarlett frowned.

Another ring.

She zeroed in on Sal. Before she could ask why he'd brought

his phone with him, he stepped away to the far side of the basket, turned his back to her, and answered the call.

FITZGERALD STOOD ATOP the large kopje, watching the hot air balloon drift slowly away until it was nothing more than a dot in the rapidly clearing sky. Below, speeding across the African veldt, the pickup truck followed the balloon's progress. Then both balloon and truck disappeared from sight. He started down the steep-sided rocky hill toward the safari camp. What he had planned wouldn't take a minute.

"IT'S ME," DANNY said. "I'm with our guy."

Sal's blood boiled at the mention of the man who'd tried to kill him. The fact that this particular man was rich and powerful himself, revered as a god in parts of Asia, made the attempted assassination only slightly less insulting.

"Put him on," he said.

Raspy breathing sounded on the other end of the line.

"Hello, Don," Sal said.

Silence.

"I want a name."

More silence.

"Danny!"

Seconds later: "I'm here."

"I told you I wanted him in a talking mood."

A few muffled words followed. What sounded like a sob.

"Yao Wang," Don Xi said weakly.

"Who is he?" Sal demanded.

"I don't know."

"You hired him."

"I never met him. That's not how it works."

Sal cursed under his breath. But at least he had a name. "Is he going to try something again?"

"No."

"Give me Danny."

"Yeah, capo?"

"You heard all that?"

"Yeah."

"Is he lying?"

"I don't know. He's a tough old nut. Wouldn't talk until I mentioned his boy."

"Tell him—" Sal lowered his voice. "Tell him that if we find out he's lying, we're going to…" He trailed off meaningfully. "Tell him now. Then put him back on."

Another muffled exchange. Sal glanced back over his shoulder. Cooper and Scarlett were both staring straight ahead, ostentatiously not listening.

"Please," Don Xi said. His voice was still weak, but it was as clear as it had been yet. "Let my son be. Have honor."

Honor? Sal thought. Where's the honor in trying to roast someone while they slept? "You sure there's nothing more you want to tell me about Yao Wang, Don? You heard what Danny said."

No reply.

"Don?"

A papery sigh. "There is another."

Sal's hand tightened around the phone. He knew it! Goddamn Chinese were as double-faced as a two-headed dragon. "Keep talking, man," he said.

"An Irishman. His name is Redstone. That's all I know."

*Another bloody assassin.*

"You stupid old man. Danny!"

"Yeah, capo?"

"Find out everything you can on this Redstone. Everything. I'll call you later." He punched End, then turned back around.

Cooper raised a bushy eyebrow. "You run a tight ship, captain."

Sal grunted and rejoined Scarlett at the basket rim. "Did I miss anything?"

"I don't want to talk to you right now."

"Why not?"

"Not now, Sal." She moved to the other side of the basket.

He frowned. He'd chosen his words to Danny carefully. She couldn't have gathered much from the snippets of conversation she'd overheard. Nevertheless, he shrugged the concern aside. It wasn't important right then. What was important was what he'd learned.

*There is another… An Irishman. His name is Redstone.*

Sal said to Cooper, "This thing's safe, right?"

"The balloon?"

"It can't somehow catch fire or anything?"

"The skirt's made of Nomex. Completely fire retardant."

"What about these things?" He kicked a propane tank. "Stable?"

"I've never known one to blow up, if that's what you mean."

Sal noticed Scarlett shift her weight from one foot to the other nervously, as if she were suddenly uncomfortable to be hanging out in the sky in a basket. She knew what he was getting at. But she'd already taken her stand. She was mad at him, didn't want to talk to him. Wouldn't break that silence, even now, even when she thought they might be in danger.

Cooper fired the burner in a continuous stream, explaining that they had to clear the herd so they could land and so Kit could meet up with them. As the balloon floated upward, the wildebeest once more dissolved into a dark splash on the earth. At five hundred feet they caught an eastwardly wind and changed course.

Sal's thoughts returned to Don Xi. He hadn't sounded very well on the phone. In fact, he'd sounded as though he was holding onto life by a thread. Sal felt no remorse. *And where the offence is, let the great ax fall.* He didn't know which work of Shakespeare that was from—he'd never been a big Shakespeare guy; life was too short, time too precious, to be reading four-hundred-year-old texts—but he knew that particular verse because his Uncle Frank had told it to him. It was a family motto of sorts.

Sal's great-great grandfather, Rocco, had been part of the original Mafia, or what eventually became known as the Mafia, which arose in the chaotic years after Italy annexed Sicily in the 1860s. By the turn of the century Rocco had become capo of the largest and most influential family in Palermo. When Mussolini tried to wipe out the Mafia and their political allies, Rocco and his wife and son fled to New York City, where he got right back in the protection/racket game.

When the Castellammarese War ended in 1931, and the new boss of bosses created the Five Families of New York, Rocco's son, Bernardo, was made boss of the Monrealesi family. Soon after "Beautiful Bernie"—a nickname he got when a gangster from a rival family dunked his head into a fish tank alongside a housecat with very sharp claws—was murdered thirty years later in his Park Avenue office, his son, Frank, was installed in the vacant post. "Crazy Frank"—whose nickname was self-explanatory—was a shrewd businessman, and before anyone else was doing it he staked out major interests in a casino in Havana, Cuba, and the Riviera in Vegas. Skimming the winnings became the family's most lucrative business. But then everything changed in the seventies. Hippies and free love cut into strip club profits. Off-track betting picked up, taking a chunk out of the bookkeeping operation. And the Feds finally started cracking down on organized crime. To top it all off, big business was moving into Vegas, squeezing the gangsters out. So by the mid-eighties Frank was running a pretty clean shop: waste disposal, restaurants and bars, vending machines, trucking.

During this time Sal had just graduated from college and was working in his father's restaurant. When Frank came by for dinner one night, and mentioned he was looking for a bookkeeper for The Cleopatra, his Atlantic City casino, Sal jumped at the opportunity. After several dull months of analyzing the gaming revenue journal entries, Sal pitched Frank a plan that involved leasing slot machines to third parties, issuing mortgage bonds, and using equity financing to free up capital to reinvest in the casino and improve profit margins. A gambler by nature, Frank went with the suggestions.

Two years later The Cleo's revenue was up forty-four percent while room occupancy had rocketed from sixty-three to ninety-five percent. Sal was promoted to vice president of finance. Over the next ten years he championed a string of successes, which included securing a seventy million dollar long-term mortgage investment from a life insurance giant, the first deal of its kind in the country, to build the largest and glitziest casino in Atlantic City.

Following this, Sal was the driving force behind the creation of the luxury management company Star International, which put up five-star resorts in Mexico, the Bahamas, and Jamaica. In the summer of '95, after the president and CEO of Star suffered a stroke on the seventh hole of Poipu Bay Golf Course in Kauai, Frank, who was chairman of the board, nominated Sal for the top position. The vote was unanimous. At thirty-three years old Sal became the youngest CEO of any company to earn a ranking on Fortune 500 that year.

Then disaster struck. Police found Frank's mutilated body in a dumpster in Manhattan's Little Italy. Sal interviewed nearly fifty ex-soldiers before settling on Danny Zamir as his "security advisor." Danny tracked down Frank's killer, a Columbia Law student named Giuseppe Adamo who was the son of a gangster Frank had knocked off back in the early eighties. Danny took Sal to a ramshackle building on the Lower West Side where the punk was being held. The room smelled like a monkey house. Adamo was lying on the floor, dehydrated and emaciated, surrounded by his own excrement. Sal rolled him over so he could look him in the eyes. Then he left, to let Danny do what he had to do.

Sal kept Danny around as his security chief, but he never again used him for anything resembling the Adamo thing. Until now, that is. Because Don Xi had tried to kill him, and that was simply something he couldn't forgive and forget.

Rocco, Beautiful Bernie, and Crazy Frank would have all concurred.

"We'll land over there," Cooper announced suddenly.

He told Kitoi their coordinates over the radio, then pulled the cord that opened the parachute valve. He remained holding it as the balloon sunk through the air. They came at the ground surprisingly fast, but Cooper bounced the basket across the flat savanna like a stone skipping water until they slowed to a gentle rest.

"Try that in a herd of wildebeest and see what happens," he bellowed. "Lo! There's our ride."

Sal followed Cooper's finger and spotted the Hilux angling toward them from the southwest, shooting up a contrail of dust. When the truck arrived two minutes later, they packed up the balloon and loaded it into the flatbed.

Sal and Scarlett didn't say a word to each other during the long trip back to camp.

# CHAPTER 11

*Wednesday, December 25, 6:38 p.m.*

*Dar es Salaam, Tanzania*

"YOU CAN LEAVE us now," Qasim said to his wife in Arabic.

Raja, dressed in a colorful hijab, picked up an ashtray overflowing with cigarette butts and went inside. Jahja did not know what her body looked like beneath the long garment, but she had a beautiful face. He had thought that for as long as he had known her, though he had never told Qasim this, of course. As a devout Muslim he shouldn't have had such thoughts about his brother's wife. Yet he was a man, and men had thoughts like that, regardless of how strong their faith was.

Jahja and Qasim were sitting on the second-floor veranda of Qasim's house in the Kinondoni District of Dar es Salaam. It was not a bad neighborhood, but it was not a good one either. To the east, Jahja could see the vast expanse of the Indian Ocean; to the north and west, the sprawling buildings of the city. Across the street, on the corner, was a branch of the American Subway restaurant chain. Two men stood outside it, laughing loudly.

"Tell me, brother," Qasim said. "How is Hana?"

"She is good."

"And Sara?"

"She is also good."

"She believes you are in Germany again?"

Jahja nodded. He was a salesman for a German pharmaceut-
ical company. In the past he had often traveled for business to
visit clients. Those trips had ceased after he was burned. The
sales director had never told him the burns were the reason for
keeping him at the London office, hidden away, out of sight. But
a lot of people no longer told him what they were really thinking. Regardless, the decline in business travel coincided with an
increase in personal travel, most of which was to come here, to
Dar, to visit his brother and his associates.

Sara was never the wiser.

"You will see her again," Qasim said.

"Do you believe that?"

"If Allah wishes it, yes." He stabbed out another cigarette in
a fresh ashtray. "You are not having second thoughts, are you,
brother?"

For a moment images of London—the good times in London
—flashed through Jahja's mind. His wedding at Tan Hill Inn in
North Yorkshire, the birth of Hana at St. Bartholomew's, Hana's
first steps at their South Bank flat. Then, as always, those images
vanished as quickly as they had come, replaced by scenes from
the day his life changed forever.

He had been in Algeria, visiting his parents in his ancestral
town of Tamanrasset. They had all been at Friday evening service at the mosque he had attended since he was a child. He and
his father were in the main hall, a barren room devoid of furniture, statues, and pictures; Islam did not condone any form of
representation of Allah. Sara, Hana, and his mother were with
the rest of the woman in a separate area closed off with panels
of fabric. Everybody, however, was faced toward the niche in
the wall that denoted the direction of Mecca. They were reciting the first chapter of the Qur'an when there was a thunderous
explosion and the high ceiling blew inward. Jahja was knocked
unconscious. He woke up in a hospital sometime later, where he

received news that his father had perished—and where he saw himself in a mirror for the first time after the bandages were removed.

Multiple Arab-speaking television networks reported that the destruction was the result of a stray American cruise missile. They cited twenty-three dead and forty-seven injured. Jahja knew this to be the truth because he knew many of the victims personally. The Pentagon and US mainstream corporate media dismissed this reality with "the claims of civilian casualties could not be independently verified."

An all too familiar rage churned inside Jahja.

"No," he told his brother. "I am not having second thoughts."

"Come then," Qasim said, standing. "Let me show you what you have no doubt been waiting to see."

They went downstairs to the attached garage where two white vans were parked side by side. Both were several years old and slightly beat up. Qasim handed Jahja a set of keys and pointed to the van on the left. Jahja unlocked and opened the tailgate doors. The entire cargo body was packed with oxygen and acetylene tanks, bags of aluminum nitrate and ammonium nitrate fertilizer, and truck batteries. Nestled in the center of it all was a small detonation device. The bomb was nearly identical to the two used to destroy the American embassies in Dar es Salaam and Nairobi exactly ten years ago, which killed 224 people, blinded 150, and injured thousands more.

Jahja nodded his approval. "Everybody else is ready?"

"Everybody is ready."

"So what do we do now?"

"We wait until tomorrow," Qasim said, smiling.

# CHAPTER 12

*Wednesday, December 25, 7:33 p.m.*

*Serengeti National Park, Tanzania*

A S SOON AS Scarlett stepped inside the tent she whirled on Sal. "Are you going to explain yourself?"

"Depends," he said, doing the lip-shrug thing.

"That's not the right answer."

"What's gotten you so worked up?"

"You know damn well. But if that's how you want to play it, fine. 'I wanted him in a talking mood,'" she said, repeating what he'd said on the phone word for word. "Or how about, 'Tell him if we find out he's lying, we're going to...'" The words still made her skin crawl.

*Had Sal threatened to kill someone?*

It was unreal. And Danny would do it too, she thought. Whatever Sal told him to do, he would do. She was positive about that. He would kill someone's grandmother if Sal told him to.

"Going to what, Sal?" she demanded.

He met her glare evenly. "Don Xi is a stubborn old mule. I had Danny smack him around a little. If he was lying, Danny was to smack him around some more. It's as simple as that."

She shook her head. "No, what you said, the *way* you said it, was worse than that."

"You make it sound like a big conspiracy, Scarlett. Christ, if I sounded clandestine, it was because I didn't want you or Cooper to overhear. Because one, it's none of Cooper's bloody business. And two, I knew it would only get you all worked up, like you are now."

"I know what I heard," she said stubbornly.

"You're going way overboard here."

"What did Don Xi tell Danny?"

"The name of the man who set the Prince Tower on fire."

"And you wanted this information so you could . . . ?"

"What are you implying?"

"Danny's going to kill him, isn't he?"

"Don Xi?"

"Someone!" Scarlett blurted. "Don Xi. The man who set the fire. I don't know! Don't play dumb with me."

Sal stared at her for a long moment, then turned away. He shrugged out of his jacket and microfleece pullover, messed leisurely through the clothes in his suitcase, chose a cashmere sweater, and pulled it on over his white undershirt. Finally he looked at her again. "I'm going to the other tent," he said in an all-too-reasonable tone that infuriated her.

She stepped in front of his path. "You're not walking away."

"I'm not discussing this with you right now. You're not thinking straight. Why don't you go and lie down for a while?"

"Don't patronize me, Sal," she said icily. "Who are you?"

"Who am I?" he snapped, and something dangerous sparkled in his eyes, something she had only seen in their darkest fights. "You want my street name? My secret identity? Maybe you want to see the costume I wear at night when I go around having affairs and killing people? Because that's what this is all about, isn't it? The affair? You won't drop it, will you? You'll never drop it. You'll never trust me again. Anytime something comes up—a late night at the office, a business trip, a phone conversation with Danny—you're going to automatically think the worst. Well, fuck that. I don't think I can deal with that."

He shoved past her. Scarlett didn't turn around. She heard him unzip the tent door and walk outside. Then she heard him stop.

"The reason I wanted the name of the man Don Xi hired to kill me," he said over his shoulder, tersely, "was so I could turn him over to the police."

He started walking again.

Scarlett frowned. As soon as she'd overheard Sal tell Danny that he wanted Don Xi in a talking mood, half a dozen images of cruel interrogation techniques had popped into her head. Now she was suddenly unsure. Had she misunderstood? What Sal said made sense. It was simple and logical. In fact, it was so simple and logical she wondered why she hadn't thought of it herself.

"Wait," she said, turning.

Sal stopped, faced her. The sun was low in the sky, silhouetting him against a furnace-orange background.

"What about Don Xi?" she pressed. "What's Danny going to do with him now that he has the name of the man he wants?"

"Let him get some sleep? How am I supposed to know?"

"Don Xi's at his home?"

"Sure. Danny went to his house. Where did you think he was?"

Scarlett didn't know. Hanging upside down by his feet from the top of a building? God, she didn't know anything anymore. She felt suddenly exhausted. "Danny was smacking Don Xi around in front of his family?"

"He's seventy-six. He lives alone."

The last of her anger and suspicion seeped away.

"Anyway," Sal went on, his tone business-neutral, "I'm going to get a drink. Dinner will be soon. Join me, if you'd like."

Scarlett stared after him as he made his way through the lengthening shadows to the mess tent. Never in her life had she been so happy to be wrong. Sal was Sal. Not the leader of some two-man vigilante squad, dishing out vengeance where he saw fit. Of course he wasn't.

What had she been thinking?

She shook her head. Sal had been right. She was using the past to explain the present, which wasn't entirely fair. He'd screwed up—big time—but he'd apologized sincerely both in private to her and publicly in front of the media. He wanted a fresh start. After a lot of soul searching, she'd decided she did also. To continue holding the affair over his head was wrong. She needed to commit to him one hundred percent or not at all, and she needed to decide that very soon.

With these thoughts in her head, she followed him through the dying light.


THE MESS TENT glowed from within with warm candlelight, while outside the six-foot-tall tiki torches burned orange and jittery flames. The sun had set fully and the stars had come out, twinkling like a spill of diamonds on black velvet. The air smelled raw and primeval and invigorating. Classical music played from a stereo system somewhere, what sounded like a Bach sonata in F-sharp minor. It was welcoming and relaxing, exactly what Scarlett wanted to hear right then.

Sal was standing beneath the overhanging branches of a large tree. With a glass of Scotch in one hand and a cigar in the other, he looked cool and in control, like a man who didn't allow anything to faze him, not even a wife who accused him of torture and murder.

God, she was a fool.

Cooper was working the smoking barbeque. His long white apron read: "Don't Mess with the Chef!" When he told Scarlett and Sal to take a seat at the table, she impulsively suggested they eat together. It was Christmas day, after all. Cooper said that was a grand idea and added another folding table and two stacking chairs to the dining setup. Kit dished out huge servings of spicy braised chicken, yogurt, and couscous. He opened a five-year-old Chardonnay and, at Scarlett's request, a bottle of local Kinyagi gin.

In his swashbuckling way Cooper led the conversation, re-counting his adventures abroad, from the deserts of Australia and Asia to a two-month stint on the barren ice shelves of Ant-arctica. When he was halfway through a story that had him climbing a frozen waterfall in Switzerland, Sal excused him-self to use the bathroom. Scarlett noticed Cooper watching him leave.

"He's had some disturbing news these past few days," she said by way of explanation for Sal's aloof demeanor. "He hasn't been himself."

"I gathered that much from his phone conversation in the balloon."

"Yes, well, that was part of it."

"How long have you been married, if I may be so bold to ask?"

"About four years."

"He's much older."

"Thirteen years. How about you, Cooper? Are you married?"

He grinned. "Would you marry this ugly mug?"

"I, too, am not married," Kit said. "So if any of your movie star friends are looking for a strong husband and the son of a chieftain, please tell them about me."

Their laughter was broken by a cry.

It was Sal.

Everybody shot to their feet. Scarlett was the first out of the tent. She looked wildly around but couldn't see anything be-yond the firelight of the camp.

"Sal!" she shouted.

He didn't answer.

"Sal!"

Kit and Cooper exchanged a quick look. Kit dashed back in-side the tent and returned carrying two rifles and a heavy-duty Eveready flashlight.

Cooper snatched one of the rifles. "Stay here," he told Scar-lett. "We'll check it out."

"No!" she protested. "I'm coming."

"You'll be in the way."

"He's my husband!"

Cooper started away, Kit beside him.

Scarlett ran to catch up.

"Lord, woman!" Cooper grabbed her wrist and pulled her between himself and Kit. "If you must come, stay in the middle and do exactly as I say."

They moved at a brisk pace in the direction they'd heard Sal cry out. Kit took the lead, playing the beam of the flashlight over the ghostly trees as they moved deeper into the forest that surrounded the camp. Scarlett stuck right behind him, a hand on his shoulder. The ground beneath her feet was spongy and invisible. She stumbled twice. Cooper, taking up the rear, yanked her upright both times.

"Sal?" she shouted again, her thoughts racing. Lions? Hyenas? Assassins?

"Mr. Brazza?" Cooper called urgently.

"Here." The reply was a harsh whisper, surprisingly close.

Kit swung the flashlight around. Sal was less than ten feet away, his back pinned to the trunk of a tree, his eyes fixed straight ahead.

"Sal!" Scarlett ran to him and threw her arms around his neck.

"There," he said, pointing.

She turned. Kit redirected the light.

Numerous pairs of yellow eyes reflected back at them.

"My God," Scarlett said, her breath hitching in her throat. Her legs felt suddenly weak. "What are they?"

"Lions," Sal stated.

"They're just cubs," Cooper said.

"No," Sal told him. "I saw a fully grown one, a lioness."

"Their mum." Cooper nodded. "She wouldn't have left the cubs alone. We better get out of here, slowly. If you see the mum, whatever you do, don't run. She'll be on you in seconds."

They set out in a tight line. Kit in vanguard again, Scarlett and Sal bunched in the middle, Cooper, the rear. Kit forced a much slower path out than the reckless charge in.

"There she is," Kit whispered suddenly, aiming the flashlight to the right.

Two devilish eyes shone back, twenty yards away.

*Good lord, it's following us*, Scarlett thought. No—it's *stalking* us.

Her breathing sounded absurdly loud in her ears, and she wondered if the cat could smell her fear, the way dogs supposedly could. Her heart beat like a tribal drum in her chest.

Several paces later Kit stopped. Scarlett peered anxiously over his shoulder.

The lioness was directly ahead of them now, much closer than before. Powerful and sinewy muscles bunched and knotted beneath the silky flank as it slinked between the trees, silent, ghost-like. The thin tail, the tip marked by a black tassel, snaked back and forth in rhythm to its imperial stride. Faint rosettes spotted the hind legs, tapering down to the paws. Then abruptly, dramatically, the beast swung its head to look directly at them. It snarled in a rictus of menace, baring its yellow fangs and a flash of pink tongue, before turning away again, apparently bothered by the glare of the light in its face. It growled, a low and rumbling sound that came from deep within its throat. Scarlett didn't know whether that was a warning sound or a hungry sound, only that it was blood chilling either way. A second growl answered the first, from somewhere to the left of them.

*There were two lionesses.*

Cooper understood the danger. "Cover your ears!" he ordered, then fired a round from the bolt-action rifle into the sky. The muzzle flash was as bright as daylight. The sound was deafening. The acrid stench of cordite filled the air.

Scarlett searched the trees for either lioness. They appeared to be gone. "Monsters be gone," she breathed. It was a line from a fairy tale she'd read as a child, and she repeated it over and over in her head now, a kind of mantra that would keep the creatures from returning.

Kit pressed forward, moving at the same dreadfully slow

pace. Scarlett wanted to run, but she remembered what Cooper had told them. *She'll be on you in seconds.* Another tense minute passed with still no glow from the tiki torches. It seemed to be taking them a hell of a lot longer leaving the forest than coming in, and she began to question whether they were going the wrong way. God, if that was the case, and they got lost—

There was a commotion to the left of them.

Kit swung the light. Scarlett's jaw dropped. A lioness came barreling toward them through the trees, huge and pale as bone, grunting and snorting.

It seemed to be coming straight for her.

Because she was the smallest?

The weakest?

"Don't run!" Cooper ordered.

"Shoot it!" Sal bellowed.

"Don't move!" Cooper repeated.

Shoot it! Scarlett screamed. But the words never escaped her locked throat. Nothing did except a harsh whistle.

The lioness didn't slow.

It *was* coming straight for her.

*Why isn't anybody shooting it?*

At the last possible moment the lioness skidded to a halt on muscular front legs. It glowered at them, still snorting. It was so close that Scarlett could see the stiff white whiskers, the wet black nose in the shape of an upside-down triangle, the tuft of beard. Its eyes shone like gold-flecked quartz, the pupils rounded to perfect black dots. A killer's eyes. Emotionless, without mercy. The power the cat exuded was tangible. She waited in horror for it to lunge forward and claw off her face with one bat of its oversized paw. But it only snarled, flicked its head, then trotted back into the forest.

The world seemed to tilt crazily before righting itself. Scarlett had to grab hold of Cooper's shoulder to keep from falling over. Still, she felt oddly okay. Terrified, yes. Woozy even. But the fear was tempered by an unrealistic calm, and she knew she must be out of her mind on adrenaline.

"Why—?" she began.

"Later," Cooper said.

The group continued in strict formation through the picket of trees. Sounds Scarlett hadn't realized she'd tuned out returned in a wall of noise. Cicadas, toads, the crunch of their footsteps on the leaf litter, the faint melody of classical music.

The camp.

Scarlett glimpsed the soft yellow light in the distance. The elusive music—Vivaldi's "Summer"—became louder. Given the danger that had just passed, the delicate staccato notes of the violin concerto sounded absurd, like a wedding march at a funeral. Then again, she thought, they also sounded very civilized. Wherever you had Vivaldi playing, you had hors d'oeuvres and wine and doctors and philanthropists. You certainly didn't have a crazy lioness charging you down.

They reached the relative safety of the mess tent without further incident. Stepping into the light was a feeling like no other. The light represented safety and order and control—control over nature and all the deadly things that hid within her nighttime embrace.

Scarlett's adrenaline ebbed, her nerves kicked in, and she began to shake uncontrollably.

"Would you like some tea?" Cooper asked her.

"Why didn't you shoot it?" she demanded.

"She was only protecting her cubs."

"Protecting, my ass," Sal said. "The bitch bloody well charged us."

"If you noticed," Cooper said, "she was flicking her tail back and forth during the charge. That means she's only testing you out. If you hold your ground, she'll usually back down—"

"Hell of a risk," Sal interjected. "It was our lives at stake."

"If I had shot that lioness, the game department could have had my license."

"And had you read it wrong, one or more of us might be dead."

"We wouldn't have been in that predicament, Mr. Brazza,"

Cooper said, getting riled himself, "had you not been out there on your own. What in the Sam hill were you doing?"

Sal didn't reply.

Suddenly Scarlett knew. "You were on your phone."

He shrugged. "I needed to touch base with Danny."

"Why'd you need to go off into the forest?" she said, feeling herself sliding back into the black world of lies and conspiracy. "What's the big secret? What are you not telling me, Sal?"

"I was simply walking as I talked. I had no idea how far I'd gone."

"You're a liar."

"Watch it, cara mia."

"You know," she plowed on, "I was ready to put everything in the past and move on, ready to start over, fresh. How can I do that when you won't be honest with me?"

"I told you, I was walking—"

"I don't care about that! I don't care about that. I don't care about anything anymore. Christ! This is unbelievable."

Sal stared at her, his eyes dark and defiant.

Scarlett turned on her heels and stormed off.

AFTER A FEW minutes of silently venting her anger, Scarlett got herself under control. Cooper, who had followed her into the mess tent and made her tea, was now sitting on the other sofa.

"I'm sorry you had to see that," she told him. "It's not your job to babysit dysfunctional couples."

"Listen, love. I don't know what the two of you are chomping at each other's throats over. Not exactly anyway. And I don't care to know. It's none of my business. But if you don't want to go to the airstrip tomorrow together, I'll have Kit make two trips."

"Thank you, Cooper, but that's all right. Besides, I'll be sitting next to him on the plane."

"Would you like to sleep in here tonight then?"

"Would you mind?"

Cooper retrieved a set of folded sheets and a wool blanket from a chest and gave them to her. "Good night, Miss Cox."

He fastened the three zippers of the door flaps behind him, grabbed a tiki torch that was planted into the ground outside, gave her a final salute, then wandered away into the night.

Sitting there on Christmas day, staring into her cup of tea, Scarlett thought about everything that had happened recently, and slowly, inevitably, she began thinking about a future without Sal.

# CHAPTER 13

THE WEATHER THE following morning was gray and overcast and suited the somber mood that permeated the Safari Moving Camp. It was the kind of mood you experienced at a wake, where nobody wanted to talk to anyone else because there was nothing to say.

Kit offered Scarlett some breakfast. She declined. Her stomach was in knots. That invisible something that held couples together, that made you feel guilty for arguing once tempers died down, that made you want to make things right again...well, that something had shattered, and she didn't think it could be repaired. After everything she and Sal had been through with the affair, she needed more than anything else to be able to trust him again. But she didn't, not after last night. That was a very big problem.

Kit brought her a mug of coffee, which she did accept. It was full-bodied and good. He told her it was made with beans grown on the high plateaus of Mt. Kenya. She told him he should think about quitting the safari thing and open up a café of his own. He smiled but didn't laugh. No one, not even Kit or Cooper, was in a jovial mood that morning.

She returned to their green-and-tan canvas tent to make sure she hadn't left anything behind. Sal was there, packing his suitcase. As soon as she entered he stopped folding the microfleece pullover he'd worn the night before and looked at her. She opened the wooden wardrobe, peeked under the bed, gave the room a final sweep with her eyes.

"If you're looking for me," he said, "I'm right here."

She left without saying a word. Back at the mess tent, Cooper pulled her aside to give her a three-inch curved claw that was fitted with a bronze cap and black string to form a necklace. "It's from a lion I came across a few months back," he told her. "He died of old age. The hyenas got to him long before I did. Anyway, it's not much. But after the excitement in the bush last night..." He shrugged. "I don't know. I thought it would make a good trophy of sorts. Merry Christmas, love."

"Thank you, Cooper," she said, touched. "But I'm afraid I don't have anything for you."

"I have my looks. What more do I need?" He winked at her. "It seems like you're holding up the caravan. Better get a move on."

Scarlett looped the necklace around her neck, gave Cooper a quick peck on the cheek, then went to the Hilux where Kit and Sal were now waiting inside. She climbed in the backseat, next to Sal. Kit hit the gas and they lurched forward. She waved goodbye to Cooper, finding she already missed him.

The off-roading through the forest of strangler figs was just as rough going out as it had been coming in, forcing Scarlett and Sal to once more brace themselves inside the cab. At the east-west dirt trail they turned east. Forty minutes later they arrived at the airport—though it would be a stretch to call it such. Even "airstrip" seemed inappropriate, considering it was nothing more than a belt of dirt lined with white rocks. Ten people stood off to the side of the runway, next to a stack of luggage. Scarlett and Sal waited with them. At a few minutes before ten o'clock, a boy pointed to a silver glimmer in the gunmetal gray sky, which eventually resolved into a plane. The pilot did a low fly-by, likely checking for animals on the runway, then swooped back and taxied to a stop.

Kit came over from the Hilux. "I will be leaving you," he announced.

"Thank you for the lift, Kitoi," Sal said, stuffing some folded bills into the front pocket of the man's shirt. "Aside from nearly letting a lioness eat us, you did a fine job."

He joined the queue to get on the plane.

"Ignore him, Kit," Scarlett told him. "You and Cooper were fabulous hosts."

"*Akipenda chongo huita kengeza.*"

"What does that mean?"

"When in love, a person will always find excuses for their lover." He glanced momentarily at Sal. "I wish you wisdom and prudence, Miss Cox."

Scarlett watched him go, considering his words. Then she climbed the three-step ladder and boarded the plane. It was a twelve-seat twin turbo-prop Beechcraft. Sal called these things pond jumpers; she called them coffins with wings. Even when she was seated her hair, which she'd pulled back into a messy red bun atop her head, barely cleared the roof.

After the pilot loaded the luggage into the cargo hold, the little plane shot down the runway and wobbled into the air. There was no cabin crew, which meant no inflight service. Scarlett still wasn't hungry, but she would have gladly settled for a coffee or tea, simply for want of something to distract herself. She felt awkward and uncomfortable sitting beside Sal, fully aware he was there, pretending he wasn't. It was as bad as riding an elevator with a stranger. She kept expecting him to say something, to break their unofficial non-speaking arrangement. She didn't know what she would do if that happened. Listen to what he had to say? Get into it with him? Ignore him completely?

The ruminations, however, turned out to be pointless. Sal was apparently content to sit there and play by the rules of the game—and he was better at it than she. In fact, he seemed completely indifferent to the negative energy she felt, stretching nonchalantly several times, crossing his legs, even yawning. When he closed his eyes, she couldn't help but wonder if he was taking a nap. She shoved his arm off the armrest they shared and took it over.

Twenty minutes into the fifty-minute-long flight, her rear started to go numb. She shifted her position in the seat and felt something small and hard in her pocket. She took it out. It was the compass-pendant she'd bought at the Arusha market. That's when she realized she was wearing the same zebra-print dress she'd worn on the first day of the safari. It had been simple and easy and the first thing she'd pulled out of her suitcase that morning. She turned the pendant over in her hands, then looped it around her neck, next to the lion claw.

When the plane landed at Arusha Airport, she and Sal collected their luggage and went out front of the blue-trimmed building to hail a taxi.

"Do you need a car, sir?" a black man said, walking quickly toward them.

"We're going to Kilimanjaro Airport," Sal told him.

"No problem, sir. Come with me, sir."

The man led them past well-manicured shrubs and around a corner to a parking lot, where three cars were parked.

Scarlett stopped. "Where's the taxi?"

The man pointed to an idling beige Mercedes. "See?"

"That's not a taxi."

"Don't worry, ma'am. It is a good car. It will get you where you need to go. No problem."

"It's not a taxi."

"Don't worry. It's a good car. No problem."

"You heard him," Sal said. "It's a good car." He got in the back.

Scarlett hesitated. She didn't want to get into an unlicensed taxi. But she didn't see any other option. The other passengers on the plane had already commandeered the two legitimate taxis that had been waiting. She climbed in, wincing as the trunk slammed shut.

The man drove them through the grimy yet colorful streets of Arusha with frightening aggression, honking and swerving and mumbling in Swahili to himself. At one intersection they were almost sideswiped by a truck. Nevertheless, they made it out of the city alive, the buildings giving way to sprawling maize and wheat estates and coffee plantations.

Scarlett broke her day-long silence and said, "I'm not coming to Dubai."

Sal studied her. "Where will you go?"

"Back to LA."

Silence.

"Listen," he said, clearing his throat. "I think we need to talk about—"

Suddenly the driver swerved to the shoulder of the road and slammed on the brakes, throwing Scarlett and Sal forward in their seats. He jumped out of the front, yanked open the back door, and yelled at them to get out.

"What are you—?" Sal cut himself off. "Hey. Okay. Take it easy."

Scarlett leaned forward so she could see past Sal. She gasped. The man was pointing a snub-nosed revolver at them.

Hands raised, Sal got out. Scarlett followed.

"Give me your wallets!" the man said. There was intensity in his eyes that hadn't been there before. Fear or lunacy or bravado or all three. "Fast! Or I shoot you!"

Sal reached into the inside pocket of his blazer and handed over the croc-embossed calfskin wallet Scarlett had bought for him on their honeymoon. She'd chosen it because the designer's name—Salvator—was so similar to his own. For a moment she was furious. Who was this jackass to take it from her husband? But when the jackass pointed the revolver at her, the fury vanished in a heartbeat.

"You too!" he said. "Your wallet. Now!"

Scarlett fumbled around inside her handbag.

"No! The whole bag. On the seat."

She did as he asked.

"Walk away. Go!"

Hands raised again, Scarlett and Sal back-stepped. Good obedient victims, she thought. No one's getting shot over a few dollars here. Take what you want. We got plenty more where that came from.

The man ducked back behind the wheel, slammed the door, hit the gas. The Mercedes' tires spun on the loose gravel, then the car shot away, leaving a cloud of blue smoke and gray dust behind it. Scarlett pictured the scam artist grinning greedily when he went through her wallet later. She must have had five hundred dollars in it.

"Perfect," Sal quipped, waving his hand in front of his face. "Bloody well perfect."

"It's not such a big deal," she said, her voice unsteady.

He arched an eyebrow. "Oh no?"

"No. We'll just cancel our cards."

"I don't know about you, cara mia, but my passport was in my suitcase. And the suitcases are in the trunk of that Mercedes."

She hadn't thought of that. "What do we do?"

"We'll have to get to the nearest US Embassy. I'm guessing that's in Dar es Salaam."

"Will they let us on the flight? I mean, without ID or anything?"

"Grab a magazine and point to your goddamn picture."

Rolling her eyes at him, Scarlett looked around. Mt. Kilimanjaro towered to the north while fields stretched away in every other direction. "Even if they do let us on the flight," she said, "we still need to get from the airport to the embassy. I don't have any money—"

"Do you have your phone?"

"Who do you want to call? *Danny?*" she said, taking a cheap shot. "Think he can get you out of this mess too?"

"Do you have your goddamn phone or not?"

"Do I look like I have my phone, Sal?" She turned in a circle. "Where do you think I keep it? In my bra? My garter belt?" She shook her head. "I knew getting into that car was a bad idea."

"You're saying this is my fault?"

"As a matter of fact, I am. That's exactly what I'm saying."

"The airport can't be more than ten miles away," he said, shading his eyes and looking in the direction the Mercedes had gone. "I'll call the office from there. Get something worked out. Can you keep up?"

Not, "Do you think you can make it?" Not even, "Can you make it?" Just, *Can you keep up?*

That was the last straw. "I've had enough, Sal," she said. "This is too much. Everything. I thought I could cope. I thought we could fix things. I thought we should at least *try* to fix things. But I was wrong. It's not going to work." She took a deep breath, bracing herself for his reaction. "I want a divorce."

He didn't react. Didn't say a word. He simply stared at her for a long moment, then turned away and started walking in the direction of the airport.

Scarlett watched him go, full of mixed emotions. When he was far enough ahead that he began to shimmer in the heat haze, like a mirage that would disappear at any moment, she followed.

# CHAPTER 14

T HE THIRD CAR Scarlett thumbed was a cherry-red Toyota Rav 4. It pulled over twenty feet ahead of her. She caught up to it and opened the passenger-side door, surprised to find a handsome Western man inside. "Thank you so much for stopping," she said above the song on the radio, something funky with an African beat and an Arabesque melody. "I'm going to Kilimanjaro Airport. There's a turnoff just up ahead. If you could take me that far, I would really, really appreciate it."

"No worries," the man said in an Australian accent. "Hop on in."

Scarlett got in, fastened her seatbelt, and they were off.

"I'm Thunder." He offered her his hand, which dwarfed hers.

"I've never heard that name before," she said, shaking his hand. "I'm Scarlett."

"Thunder from Down Under. Thor. I've gotten it all." He shrugged. "Better, I reckon, than Rain or River or Greenland. My mum was a self-confessed flower child back in the sixties."

"Thunder's very nice."

"Thanks." He nodded ahead. "Pretty far walk to the airport."

"I was robbed."

He slanted her a look. "You're having me on?"

"He took everything—wallet, passport, luggage. God, there's my husband!"

She pointed to Sal, who was walking along the same shoulder

she'd been on. For a moment she considered telling the Australian named Thunder to keep driving. Then she considered telling him to slow down so she could flick Sal the bird. In the end she said, "I'm sorry about this, but would you mind giving him a lift as well?"

"Anything for a damsel in distress." He rolled to a crawl to pace Sal.

She hummed down the window. "Get in, Sal. He's giving us a lift to the turnoff."

Sal barely glanced at her. "I think I'll walk."

"Don't be ridiculous."

"I'll see you at the airport."

She shook her head in frustration. "You heard him," she told Thunder. "He's enjoying the exercise."

As Thunder accelerated away, she watched Sal shrink and vanish altogether in the side mirror.

"Is he going to be all right?" Thunder asked.

She shrugged. "He's a big boy."

"Seemed a bit of a grumpy bugger, you ask me."

"We had a fight."

"About the robbery?"

"Among other things."

"Ah, right-o. Personal. Won't say another word."

Scarlett studied the Australian. The top of his head almost touched the roof of the car, and he seemed to be hunched over the steering wheel, like a kid who'd outgrown his Big Wheels. He was well built, lean rather than bulky. His skin was about as dark as Sal's, but from the sun rather than natural pigmentation, which was obvious enough given his neatly brushed blond hair and bright, almost electric blue eyes.

"You know," she told him, "you look like a stereotypical Australian."

"You reckon? Well, I've been called worse things than a stereotype."

"I didn't mean it in a bad way."

"I'm just having a go, hey."

The song on the radio ended and was followed by another with a heavy drum beat.

"You like this stuff?" she said.

"Wouldn't mind some good old Acadaca, tell the truth."

"Aca who?"

"You know. 'Back in Black.' 'Highway to Hell.'"

"You mean AC/DC?"

"Sure. Acadaca."

Scarlett smiled. She liked Thunder.

"I have a few Australian friends," she told him.

"Stereotypes like me?"

"Unfortunately not."

He grinned at her. "Should I take that as a compliment?"

"Take it any way you like," she told him, and felt a sudden flush color her cheeks.

*Was she flirting?* A whole five minutes after telling her husband she wanted a divorce? Nonsense. She was merely having a little fun, letting off some steam. She deserved it after the week she'd had. She'd almost died in a car crash. Learned someone had tried to kill Sal. Was nearly eaten by a lioness. And, if that all wasn't enough, she was now looking at a divorce. So why not have a few laughs with the Australian if it made her feel a little better about everything?

"What do they do?" Thunder asked. "Your Aussie mates?"

"Two of them are actors."

"There's a good gig, I reckon. Read a few lines, blow a few things up, and get paid for doing it."

"Admittedly, I've never heard of acting described quite like that."

"How about the others? Your Aussie mates again. They can't all be actors."

"Just one more. She's a singer."

"Actors and singers." He whistled. "Bloody hell." He peered through the windshield at a passing road sign. "How far is the airport from the turney?"

"The turnoff? I'm not sure. Maybe five miles."

"Tell you what. I'll drive you there myself."

"It's out of your way."

"No dramas. You're the best conversation I've had all arvo."

"You had better conversation this morning?" she teased.

"There was this woman back at the hotel in Arusha. Only had a few teeth, could barely speak English, but she swore she was an aristocrat."

"You were in Arusha?"

"It was base camp for the climb up Kili." He nodded out the window at Kilimanjaro.

"Oh wow." She craned her neck to stare up at the massive snow-capped mountain. "Was it dangerous?"

"Nah. The fourteen in the eight-thousand-meter club are the ones you have to be careful with. Everest, Lhotse, K2..."

"Have you climbed any of those?"

"Not yet. But I reckon I've just found a new hobby. How about you? Safari?"

"How did you know?"

"Every foreigner up this way is either climbing Kili or going on safari. That, or they're with some church group spreading the Good Word."

"Where are you going now?"

"Dar es Salaam."

"You're not flying?"

He jerked a thumb at the backseat. Scarlett turned and saw it was piled high with climbing gear, so much so Sal would have had a tough time squeezing in back there. "More in the boot too," he said. "They barely let me take it on the jet from Brizzie. No way it was all getting on one of those rinky-dinky things that fly up here. Where do you reckon I turn?"

"Not much farther," she told him. "Do you do this a lot? Climb mountains and stuff?"

"I'm a lawyer actually."

"You're kidding."

"Can't see me in a suit?"

She eyed his board shorts and flip flops. The slogan on his T-shirt read: "Kimchi Cures Bird Flu."

"No, I can't," she said with a smile.

"That the turney?"

She made an impulsive decision. "Keep going."

"Wait, there's a sign. This is it." He flicked the blinker.

"Keep going," she repeated.

He gave her a curious look, but didn't slow.

"I'm going to Dar es Salaam as well," she explained.

"You want a ride all the way there?" he said, surprised.

"If you don't mind?"

"Not at all. But what about your flight?"

"Screw it."

"And your husband?"

She shrugged. "Screw him too."

SCARLETT WAS PLEASED with her decision to remain in the car. Not only was Thunder a much needed breath of fresh air, he was genuine, a rare find among her Hollywood crowd. And apparently he didn't recognize her, which was also a refreshing change. She felt like she could be herself, without the pressure of meeting the impossible ideals that people expected movie stars to meet. Indeed, instead of Thunder telling her what she wasn't, he was accepting her for what she was. Moreover, she no longer had to worry about negotiating her way onto the plane, getting from the airport to the embassy, and most of all, Sal. In short, she couldn't have asked for a better stroke of luck than for the Australian to have come by when he did.

During the ride, Scarlett told Thunder a little about the safari, purposely omitting the hot air balloon ride and the lioness attack. The balloon ride was personal. The lioness attack was just plain disturbing to recount, even now, in the light of day.

Then she asked him about his climb up Kilimanjaro. She'd never known someone who'd climbed a mountain before, certainly nothing the size of Kilimanjaro—the only thing most of her friends climbed, including herself, were stair climbers—and she was both fascinated and impressed. According to Thunder, there were a number of routes to the summit. He had taken Lemosho, the longest and most scenic. Seven days of hiking through terrain such as rainforests and snowfields and ice cliffs. He'd hired two porters—a cook and a guide—and they were the ones who'd told him the tales concerning the eight-thousand-meter club, tempting him to give one of them a go. He told her if he ever made it to the top, he was going to hit a golf ball off it, to get into the *Guinness Book of World Records.* She still wasn't sure whether he was kidding about that or not.

"Why did you come to Africa in the first place?" she asked him.

"Short and long of it, my dad died, which made me sort of pause and evaluate my life. And to tell you the truth, I didn't like the direction it was heading."

"You mean as a lawyer?"

"I worked my arse off for the past ten years. Put in the hours, moved up through the firm. But I realized the next ten would be more of the same, and the ten after that. More money, I reckon, more prestige, but nothing new. So I left."

"So you're not on vacation? You actually quit?"

"Best decision I ever made. I finally feel free. Climbing Kili, all I thought about was getting to the top. Nothing else. No deadlines, no clients, no contracts, nothing."

Scarlett realized she was envious of him. "What are you going to do now?"

He shrugged. "No idea. But I've saved up enough to last me a while until I figure it out."

Scarlett wondered if she could ever quit acting just like that. For so many years it had been all she'd wanted to do. Recently, however, the glam was wearing thin, and it was starting to feel more and more like hard work. The early mornings and long hours in the makeup chair, the charity dinners and interviews and photo shoots, the constant pressure of shouldering multi-million dollar productions. Then again, if she ever did quit, what would she do with her time? Sleep in late every day? Climb mountains? Sail around the world?

Sure—why not?

A Swahili hip hop song spliced with an English chorus came on the radio. It was pretty catchy, and they listened to it in silence for a while. She saw another junked car on the side of the road, bringing her number count to twelve so far. Five miles farther on Thunder mentioned he needed gas and pulled into a Shell station.

"*Petroli? Dizeli?*" an attendant said, rushing over as they got out of the car.

"Do whatever you need to do, mate," Thunder told him.

The attendant shook his head, not understanding. Thunder wrapped his arm around the much smaller man's shoulder, pointed to the gas cap, and pantomimed filling the tank. The little guy grinned and got to work. Thunder went to the small service station to pay, and Scarlett, alone for the first time in hours, found herself wondering about Sal. Namely, where he was right then. Probably already at Julius Nyerere International Airport. But so what? Once she reached the US Embassy, she'd get an emergency passport issued, get her manager to wire her some money, then buy a ticket on the first flight back to LA. She'd be home soon enough. She didn't need Sal. She'd made the right choice leaving him back there on the highway.

Thunder returned a few minutes later and said, "Any idea what time your embassy closes?" He handed her an orange juice. "This is the main highway to northern and eastern Tanzania. If it's anything going into the city like it was coming out, then there's going to be heaps of trucks. Traffic's going to be killer."

Scarlett checked her wristwatch. It was two o'clock. Was there a duty officer or someone on staff 24/7 in case of emergencies? She didn't know, and she wondered what would happen if she missed getting to the embassy before it closed. She didn't have money to rent a hotel room anywhere, which meant she would have to find a twenty-four-hour coffee shop and stay awake all night. At least she didn't have to worry about getting robbed again: she had nothing more to give. No, that wasn't true. She still had her watch and jewelry. Could she pawn some of it? Her engagement ring alone would get her a week in the city's top hotel with plenty of change to spare.

"I don't have a mobile," Thunder went on. "But there's a payphone over there. Why don't you ring the embassy?" He handed her a phone card. "I picked this up inside. The phones don't take coins."

Impressed by his thoughtfulness, Scarlett hurried past the pumps to a payphone in a yellow-and-white booth. She scanned the plaque titled "Welcome to Rafiki User Instructions," picked up the receiver, and found the instructions to be redundant as a recorded voice prompted her to choose between either English or Swahili.

Two minutes later she was back at the car. "The embassy closes at six," she said.

"Then let's get cracking," he said. "It's going to be tight."

# CHAPTER 15

THE NEWLY REBUILT Dar es Salaam American Embassy was located along Old Bagamoyo Road at Msasani Village. It was a massive twenty-plus-acre compound, trapezoidal in shape, and gently sloping to the north. The tops of the Chancery and other buildings could be seen above the stone perimeter security wall. Thunder pulled into the staff and visitor parking, stopping next to a land bank that looked as if it was reserved for future development. It was 5:30 p.m., giving Scarlett thirty minutes to spare.

"Thank you so much, Thunder," she said. "You're a life saver."

"You going to be right?"

"If these guys can't help me, who can, right?"

He handed her two yellow fifty dollar bills. "Take this."

"Looks like Monopoly money."

"Aussie money. I've had no problem using it."

"Did you enjoy my company that much?"

"Even if you get an emergency passport issued, you're going to need a place to stay tonight."

"I'll get money wired."

"Banks are closed now."

"Surely the embassy has some service that deals with situations like mine. They'll figure something out."

"And if they don't?"

"I can pawn my watch."

"Don't be daft. I might be unemployed, but I'm not broke yet. Take it."

Scarlett reluctantly accepted the money. "Thank you again, Thunder, really."

She leaned across the seat and kissed him on the cheek, letting her lips linger for a moment or two longer than appropriate.

A loud pop, like a blown tire, startled them apart.

Scarlett snapped her head toward the embassy gate. A Marine was lying on his side, next to an idling white van. Suddenly three more vans screeched around the corner, pulling up behind the first. The tailgates burst open and six men spilled out. They all wore scarves around their faces and carried AK-47s. They immediately sprayed the gatehouse with bullets. One of them lobbed a grenade.

Thunder yanked Scarlett down against the seat and covered her with his body.

The spitfire cadence of the assault rifles on full automatic continued. There was a loud bang—the grenade going off—followed by a motor revving and roaring away in the direction of the embassy.

All of this happened in the space of a few seconds, not more than a hundred feet away. Scarlett was crazily thinking she was on a movie set—the Marine on the ground an actor, the machine guns shooting blanks—only she knew what blanks sounded like, and it wasn't anything like the screaming, angry roars of those automatic weapons.

A thunderous second explosion dwarfed the first. Vibrations burrowed up through the seat, rattling her teeth and bones. She squeezed her eyes shut as a shockwave imploded all of the Rav 4's windows. Gummy shards of safety glass rained down on them.

*That* was no pyrotechnics.

"My God!" she exclaimed.

"Quiet," Thunder said.

He pushed himself up and off her. She tilted her head and saw

him peering over the dashboard, through the open space where
the windshield had been. She sat up. The remaining three vans
were speeding through the embassy gate. One wall of the gatehouse was in rubble. A funnel of black smoke curled into the air,
beyond the perimeter wall.

Thunder said something.

"What?" Her ears were ringing loudly.

"Stay here!"

"Where are you going?"

"They might still be alive."

"Who?"

He said something else, but she didn't catch it. The low
whine in her head was like electricity whistling along a wire,
driving her crazy. He shoved open the door and took off, keeping his head low, running toward the Marine lying prone on the
ground. She followed, not sure what she was doing, only that
she wanted to be doing something. She stopped next to Thunder, her eyes widening in horror. The head of the young man
in the desert battledress uniform at her feet was surrounded
by a pool of blood. Half his face was missing. She spun away
and vomited everything that was in her, which wasn't much.
She wiped her mouth with the back of her hand while looking
around through blurry eyes for Thunder, who was nowhere in
sight.

"Thunder!"

He appeared through the hole blown in the wall of the gatehouse. He shook his head.

*They're all dead,* she thought, feeling sick again. *That's what he
means. The guards are all dead.*

Through the open gate Scarlett saw a large crater dug into
the ground in front of the Chancery building. Wreckage from
the suicide vehicle was scattered over the green grass and
among the flame trees. Aside from the broken windows and the
black blast marks on the stone façade, the structure seemed
largely undamaged. The American flag atop the twenty-five-
yard flagpole flapped undaunted in the wind. Then the front

doors to the main entrance flung open and four gunmen herded a group of men and women into one of the waiting vans.

Scarlett's instincts told her to run, but her feet remained soldered to the ground. She watched what played out dreamily, as if it were all happening in slow motion.

*A terrorist attack*, she thought, the reality of the situation clubbing her over the head with an almost physical force. *I'm witnessing a terrorist attack. Not on the news. Right here, right now.*

Three more gunmen emerged through the doors, herding more hostages.

One of them was Sal.

Before she could think better of it, she shouted his name.

A terrorist pointed at her.

That slapped her out of her dazed stupor. Time slung-shot forward. Her vision returned to normal. Sound bubbled back. Shouts in Arabic, cries in English. A burnt, chemical smell hung over everything.

The same terrorist leveled his gun. Red fire erupted from the muzzle.

Thunder snagged Scarlett's hand and they fled back to the Rav 4, scrambling inside. Thunder threw the transmission into reverse. The tires squealed as the car shot backward. As they neared the gatehouse, he hit the brakes, tugging the wheel to the right. The front tires skated across the asphalt in the opposite direction, coming to rest pointed toward the street. He shoved the gearstick into first and stamped the gas again.

Before he switched to second, however, there was a jolting crash. They didn't have their seatbelts on and Scarlett slammed forward against the dash while Thunder shot up, cracking his head on the roof. She swung around in her seat. One of the vans was right behind them.

"Go faster!" she shouted.

The van swerved to the left, pulling parallel to them, its engine roaring.

Metal screamed as the two vehicles traded paint.

Scarlett could see the driver only a few feet away. He stared at her, his eyes narrowed slits filled with black hatred. His scarf blew away in the wind, revealing a horribly burned face.

"Faster!" she urged in a voice she scarcely recognized as her own.

The van swung hard to the right, sideswiping the smaller and lighter Toyota, causing the steering wheel to spin wildly in Thunder's hands. The car careened off the road and collided head-on with the trunk of a palm tree.

Scarlett saw a burst of white moments before the airbag exploded in her face.

A snowy darkness faded to black.

# CHAPTER 16

*Thursday, December 26, 7:33 p.m.*

*Dar es Salaam, Tanzania*

F ITZGERALD SNAPPED OFF the television and remained seated on the bed for a long time, thinking. His job, it seemed, had just become a hell of a lot more difficult.

He wasn't surprised the terrorists had attacked the American embassies on the tenth anniversary of the original Nairobi and Dar es Salaam bombings. He was well aware of how history, and warfare by extension, repeated itself. What did surprise him, however, was that the man he'd been hired to kill had somehow gotten himself tangled up in the whole bloody mess.

Nevertheless, to keep things positive, Fitzgerald's earlier foresight was now proving to be more important than ever. Back in the Serengeti, when he'd surveyed the safari camp from the kopje, he'd realized he wouldn't get another chance at Brazza, not there anyhow. The camp had been too small. Too many potential witnesses for him to have pulled off something unnoticed. And taking them all out would have been suspicious. You could murder lowlifes with little thought to circumstance and consequence, but he didn't take out lowlifes. The privilege of his clientele often extended to their deaths. So when Brazza and Cox and the stocky fellow had gone off in the balloon, and the cook had followed on the ground, Fitzgerald had slipped two tracking devices into Brazza's belongings—one in his suitcase, another in his blazer. The reasoning was simple. If he couldn't get Brazza in Africa, then he'd get him in Dubai or LA or wherever he went to next.

Which, as fate would have it, was now going to be some Al Qaeda stronghold.

Fitzgerald flipped open his MacBook, attached a white receiver about the size of an external hard drive to a USB port, and used his Wi-Fi enabled thumb drive to connect to the internet. The two tracking transmitters sent signals to the twenty-four Department of Defense satellites orbiting the earth. The receiver could triangulate the transmitter's location to within eight inches and one-quarter mph. He frowned at the screen now. There were two dots on the map. One was in Moshi, a town in the northeast of Tanzania. The other was on the B129, between Dar es Salaam and Dodoma, Tanzania's capital.

He watched and waited. The one in Moshi remained immobile while the one on the B129 moved west. He reviewed the archives and discovered that from the time he'd activated the transmitters in the Serengeti, both had stayed together until Arusha, when, on the highway near Mt. Kilimanjaro Airport, they'd diverged. Had Brazza and Cox split up then? That couldn't be right. They'd both been at the Dar embassy. Since that was the case, he ignored the tracker in Moshi and focused on the one that had gone through Dar and was now heading west. He spent another minute watching more of the same, then went to the window and lit a Kent.

He inhaled deeply, exhaled through his nose, and stared absently at the traffic far below him. By the time the tobacco had burned to the filter, he had come to the conclusion this new twist of events might actually be to his advantage. Because now he wouldn't have to bother with making the kill appear accidental. Who would suspect an assassin's bullet when Salvador Brazza was in the hands of Al Qaeda fundamentalists?

He snubbed out the fag on the window ledge, returned to the bed, and looked to the part of the laptop screen where the program monitored the battery life remaining in the transmitters.

He had exactly two days, eleven hours before he lost the signal.

# CHAPTER 17

*Friday, December 27, 12:01 a.m.*

*Macau, China*

"**M**ANYAK," DANNY ZAMIR swore under his breath in Hebrew as he skipped through the television channels. He exchanged the remote for his cell phone and dialed Sal's cell number. He didn't expect an answer and didn't get one.

He paced the hotel suite.

The last time he'd spoken to Sal had been approximately twenty-four hours before. He'd told him that Don Xi was dead and gave an update on what he'd learned about the Irishman named Redstone, which, as it had turned out, hadn't been much. Even Danny's shadiest contacts had heard only rumors about the man. One was that his alias, Redstone, was chosen after the first man he'd killed, a Malcolm Ruby. Another was that he was the son of a late London crime lord. Another still was that he'd single-handedly taken out an entire Russian mob.

According to that last rumor, after the Irishman had put a half-inch-wide bullet from a Barrett M107 through the heart of a high-ranking member of a Moscow-based mob, the mob's boss, Alexander Noukhaev, tracked the Irishman down to a small house on the coast of Northern Ireland.

The Irishman wasn't home, but his wife and daughter were. They were found by police dismembered, their limbs pinned to the living room wall like some kind of macabre art exhibit.

Less than a month later, the severed heads of Noukhaev's three sons were discovered in a garbage bag in the center of Cathedral Court, in the heart of the Kremlin. Over the next two years the rest of the mob was systematically picked off one by one—big daddies, little sixes, thirty-three men in total—until only Alexander Noukaev remained. Then one day he simply disappeared.

Regardless of whether that tale was true, Sal had not been cheered to hear any of it. The initial plan Danny had devised had called for his boss to skip the Prince Tower's opening and return to the US, pronto, avoiding all public events, while Danny stalked the stalker. Now, it seemed, those concerns had become secondary.

*Kidnapped in Africa,* he thought. *Christ, capo.*

He punched another number into his cell. "Yeah, I saw it," he snapped. "Why do you think I'm calling? Round up six of our guys and meet me at the hangar at first light." He paused. "And bring some sunscreen. Africa's going to get hot."

# CHAPTER 18

*T*HUMP, THUMP, THUMP.

Scarlett opened her eyes. Blackness. The thumping continued, loud and hollow, from somewhere above her. She heard the hum of tires, felt the sense of speed. "Hello?" she said.

"Scarlett?"

"Sal?"

Suddenly hands cradled her head, fingers brushing her hair back from her face. She smelled the spicy-rose scent of Sal's cologne. She struggled into a sitting position and hugged her husband fiercely. "How?" she mumbled into his shoulder.

"You're all right," he said.

"That noise? The banging?"

"It was me. I was kicking the damn door."

"Where are we?"

"In a van. They took us."

She recalled the explosion, the dead Marines, the car crash. Her gut knotted with reawakened fear. "Thunder?" she said. "Where's Thunder?" She looked around, but couldn't see anything in the dark.

"Big fellow? He's here. They brought you in together."

Scarlett crawled blindly forward and discovered an inert body lying in the center of the van's cargo body. Thunder. She traced her fingertips up his shoulder to his face and felt something sticky on his forehead that had to be blood. She probed gently, finding a gash just above the left eye. She pressed the pads of her index finger and middle finger in the hollow between his windpipe and the large muscle of his neck. Relief filled her. His pulse was strong, the rhythm regular. She settled down beside him, resting his head on her lap.

"Who is he?" Sal asked. She heard him shift, as if he was settling down as well.

"The man whose car you wouldn't get into."

"*Him?* He drove you all the way to the embassy? What were you thinking anyway? I had no idea where you went—"

"Not now, Sal. Please." It still sounded as though she were hearing everything through cotton. "How long have I been out?"

"Only a few minutes," a woman said.

Scarlett jumped. "Who are you?" She spun her head. "How many people are in here?"

"My name is Joanna Mills." Her voice came from where the cargo body met the cab. "I'm the vice consul at the embassy."

"I'm Miranda Sanders," a soft, barely-there voice said. "I'm a clerk in the passport office."

"They were in the atrium with me when the blast occurred," Sal explained. "We were thrown to the floor. Then the gunmen came in and took us outside. That's when I saw you at the gate. What the bloody hell were you doing just standing there?"

"Thunder and I had just arrived. We saw a bunch of men in scarves shoot the Marine at the gatehouse. Thunder went to see if any of them were alive and I followed." She swallowed. "Who were they anyway? Al Qaeda?"

"I'm afraid so," Joanna said.

"How do you know?" Miranda asked. She sounded young— young and scared.

"Who else blows up American embassies?" Sal quipped.

"Watch how you speak to her," Joanna said sharply.

"I'm in no mood for imbecilic questions right now."

"1965," Joanna said authoritatively, "the Viet Cong detonated a car bomb outside the US Embassy in Saigon. 1979, Iranian students stormed the US Embassy in Tehran and held fifty-two American hostages for 444 days. 1983, two truck bombs, this time Hezbollah, against the American barracks in Beirut—"

"And in 1998," Sal cut in, "Al Qaeda terrorists blew up the embassies in Nairobi and, guess what, this same city. Last I checked it was 2008. That makes it exactly ten years after the original bombings. Anniversaries, as you should know, are big for these guys. So unless you're telling me this is all some grand coincidence, and in fact some Viet Cong who's just woken up from a coma—"

"Shut up."

"—and still thinks Johnson is president has decided out of all places to bomb why not—"

"I said shut up!"

"I just want to make it clear that, yes, it was a very imbecilic question."

"Enough!" Scarlett shouted. "Enough. Everyone's stressed. Okay. But we need to think this through. Figure out what's going to happen next."

"I'll tell you what's going to happen," Sal said, still using his boardroom tone, authoritative and in control, as if he were talking about quarterly forecasts. "They take us somewhere, call up the most important politician they have the number for, and start ransom negotiations."

"That's if they want money," Joanna said.

"What else would they want?"

"You said so yourself, Mr. Brazza. This is Al Qaeda. Not some South African syndicate going after children and businessmen. Nor Somali and Sudanese tribal clans snatching up journalists and foreign aid workers."

"It's not political," Sal stated flatly.

"How can you say that? They bombed an embassy."

"Bombings, assassinations—that's political, sure. Kidnapping is all about money."

"How can you know that? How can you possibly, categorically know that?" Joanna sounded half flustered, half incredulous, like Sal had just told her Mars was pleasant to visit in the spring. "Maybe they want to put us on the internet and—" She bit back the words.

"Cut off our heads?"

"My lord, you're a horror! Don't you know Miranda is just a girl?"

"She better grow up fast."

"Stop it!" Scarlett shouted again. "Would you two please stop? We're on the same side here."

Silence fell. Scarlett found it almost as bad as the infighting. She could taste despair in the coffin blackness.

The van lurched around a corner, throwing her onto her side. She pushed herself back upright, repositioning Thunder's head on her lap. The engine made a dirty, revving sound, as though the driver had left his foot on the clutch for too long. She prayed the bastard would get a speeding ticket, or the van would blow a tire and flip—or swerve to avoid a pothole and shoot through a cable-and-post guardrail. Ironically, she would have welcomed such a fate right now. God, how quickly one's fortune could change.

Scarlett cleared her throat. "Let's stick to the facts, okay?" she said, trying to remain rational. "Have there been any other Al Qaeda kidnappings in Africa?"

"There were those eleven Europeans in Egypt," Miranda said.

"No, hon," Joanna said. "Militiamen from Darfur were responsible for that."

"The Salafist Group for Preaching and Combat," Sal said.

"Who are they?" Scarlett asked.

"A rebel group that's been fighting the Algerian government in a civil war for the past decade or so. When they couldn't win support at home, they started looking global. With Al Qaeda's support, they've become an umbrella for radical Islamic factions in neighboring countries like Morocco and Tunisia. They run training camps in the Sahara and ship fighters off to Iraq, where they make up as much as thirty percent of the foreign fighters there. Recently they've become known as the Al Qaeda in the Islamic Maghreb."

"You know a lot about terrorists, Mr. Brazza," Joanna said, and it was tough to tell whether there was suspicion or deference in her voice.

"They fascinate me," he said simply.

The truth, Scarlett knew, was that before settling on Mauritius as the site for a future hotel-casino, Sal had looked into several other African nations, and he would have received regular reports on their political and economic environments. "Are these Salafist guys involved in kidnapping?" she asked.

"Yes," Joanna said. "In 2003 they kidnapped thirty-two Europeans. I believe the German government paid a five million ransom. Last year, again, they kidnapped two Austrian tourists in Tunisia. Eight million ransom that time."

"You see," Sal said. "It's all about money."

"But remember," Joanna said. "Salafist is North African."

"Who was responsible for the East African embassy bombings ten years ago then?" Scarlett asked.

"The Jihad Organization. They've been around since the late seventies."

Sal grunted. "It's all the same thing. They all follow bin Laden."

In the silence that followed, Scarlett thought about everything that had been said. It made her head spin with incredulity. Cold and bleak depression washed over her in waves.

She saw the black smoke curling above the embassy.

She saw the young Marine's half-missing face.

She saw the crazy bastard with the third-degree burns staring at her madly before running her and Thunder off the road.

She shoved the images aside decisively and forged her resolve. Sal was right. The kidnappers likely only wanted money. No problem. Name a price. One million? Ten? God, when they found out how much Sal was worth... "They're going to wants tens of millions, Sal," she said.

"Will you pay them?" Miranda asked. "Whatever they ask?"

"Of course," Sal said shortly. "What good is money if you're dead? Besides," he added, "I'm insured against this type of thing."

A new thought struck Scarlett. Maybe in a normal kidnapping-hostage situation, the kidnappers wanted money. But this wasn't a normal situation. She and Sal were one of the most famous couples in the US. Al Qaeda was well-funded. Money was secondary to them—a means of achieving the end goal of spreading propaganda and terror. So what if whoever was calling the shots decided that no amount of ransom would be worth the coverage their deaths would bring?

It was a chilling possibility, one which she kept to herself.

SEVERAL HOURS LATER the van stopped. The rear doors swung open, letting inside gray light. Three gunmen dressed in drab-colored clothing, including the driver with the burn marks on his face, shouted at them to get out. Scarlett gently moved herself out from beneath Thunder, whose head was still resting on her lap, and got to her feet. She followed Sal and hopped to the ground. Her cramped legs immediately gave out and she almost toppled over. The nearest gunman laughed at her; she resisted the urge to spit in his face.

She looked around. It was dusk, but the dying light seemed bright compared to the complete blackness of the van's cargo body. The air was fresh and earthy, with not a trace of civilization in it.

They were in some sort of forest clearing. Tall, foreboding trees surrounded them on every side. Two primitive huts faced each other across an open hearth. They were constructed from sturdy wooden poles, thin branches for horizontal tie-beams, and thatch. In fact, they resembled crude facsimiles of the villa Scarlett and Sal had stayed in up on the rim of Ngorongoro Crater, only she didn't think these would boast interiors flush with long-stem roses and Persian silks. Definitely no bathrooms with hand-beaded chandeliers and views of Africa's Eden.

The gunman who'd laughed at her ran his grubby hands up and down her arms and legs and fondled her crotch and breasts. She gritted her teeth and endured the harassment. He stuck his knobby fingers into the pockets of her dress and found the two Australian fifties Thunder had given her, which he kept. Next he examined the lion claw and compass-pendant around her neck. Apparently he decided they were worthless and left them where they were. He ordered her to take off her wristwatch. She fumbled with the clasp and handed him the gold jewelry piece. He held it up in front of his face for inspection, then dropped in it the same pocket that held the fifties. Finally he pointed to her engagement ring and wedding band.

Scarlett glanced over at Sal. He was surrendering his three hundred thousand dollar Patek Philippe wristwatch to the gunman with the burns. Joanna and Miranda were also shedding their valuables. It was the first time she had seen the two embassy women. Joanna was somewhere in her fifties with a sharp, intelligent face and short-styled hair. Miranda was the complete opposite—early twenties, mousey features, long, flat hair. Her cheeks were streaked with tears, and she was biting her lower lip.

The gunman in front of Scarlett barked something at her. She returned her attention to him and quickly twisted off the diamond engagement ring and platinum wedding band. She dumped them into his greedy, outstretched hand. He grinned at the size of the diamond and made a crack in Arabic to his buddies. They laughed. He tied a black piece of cloth around her eyes. Blinded, Scarlett felt a renewed surge of panic. He gripped her roughly by the shoulder and steered her across the clearing. She stumbled and fell to her knees twice. Thirty or so steps later he shoved her inside what she thought was one of the huts and tied her hands behind her back to a thick corner post. She heard more movement and grunts. Booted footsteps left the hut and the door clattered shut.

"Sal?" she said.

"I'm here."

"Joanna? Miranda?"

They answered as well.

Scarlett tested the rope binding her wrists. There seemed to be about two feet of slack. Enough to lie down, enough to touch feet with the others, but that was all. She listened for the terrorists, but didn't hear them. Even so, that didn't mean they weren't right outside, standing guard. She swallowed hard. She hated not being able to see. She felt perfectly exposed and vulnerable. What if the bastards decided to rape her? What would she do then—what could she do? She imagined their hot, smelly bodies rubbing against hers, their rough beards scraping her face, their snorts of pleasure as they mounted her one after the other.

She would bite them, she decided. She'd rip off their goddamn noses with her teeth if they tried anything.

They didn't try anything. The hours slipped away without event. The night grew colder. She didn't speak to anyone, and no one attempted to speak to her. What was there to say really? How's it going over there? Sort of like camping, huh? Got any marshmallows?

Mosquitoes feasted on her exposed flesh, their incessant whining around her head almost as bad as their pinprick bites. She couldn't slap them away because of her restraints and had to lay there for them, a blood buffet. From somewhere not far away an owl hooted, a deep, resonant ooh-hu. It almost sounded like "who you?"

Who am I? she thought vaguely. My name's Scarlett Cox. You might have seen some of my films? No? Well, next time you're in Times Square or cruising down Hollywood Boulevard take a gander around and you'll probably see one of my billboards somewhere. Maybe the Estée Lauder one. It's right across from the Kodak Theatre. You can't miss it.

More minutes ticked away. More silence. Scarlett's shoulder muscles began to stiffen and her wrists ached. She stretched out on the lumpy dirt floor and remained like that until her left arm went numb below the elbow, then she shifted to the other side.

She heard the others tossing and turning as well. At some point —by then, time had ceased to mean anything to her—she ended up going over everything that had led to the current nightmarish predicament.

The safari had started out well enough. The morning in Arusha had been nice. Ngorongoro Crater and the Serengeti had been fun too—until she'd overheard Sal on his phone in the balloon. That's when it all started to go downhill, wasn't it? Yes, because if she hadn't overheard him in the balloon, she wouldn't have confronted him about Don Xi later on. He wouldn't have felt the need to go off into the forest to make another call during dinner. If he hadn't done that, he wouldn't have stirred the lionesses. They wouldn't have gotten in the subsequent argument. They wouldn't have been on non-speaking terms during the flight back to Arusha the next day, and they likely would have sat down for coffee or tea while waiting for a legitimate taxi to show up.

She wondered what was going to happen between them if they got out of this mess alive—*when* they got out of it. This morning she'd told Sal she wanted a divorce. Had she really meant it? She wasn't sure. How could you worry about divorce when you were kidnapped and being held hostage by the most infamous terror group on the planet? Right now there was no future. It was day by day, night by night.

Scarlett heard sobbing. It was the girl.

"It's all right, Miranda," she said.

"No, it's not."

"Just hang in there."

"I want to go home."

"We'll go home. Soon. All of us."

Silence. More tossing and turning. Sal began snoring softly. Scarlett couldn't sleep. It was too cold. She was too uncomfortable. Thoughts kept squeezing into the blankness she was attempting to create.

At what might have been around midnight she heard the faint ring of a cell phone. She quickly worked herself into an upright position. The ringing continued, shrill and unnatural in the stillness. She guessed it was coming from the other hut. It stopped. Muffled Arabic followed.

A distant door banged. Footsteps approached. The door to her hut rasped open.

"You are Scarlett Cox? The actress?" a voice said—a voice that could speak perfect Oxford English.

"Yes, I am."

"And you? Salvador Brazza? The hotelier?"

Sal answered in the affirmative.

"May I ask why neither of you were carrying identification?"

"We were robbed," Scarlett told him simply.

"What an unfortunate day you are having."

She didn't say anything. He might find her predicament amusing, but she certainly didn't.

The door clattered shut.

Scarlett let out the breath she'd been holding, but her heart continued to knock rapidly against her ribcage. Now the terrorists knew who Sal and she were.

Was that a good development, or bad?

"Can you believe that?" Sal said. "Did you hear him? The man's a bloody British national—"

"Shhh," Joanna said. "Listen."

More Arabic was being spoken. The conversation sounded one-sided, like the man was on the phone with someone again. "Yes, I've confirmed it is indeed Scarlett Cox and Salvador Brazza," Scarlett imagined him saying. "Where would you like us to drop them off? Certainly. And we do apologize for the embarrassing mix up."

That, of course, wasn't how it played out. Instead, one of the gunmen reentered the hut and untied her from the pole. He yanked her to her feet, rebound her hands behind her back, and marched her across the clearing. The others were being moved as well. She wondered briefly where Thunder was. Had he been in the hut with them, lying a few feet away, unconscious? In the van? In the other hut?

Miranda was crying. Sal was negotiating, offering money. Joanna was reciting a prayer.

*This is it,* Scarlett thought. *This is the end. They're taking us to a firing squad, or a butcher with a sword.*

God, she didn't want to die. Not now, not at thirty. Not like this.

A click and a squeal as something opened. An oven? Mother Mary, they were going to cremate her alive. They were going to cremate her and—

She was shoved forward. She banged her knee against cool metal. Not an oven. The van's bumper. *The van.* She ignored the pain and scrambled into the cargo body. Someone stepped on her heel, tripping her up. She had no free hands to break the fall and landed flat on her face. Coppery blood filled her mouth. But that was okay, that was just fine, because she wasn't crawling inside an oven, just the van. The others clambered inside as well. The tailgate slammed shut.

As Scarlett struggled back up into a sitting position, she bumped an inert body. Thunder? Had to be. They'd left him in the van after all.

"Where are we going?" Miranda asked between hiccups.

"Likely somewhere a little more secure," Joanna told her. Her voice was calm, but a fragile terror soaked her words.

"So they can keep us for a lot longer?"

"We don't know that."

"It's true! And it's all because of you!"

Scarlett couldn't see Miranda, but she knew the girl was speaking directly to her.

"They know who you are now!" Miranda went on. "They're not going...going to let you go. They're not going to let any of us go anymore."

She burst into fresh tears.

Scarlett didn't know what to say. Any words of comfort would sound empty. Because that was one of the possibilities she'd drawn herself six or seven hours earlier.

# CHAPTER 19

**A**FTER THE INITIAL relief that came with the knowledge they weren't going to be summarily executed, Scarlett's confusion and anger returned in full force. There were still so many unanswered questions. What had happened to the other Americans who'd been whisked away in the other vans? Had any of them been rescued? What were the US and Tanzanian governments doing to get all the hostages back? Scarlett had overheard the Secretary of State speaking to someone about Iran at a White House dinner a few months back, and the woman's words came to her now, clear and clipped: *The United States does not make concessions or ransom payments, period.*

Well, gee, thanks, Madame Secretary, she thought. Maybe if you were sitting in the back of some lunatic's van, tied up and blindfolded and bleeding, you might think twice about that blanket statement. But whatever, fine, you don't make ransom payments. That's all right. Because I don't think these guys want money anyway. So how about sending in a strike team? The Delta boys would do just fine, thanks. Maybe throw in a few sharpshooters as well. Can you at least do that, Madame Secretary?

The van started to heat up. Scarlett felt it first in the air, which became thick and stuffy, then in the metal floor, which became hot to the touch. It was morning.

She did a quick calculation and determined that since leaving the clearing they'd been driving for six, maybe seven hours. At first she welcomed the warming temperature as it burned away the chill of the long, cold night. But gradually it became a slow roast, as if the van were not a van but the crematorium she'd feared. Her lips cracked and her mouth became so dry she couldn't work any moisture from the saliva glands. The terrorists hadn't given them anything to drink yet, and she was literally drying up from the inside out.

She began thinking about escape—attacking the gunmen when they opened the van doors, making a run for it—but she soon drifted into a weird half sleep during which time she tried to convince herself she was on an airplane going to Hawaii. It wasn't a dream because she was aware of being partly awake. Maybe a hallucination. Whatever it was, she didn't want to break the spell. The flight attendants would be coming by soon to take drink orders.

The van hit unsealed road, jarring Scarlett lucid. She sat up, feeling worse than ever. They bumped and jolted down some rutted road, and she became painfully aware of her aching bladder. What was she going to do if she couldn't hold on? Wet herself? God, she hoped not. Hostage or not, she still had her dignity. Maybe they'd pull into a McDonald's drive-thru for a restroom break. She'd order one of those ridiculously large thirty-two ounce, four hundred calorie soft drinks she'd never considered ordering before. Mountain Dew, thanks. Free refill? Yes, please!

When that fantasy wore thin, she moved onto the next in queue: being back in her Indonesian-inspired Bel-Air home, doing laps in the infinity pool, hearing the clap of water against the tiled edges, feeling the water stream over her as she dived deep into a cool, silent world...

The van slowed to a stop. Doors opened and closed. Someone slapped the side of the van. The tailgate squawked open. Light seeped in under the lips of Scarlett's blindfold, and she was pulled outside. The fresh air was heaven sent. She heard water—

waves lapping against the shore.

Was she hallucinating again?

Someone started shouting in Arabic, probably at her.

Well, screw him, she thought. She couldn't see, could barely stand. Let him yell. Let him yell his stupid head off.

She remembered the stabbing pain in her bowels.

"I need—" She tried to work up nonexistent saliva. "I need a bathroom."

She was shoved forward. The sound of waves became louder. She detected a sedge-like seaweed smell. She stepped onto a wobbly walkway. Yes, definitely waves, below her now. Was she on a gangplank? *Walk the plank, matey.* She froze. Were they making her walk a *plank*? No. Why would they drive this far just to make her walk a plank? She wasn't thinking straight. Before she could figure out what exactly was happening that same rough, vile hand urged her forward. There was nothing to do but obey. She took one small step after another, half expecting the next one to plummet through air. That never happened and soon she was on solid ground once more. The sedge smell was replaced with the astringent reek of oil and gas.

A boat? Why were they taking her on a boat?

There was more shoving and pushing and shouting until she stumbled into a hot and humid room that felt like a sauna.

"Who's here?" she said, each word like a hairball coming up her throat.

One by one Sal, Joanna, and Miranda answered her, like kids responding to roll call at school. Scarlett wondered once again what happened to Thunder. Was he still back in the van? Had the terrorists carried him in here? She was about to call out to him when the engines coughed, then rumbled to life. Vibrations shuddered the ship's superstructure.

"Where are they taking us?" Miranda asked.

"Would you stop asking that same bloody question," Sal snapped. "You're like a broken—"

"You are a boor, Mr. Brazza," Joan croaked.

They started yelling at one another. Given their raspy and

weak voices, it sounded like a fight at an old age home. Scarlett wanted to cover her ears, but she couldn't because of the restraints.

This was hell, she thought. Forget fire and brimstone and pitchforks and the seven princes. This was close enough.

She swallowed a scream—and heard someone moaning.

Thunder?

She dropped to her knees and crawled/waddled toward the sound until she bumped a body. "Thunder?" She shouted back at Joanna and Sal: "*Would you two please stop it?*"

They went quiet.

"Thunder?" she said again.

"What the...? Can't see."

"Thunder. It's me. Scarlett. It's just a blindfold."

"Why?" She felt him try to sit up. "My hands are tied."

"Welcome to the club," Sal said.

"Who are you?"

Scarlett introduced everyone, then explained what happened, pausing every few seconds to give her baked throat a rest. When she finished there was a hushed silence.

Thunder surprised her with a dry laugh. "Well, I came to Africa looking for an adventure," he said. "Reckon I just found one."

"He's in shock," Joanna stated.

"Nah, I'm right," he said. "Just relieving some tension, hey."

Suddenly rusty hinges groaned. Heavy footsteps approached. Someone tugged Scarlett to her feet. "Let go of me!" she shouted, twisting in the man's firm and calloused grip.

"What's happening?" Sal demanded.

"They're taking me!"

"Where?"

But then Scarlett was out the door, the man locking it again behind them. The hand around her bicep directed her up a flight of circular steps. At the top she felt a muggy breeze. Her restraints were removed. The blindfold came off. The onslaught of bright light overwhelmed her sensitive eyes, and she reflexively squeezed them shut, seeing stars and feeling momentarily faint. When she cracked them open again, she was looking at worn teak floorboards and her muddy sandals. Her toenails were painted a frosty pink.

Looking up, she saw she was on the top deck of some kind of riverboat. It was maybe fifty or sixty feet long and in the middle of an iron-gray lake that spread away as far as she could see. From the sun-bleached wood and blistered paint and rusty bolts, she guessed the boat's heyday to be at least one hundred years ago. A tarpaulin overhead provided shade from the equatorial sun, while beside her stood a scarred wooden table surrounded by several chairs. Aside from the gunman at her shoulder, four more leaned casually against the iron railing. Two were the men from the van. The other three wore jungle camouflage and black keffiyehs wrapped around their heads. All five had AK-47s hanging from their shoulders, and they all had hard, cold expressions.

One man in particular—tall and thin and effeminately handsome—was giving her an odd, almost creepy stare. Like maybe he recognized her. Or maybe wanted to rape her. She turned quickly away.

There was a wheelhouse amidships. Through the open door she could make out the tiller wheel, throttle, and basic control panel. There didn't appear to be a radio or radar or anything electronic of any kind. The helmsman, who had ignored her until this point, now turned to face her. It was the man from the van that had swatted the Rav 4 off the road, the man with the third-degree burns.

Scarface.

He was wearing a long olive-green tunic, loose pants, and no headdress. He held a dainty cup of tea in his hand, which he brought to his lips, sipped, then returned to the bone-white china saucer. He walked toward her, smiling an entirely fake smile. Scarlett lifted her chin and focused on the middle distance between them. She would not be cowed by him.

At the table he pulled out a chair and gestured for her to sit. "Please, Miss Cox," he said. "You must be tired."

So he was the British national, she thought.

"I need—" She swallowed. "I need to use the bathroom."

"Of course," he replied. "It's directly behind you."

Scarlett turned and noticed a small aft cabin. She crossed the deck, forcing the urgency from her step. The cabin turned out to be just as dirty and rundown as the rest of the ship. A couple of chairs, a chest of scuffed drawers, an oil lamp, and a small table on which sat a backgammon board. A frayed hammock swayed back and forth, looking more utilitarian than relaxing. The toilet was in the water closet off to the right. The seat was yellowed with age, and there was no plumbing, just a deep dark hole.

As she did her business, Scarlett wondered about escape, but there was nowhere to go but down the hole. Back in the small room she looked for a weapon of some kind. Nothing. She reluctantly returned outside to the sweltering heat.

Scarface told her to sit, so she sat.

He saw her eyeing his tea and said, "Where are my manners?" He made a gesture to one of the gunmen, who brought her a metal mug filled with water. "It's boiled. Quite safe, I assure you."

The water was warm and tinny but tasted better than the finest champagne on ice. She gulped down every last drop.

Scarface took a seat across from her. He produced a small microrecorder from his tunic pocket, pressed a button, and set it on the table. "If you'd be so kind as to answer some questions for me?" he said, still playing the absurd good-host act.

"Go ahead then," she replied, still playing the absurd unfazed-hostage act.

"My name is Jahja al-Ahmad. You may call me Jahja."

She did not wish to do so and said nothing.

"What is your name?"

"You know my name."

He nodded at the microrecorder. "I would like you to tell it to me again."

"Scarlett Cox."

"Do you prefer Scarlett or Miss Cox?"

"Why are you speaking like that?"

"English?"

"The good manners."

"You believe because I am currently your captor, I must be some sort of savage? I am a civilized member of society, just like yourself, Miss Cox. Or your husband, for that matter. I attended the University of Cambridge. I have a wife who loves me very much and a beautiful daughter who loves me even more. The only difference between you and I is that we differ on our politics—differ greatly, I should say."

Scarlett wanted to tell him they were about as different as black and white, good and evil, chocolate and shit, but she held her tongue.

"When were you born?" he asked.

"December 13, 1978."

"Social security number?"

"Why do you want that?"

"Answer the question, please."

And then Scarlett understood, or at least she thought she did. A number of terrorist groups were likely going to claim responsibility for the bombing, and the great citizen Jahja with the dignified British accent and the loving wife and daughter wanted to prove to whomever he spoke that he was the real deal. For a brief moment she considered giving him false information, but she didn't see how that could help her in any way. She rattled off her social security number.

"License plate number?"

"Which one?"

"Of course. You are a famous American film star. You have more than one car. You must have many cars. You certainly are a lucky woman." He said something in Arabic to his henchmen. They erupted in laughter. "Let me clarify the question," he went on, returning his attention to her. "Which car do you drive the most?"

"An Aston Martin Vantage. It has a vanity plate. S-E-M-A-R-A."

"What is Semara?"

"The name of the Balinese god of love."

"Do you believe in a god, Miss Cox?"

"No."

"You are an atheist then?"

"Yes."

"Even worse than a Christian." He smiled thinly. "Tell me your passport number."

They went on like this for another dozen questions or so, and when they finally concluded, Scarlett said, "What are you going to do with us?"

"That is not for me to decide."

Her heart sank. She had been hoping he might have been the one calling the shots. "Tell whoever you work for that if they want a ransom, my husband and I will pay it. Just give us a number."

He shook his head. "I'm afraid this isn't about money, Miss Cox." He stood. "Please stand and turn around."

Scarlett reluctantly obeyed. The blindfold was replaced, her wrists bound. Her despair deepened. The light had only reminded her of how helpless being blindfolded made her feel. One of the gunmen led her back down the stairs to the main cabin.

"Scarlett?" Sal said.

"Yes, it's me."

"What happened?" Then, to someone else: "What the hell are you doing?"

"What's happening, Sal?" she demanded.

"Some chump is taking me."

"They just want to question you." She added quickly, "Ask for water."

The door slapped shut.

"The party's over here," Thunder said. "Follow my voice."

Scarlett made her way cautiously forward. She came to a wall and slumped down against it, adjusting her hands awkwardly so she wasn't sitting on them.

"They gave you water?" Joanna said. "Sweet Jesus, I'd love some. At least it's not as hot in here as in the van."

"What did they want to know?" Thunder asked.

"Personal information."

"Why?" Miranda said.

"Proof they have me, I think."

"Proof of life," Joanna concurred.

"How many blokes are up there?" Thunder asked.

"The three who were driving the van and another three dressed in camouflage. And if you're wondering, we're in the middle of some huge lake. I couldn't see land in any direction."

"There are three very large lakes along the East African Rift Valley system," Joanna told them. "Malawi, Victoria, and Tanganyika. It must be one of those."

Scarlett said, "Lake Victoria is up near the Serengeti, right?"

"Yes. It's administered by Tanzania, Kenya, and Uganda. It's also the source of the Nile."

"What about the other two?" Thunder asked.

"Tanganyika is surrounded by Zambia to the south, the Congo to the west, Burundi to the north, and Tanzania to the east. Malawi is bordered by western Mozambique, eastern Malawi, and southern Tanzania."

"Great," Scarlett said. "So we could be anywhere."

"Seems that way."

With that glum news, they fell silent for a while.

"Oi," Thunder said abruptly. "Your husband. That's Sal for Salvador, am I right?"

"Yes," Scarlett said.

"Salvador Brazza?"

"Yes."

"That makes you Scarlett Cox, the actress? Or actor..."

"Actress is fine."

"Don't know how I missed that."

"Not quite as glamorous as in real life, huh?"

"Come off it, Lettie," he said, purposely notching up his accent. "You're a right Sheila."

Scarlett couldn't help but smile. "Do you guys really say that? Sheila?"

"Fair dinkem."

Now she laughed. "Stop it."

"What?"

"Talking like that."

"It's how I talk."

"You're exaggerating."

"Okay, you got me. Busted."

"Well, you accomplished the impossible. You made me laugh. Under the circumstances, I'd stay that's pretty damn impressive."

"You sound like Crocodile Dundee," Miranda said.

"That's not a knife..."

Miranda giggled.

"How do you know Sal?" Scarlett asked, liking Thunder more and more by the minute.

"I was in the corporate side of law. Property development, specifically. My team dealt mostly with time-share resorts along the Queensland coast. Not knowing Star International would be a little like a criminal lawyer not knowing OJ. Not saying your husband is OJ..." His voice became hoarse, and he trailed off.

Scarlett didn't feel so hot either. The water had helped a little, but she still felt weak and faint, and she very much regretted not eating breakfast at the Safari Moving Camp the day before. She should have forced something down, regardless of how anxious about her marriage she'd felt at the time.

Thunder cleared his throat. "Time we get serious, ladies," he said, the levity gone from his voice. "Are you ready for the hard facts?"

"Why not?" Scarlett said.

"I've been thinking this through, and I reckon there are four possible outcomes to kidnapping. One is that the ransom is paid, and we're released. Two, we're rescued. Three, we escape. And four, we're killed."

"There's one more," Joanna said. "No ransom is paid, but we're still released."

"Fair enough. I reckon we can toss that in with the first alternative. Now, I'm going to be brutally honest here. I'm not sure how much faith I can put in a ransom payment bailing us out. Not now, not with them knowing who Lettie and Brazzy are."

That's what Scarlett had surmised, and what Miranda had spoken out loud. Hearing it from Thunder, however, who seemed to be a rock of stability and reason, made the prospect terrifyingly real.

"That leaves being rescued," Thunder went on. "Again, can't see it. These blokes are obviously taking extensive precautions to keep us hidden. I'm not about to consider the fourth alternative, so that leaves the third. Are you with me?"

Scarlett nodded, even though she knew nobody could see her. It was a bleak outlook, but she felt it was the truth. What was that verse from the Bible? *And ye shall know the truth, and the truth shall make you free.* She wished.

"So do you have a plan to get us out of here?" she asked.

"Not yet," he told them. "But it's time we start thinking of one."

# CHAPTER 20

*Friday, December 27, 3:32 p.m.*

*Stuttgart, Germany*

C HIEF MASTER SERGEANT Larry Cohen was sitting behind his desk in the United States Africa Command.
He finished off the dregs of his cold coffee, then drew
his thumb and forefinger across his tired eyes. Talk about a
long bloody day. He was the senior enlisted leader of AFRI-
COM, a newly created subcommand that was responsible for US
military operations in fifty-three African nations. Yesterday's
bombings of the Kenyan and Tanzanian embassies were its first
major crisis. Larry had just ended a secure video conference
with the White House Situation Room, and his boss, the defense
secretary, had made it very clear he wanted all twenty-three
hostages found within the next twenty-four hours. Which was
next to impossible, but which, of course, Larry had not said.

The phone on his desk rang. It had been ringing all fucking
day.

He picked up the receiver. "Cohen," he said curtly.

"*Shalom,* Chief," a familiar voice said.

Larry sat back in his chair and smiled humorlessly. "I was
expecting a call from you, Danny. Isn't this exactly the kind of

thing your man is paying you the big bucks to keep his ass out of?"

"And get his ass out of."

"This is out of even your league, my friend."

"Probably. But I'm not calling for permission."

"What do you want to know?"

"Everything."

Larry shook his head. "Christ, Danny. I don't get anything from you in six years. And now you call up and expect the works?"

"What are old friends for?"

Larry had known Danny Zamir since they were kids. Both had grown up in the same apartment building in the same sleepy Jerusalem neighborhood, where they had spent much of their free time out front San Simon Monastery smoking cigarettes and chasing girls. When Larry was seventeen, his parents moved to the US. His father was American, his mother Israeli, giving him dual citizenship. He didn't care much for university, so he enlisted in the Air Force instead, entering into active duty in 1988. Danny, meanwhile, joined the Tzahal—Israeli Defense Forces—and less than eight months later he volunteered for the Sayeret Matkal, the country's equivalent to the SAS or SEALs, an elite special operational forces unit dealing in deep reconnaissance, counterterrorism, and intelligence gathering. Despite the distance and the passing of the years, however, they had remained close friends.

"The truth is," Larry said, "I don't have much to tell you."

"Humor me," Danny said.

"They're an Al Qaeda cell that's been active in Somalia. Last year we learned that three senior members tied to the '98 bombings had popped up in Afmadow and Hayi. We hit them hard. AC-130 gunship. Attack helicopters. A dozen dead, including their leaders. We thought we shut them down."

"The media's saying there were three vans at each embassy?"

"Correct. We're working with local police to set up roadblocks along major roads. But it's like fishing for minnows with a tuna net. If you ask me, they're already out of the cities. And if they have any smarts, they'll have all split up, which is going to make finding them that much harder."

"Who's running the show?"

"A Saudi named Abdul al-Jeddawi. Grew up in Kuwait and Pakistan. He was one of the guys behind Bojinka back in '95. He and his nephew also had their hands in the original embassy bombings ten years ago. Since then he's laid pretty low, but he's been a suspect in several other international operations."

"He's not after money?"

"Not this guy. He gets all the cash he wants through backdoor Saudi charities. Nice to know where your oil dollars are going, huh?"

"Has he made contact?"

"Only one message so far. A lot of theater about the blood of Muslims being spilled, Crusaders, Holy Warriors, all that. The gist is they want a bunch of their guys released within seventy-two hours."

"Are you going to do it?"

"You know our policy on negotiating with terrorists."

"And I know you regularly ignore it."

"It's not my call. I'd say it's a last option."

"Special Forces?"

"Not off the table. But we don't even know where these fuckers are. Listen, Danny. That's all I have. It's gone to shit here. The crisis committee is pointing fingers at everybody, including yours truly. I need to get back out there."

"I'll be in touch."

"Sure. But listen. Like I said, this one is out of your league. There isn't anything you can do—"

Danny Zamir had already hung up.

# CHAPTER 21

FITZGERALD FOLLOWED THE blue sedan into the parking lot of a Victorian Turkish bath on Mawenzi Road in Oyster Bay, a posh area of Dar es Salaam where many senior foreign government officials resided. The sedan pulled into a corner spot. Fitzgerald parked three spaces down. He watched the Indian general get out, collect a black bag from the trunk, and enter the old brick building. Deciding to give him a few minutes to get comfortable inside, Fitzgerald wound down the Land Cruiser's window and lit a Kent. His mind turned to the previous evening. He'd spent much of it watching the tracker continue west across Tanzania. At roughly ten o'clock it had stopped seventy kilometers south of Dodoma before moving again at one in the morning, continuing west, eventually reaching the westernmost border of Tanzania at two in the afternoon, twenty hours after the bombing.

Then it started across Lake Tanganyika, toward the Democratic Republic of the Congo.

That had surprised Fitzgerald—and concerned him too. If AQ and the hostages had remained in Tanzania, or even crossed into Kenya or down into Mozambique, he knew he could have caught up with them easily enough. The DRC, on the other hand, covered an area of more than two million square kilometers. Or what was roughly the size of Western Europe. That was bad. Worse: years of economic mismanagement had reduced the infrastructure to ruins.

And then, of course, there were the rebels.

Fitzgerald knew the sick bastards up close and personal. Between 2001 and 2003, when most of the world had their eyes glued to the events following 9/11, he had been in Africa, making a small fortune taking out high-ranking officials from the eight nations involved in the Second Congo War—Africa's World War—as well as the twenty-five-and-change armed militia groups. The politicians in Kinshasa, the capital of the DRC, were a pack of spineless muppets who didn't want to risk their national army in the fighting. So instead they funded rebel factions with guns and other weapons to do their dirty work for them. But a lot of these well-armed, government-backed guerilla groups became consumed with their unbridled power, ultimately raping and pillaging and participating in rampant cannibalism, with a special taste for the local pygmy population. They ran unchallenged everywhere, including the Katanga province along the Congo's eastern coast—right where AQ was taking Salvador Brazza and Scarlett Cox.

Knowing all of this, Fitzgerald had initially thought bollocks to following them. Chances were good Brazza and Cox would never get back out alive. They'd be killed by AQ or the rebels or disease or the ruthless wildlife. Or some kid with a machine gun who decided he wanted to kill somebody that day.

Nevertheless, the more he thought about it, the more he reconsidered that position. AQ had a pretty sophisticated network of bad guys and rocks to hide under. If they were going into the Congo, they probably had some sort of base set up there, or at least a safe house, which meant there was still a good possibility they would broker some kind of deal with the hostage negotiators. Brazza could return home unscathed. If that happened, Fitzgerald would be back to square one. So he rang up the airlines to inquire about flights into the DRC. Not surprisingly, there were limited connections. Present-day Congo wasn't exactly Disney Land.

Kenya Airways flew to Kinshasa via Nairobi every day, but

Kinshasa was way over on the western side of the country, more than fifteen hundred kilometers from where he wanted to be. Eventually he discovered that a United Nations plane made regular stops to the eastern port town of Kalemie, to resupply the aid workers stationed at the UN base there. The next flight left the following morning. The man in charge of it was the Indian general likely steaming himself in a sauna right now.

Fitzgerald flicked the Kent away, left the Land Cruiser, and entered the Turkish bath. A black man behind the front desk smiled at him. Fitzgerald didn't smile back. "I want to look around," he said. The man started to shake his head but stopped himself when Fitzgerald dropped fifty thousand shillings on the counter. "It's okay?"

"Okay."

"Okay" was the most recognized word in the world, and Fitzgerald always liked hearing it. He passed through the changing area and emerged in a large and airy art deco room. Shafts of sunlight slipped through the slit windows near the domed ceiling, casting a chiaroscuro effect on the numerous marble statues of naked men and women frozen in classical poses. To his right was a steam room; to his left, a cold plunge pool. He stuck his head in the steam room. It was hot and dry and smelled like eucalyptus. Several men in towels and slippers sat around on the wall-mounted benches. No general.

He continued to the far end of the spa, checking each hot room he passed with no luck. That left only the body-scrub room. He pushed through the door and was greeted by humid air and colored quartz-tiled walls. Lying facedown on a raised stone platform was the plump brown general, naked and covered in suds. A young Middle Eastern attendant stood next to him, holding a branch of soapy oak leaves.

"Get out," Fitzgerald told the kid.

The attendant bowed and left.

The Indian general looked up, squinting. Gold chains dangled from his neck, while gold rings boasting oversized gemstones adorned his fingers. The fashion faux pas aside, it was a fair bit of bling for somebody who didn't clear much more than a grand a month, and it said a couple things about the general. One, he was a self-conscious materialistic fuck. And two, he was likely open to bribes. To a Western mentality, bribery was frowned upon. In Africa, it was simply the way things worked. There was a name for it here: the Dash System. Everybody—police officers, politicians, military officials—hustled for the dash. Government put up a lot of anti-bribery posters and talked tough about stamping out corruption, but it was all hypocritical bullshit. They skimmed twenty percent off the top of everything that came their way.

"General Deshepande?" Fitzgerald said.

"Who are you?"

"I was told you're in charge of the flight leaving for Kalemie tomorrow?"

"Who are you?"

"I need a seat on that flight."

"You come here, to ask me that?"

"Aye, I did."

"Why are you dressed in street clothes?"

"I don't like young boys scrubbing me down."

"Who are you?"

"We're going in circles, General."

"The flight is for UN workers." He shook his head, his double chin wobbling like a rooster's wattle. "No civilians. Call up an airline. Buy a ticket like everyone else."

Fitzgerald knew that Deshepande knew that there were no commercial flights to Kalemie. If there were, he wouldn't be chartering a plane. "One thousand dollars," he said bluntly. There was actually a certain etiquette to offering a bribe, but he had neither the time nor the patience to see it through.

"Excuse me?"

"I'm a big supporter of what the UN is doing over here, General, and I'd like to make a one thousand dollar donation to whatever cause you find worthy."

The annoyed look left Deshepande's face. It was replaced by

sly calculation. "You could make this donation into a bank account of my choosing?"

"I can do better. Cash. Tomorrow morning."

"You are a very kind man. But one thousand dollars does not go very far these days."

"Two thousand then, though I'm afraid that is all I could possibly afford."

Deshepande was silent.

Fitzgerald waited.

"Why do you need to go to the Congo so badly?"

"I'm a journalist covering the humanitarian crisis."

"You are writing a story?"

"Sure."

Whether Fitzgerald was or wasn't was a moot point. The man just wanted to get their stories straight in case someone asked why he was transporting a civilian.

"You know," General Deshepande said, nodding thoughtfully, "I believe there is room on the flight tomorrow for a journalist covering the humanitarian crisis. The flight leaves at 7:55 a.m. Be at Jules Nyerere at seven. You will find me in the departures lounge." He smiled a pudgy smile. "And it would be most convenient if your generous donation could be made in small denominations."

# CHAPTER 22

SCARLETT'S DREAMS WERE fleeting and unsettling and bizarre. Dreams of big black spaces connected by tightropes. Dreams of a ship rocking in a stormy ocean, of men wearing masks that were not really masks at all, of falling and falling and never hitting the ground. During the most recent one she came awake with a start, a lurch in her stomach, perspiration beading her skin, her heart pounding.

She couldn't see. Panic squeezed her lungs. Why couldn't she see—?

The blindfold.

It all came back. She was a hostage on a boat controlled by a band of terrorists. When that cold reality sank in, the panic became despair, and it squeezed tighter. She began to hyperventilate. But slowly—one minute? Five?—she got herself under control. Still rocking like a loony in a straightjacket, but under control.

Her arms, tied behind her back, were numb from a lack of proper circulation. They felt like another person's limbs. She shifted her position on the floor and rolled her shoulders to get some feeling back. She had no idea of the time, but it was cold, which meant it was still nighttime—or, depending on how long she'd slept, even early morning.

Her mind slipped into the past because there was nothing except blindfolds and darkness in the present to think about.

The previous afternoon had gone by very slowly. After Sal had returned from his interrogation, Joanna had gone up, followed by Miranda, and finally Thunder. They were given water and allowed to use the bathroom. They were asked the same mundane questions. And they all agreed that Jahja was one world-class prick. At some point after that one of the gunmen brought down a bowl of maize meal and another of water for them to share. Because they were tied up, if they wanted to eat or drink, they had to stick their faces in the bowls like animals at a trough. Scarlett drank some of the water, but she refused to eat any of the food. It was a foolish protest, dangerous even. She needed the calories. But she was unable to sink to that level of desperation. If she did, she would be heading down a road from which there would likely be no coming back.

Shortly after eating the meager dinner Miranda had thrown up. The wet, retching sounds made Scarlett sick as well. But she had already emptied her stomach out from the embassy, and there was nothing more to come up. Sometime after that exhaustion overwhelmed her, and she drifted into a nearly comatose sleep full of those awful dreams.

And that was that. A day in the life of a hostage.

Scarlett maneuvered herself into a sitting position, propped her back up against the wall, pulled her knees to her chest. "Anyone have a guess at the time?"

No one answered.

"Hello?"

No answer.

Was she alone? she wondered with a reinvigorated burst of panic. Had the others been taken during the night? God, she hated this stupid blindfold! The not knowing and the continued blackness were too much. Like Chinese torture. Drip-drop, drip-drop, you're going insane. Nevertheless, Scarlett forced herself to relax. Everybody was here. Of course they were here. They were just sleeping, that was all. Where else would they be? On the top deck, working on their tans? She laughed softly to herself, and to her dismay it sounded like the cackle of the homeless she'd often seen camped out on Sunset Boulevard or Beverly Wilshire.

She bit her top lip to shut herself up.

In the gloomy silence the old riverboat creaked and settled and rocked gently. Water sluiced against the hull. Mosquitoes whined and bit. Scarlett found herself wondering if escape was still possible, as Thunder had suggested. She didn't think so. Ditto with being rescued or released. Which left the unenviable fate behind door number four. Death. As much as she wanted to write that one off as well, she couldn't lie to herself. What was the point? It was impossible, like trying to forget your name. So if they were going to be killed, how would Jahja and his cronies do it? Decapitation? Starvation? A bullet in the head? Would she be first or last? Or would everybody be executed together?

Maybe going out on Laurel Canyon Boulevard would have been best after all, she thought darkly. Maybe that had been her real fate, and now God was trying to right the wrong, first with the lioness, now with this.

*Maybe, maybe, maybe! Dammit, I don't want to think about maybes. I just want to go home, go home, go home...*

Scarlett was nodding off to sleep again when she heard movement on the top deck. She jerked awake and listened. Definitely movement. Then something much louder. The anchor being raised? The engines started up with a roar like a rudely woken dragon. The entire ship rattled and shook.

She heard the others stir.

*They were here.*

Of course they were, she chided herself.

"Wonder what's for brekkie," Thunder said.

"How do you like your eggs?" she asked in jest, happy to have someone to speak to.

"Sunny, please."

"I'd die for some coffee," Joanna said, groggy.

"Pancakes," Miranda said.

The small talk was good. It was normal. To keep up the charade, Joanna asked Miranda questions about her family. Miranda told her she had a pit bull named Iggy.

Thunder jumped in, saying he'd had two dogs, a six-year-old dachshund and a fifteen-year-old golden retriever, but when the dachshund died unexpectedly of a heart attack last year, the retriever died a few days later, apparently of a broken heart.

Scarlett told them she was a cat person and got promptly booed.

Sometime later, long after the fake-happy conversation had tapered off and the gloom and doom returned, the engines slowed. The riverboat began chugging along at what seemed like half the previous speed.

"Did you hear that?" Sal said suddenly. He'd been mostly quiet since waking.

"What?" Scarlett said.

"I think it was a foghorn."

She listened, but didn't hear anything except for her own breathing. She brushed along one of the walls until she found a window. She pressed her ear against the grubby glass, but still didn't hear anything. Maybe Sal was imagining things. She wouldn't blame him. You went a little batty when you were blindfolded for this long. God knows she had.

"Lettie," Thunder said. "Try to pull down my blindfold."

"My hands—"

"Use your teeth."

They found each other in the middle of the room. Scarlett raised herself on her tiptoes, bit the cloth near Thunder's temple, and tried to tug the blindfold down. It didn't budge. She bit the cloth over the bridge of his nose and tried again, still to no avail.

"Let me try you," Thunder said. She felt teeth pinch the blindfold, then he started tugging down.

"Wait," she said. "Try to pull up."

Thunder resumed his effort. The blindfold moved a centimeter or two but got caught on the ridgeline of her brow. "No go," he said.

"No, you had it," she encouraged him. "Try again. Don't

worry about hurting me."

He gave it another shot. Once more it got caught on her brow.

"Keep pulling," she said, trying to keep the pain from her voice. The cloth dug sharply into her eyelids.

He kept at it, jerking like a dog trying to get at something, and finally the damn thing started to slip over the bony protrusion.

"It's working!" she said.

Then, all of a sudden, she could see. She let out a small cry of joy.

"It worked?" Sal said.

"Yes!"

Scarlett looked around the barren room, their prison for the past day or so. It was a dump. Rat droppings were everywhere. Chewed newspapers were piled in corners like nests, while stringy gray cobwebs dusted the low rafters. Three small porthole windows lined both the port and starboard sides of the cabin. The door and a large window faced the stern. Joanna and Miranda were standing beside each other. The vice consul looked ten years older than she had the day before. The passport clerk seemed deflated. Sal stood off by himself. His face was haggard, his jaw thatched with dark stubble, but his back was straight, his head held high.

Thunder was right next to her, seeming none the worse for wear except that his neat lawyerly hair was now a mess. The cut on his forehead was red and angry looking and had started to bruise. She found it an odd sensation to be able to see when no one else could. It was a little voyeuristic, like being the Invisible Man.

"The room's empty," she told them. "Just us."

"What about outside?" Sal said, the iron timbre back in his voice. "Are we still in the middle of that lake?"

She went to one of the starboard windows. She gasped.

"What is it?" Thunder said.

"We're on a river. Going through a town or city."

"Tell me everything you see," Joanna said quickly. "Maybe I'll recognize something."

Scarlett gave a running commentary. The river was a few hundred yards wide, the banks silted. Beyond the scattered banana trees and coconut palms, derelict buildings and billboards with faded advertisements rose up against the misty-pink morning sky. A little ways ahead a bridge spanned the river. People were walking along the pedestrian carriageway beneath the road.

"Any ideas, Joanna?" Scarlett said when she'd finished.

She was shaking her head, a frown on her face. "Not without better landmarks, I'm afraid."

"Dammit," Thunder said.

"Keep your eyes peeled," Sal told her.

Scarlett said she would and went to a different window. The orange sun rose higher in the sky, which gradually brightened to a crystalline blue. The air warmed. The buildings became sparser until there was nothing to see but virgin land. She went to the stern window for a change of scenery. It offered a panoramic view of the river behind them. The river remained on average two hundred yards across, sometimes wider, sometimes narrower, mud brown, slithering this way and that like a long, still snake. The wake churned the mocha-colored water a bubbly white, which fanned away from the stern and washed up against the tussocks of grass, lily pads, and water hyacinths that suckled the shore. The spiral staircase she had climbed the day before was directly to the right of the door. From her vantage point it was impossible to see up to the top deck. Thankfully that worked both ways. She didn't know how the great Jahja would react if he glanced down and saw her peering up at him.

Every now and then someone would ask her what she saw, and each time she would tell them the same thing: nothing new. Eventually they stopped asking altogether. For the next while the land rolled past flat and unexceptional until, quite abruptly, the riverbanks steepened.

Tall reeds, papyrus, and trees of every shade of green rose to form impenetrable walls on either side of the riverboat, broken only by occasional drainage passages that cut deep scars in the red earth. So hypnotic was the passing landscape Scarlett almost missed the village spread out on a riverfront clearing. When her brain registered what her eyes were seeing, she immediately snapped to attention. She hurried back to the starboard window. Her eyes widened. The huts were perched high on stilts, likely to avoid seasonal flooding. The walls were made from sunbaked mud, the roofs from grass and palm fronds. Fishing nets had been hung out to dry. Several pirogues—dugout canoes—lined the shores. Two African men stood at the edge of the water, watching the riverboat pass. They had perfectly black skin, scruffy Western T-shirts and shorts, and no shoes. One of them held an egg-beater fishing rod, the kind you find in any American sporting store.

"There's a village," Scarlett said. "Two men are watching us pass. Tribal people."

Joanna sighed. "We're going to need more than a couple of natives to pinpoint our location, unfortunately."

The excitement in the cabin quickly died down. Silence and frowns returned.

Scarlett, however, would not be deterred and kept post. Time dragged. Hours, maybe. Her eyelids became heavy. Her mind wandered. Her knees began to ache. Just as she was considering sitting down, a second village appeared. Children ran along the shore, pointing at the riverboat. Women stood before big cooking fires, dirty clouds of smoke billowing in the air.

Four men jumped in two pirogues, two in each, and began paddling to the center of the river, where they waited, like the pace car on a racetrack. The riverboat chugged past, and Scarlett saw that one pirogue was filled with plastic bottles of what might have been palm oil while the other was stacked with cassava, bread, fruit, fish, and meat. She stared into the eyes of the four men. They stared back at her impassively.

Then they were gone from view.

"Um..." she said uncertainly.

"What is it?" Sal said, turning his head toward her.

"I think we're about to be boarded."

Sal and Thunder and Joanna and Miranda all started talking at once, asking questions she couldn't answer. She hurried to the stern window. The Africans were now paddling furiously to catch up, bobbing and dipping in the churning wake. The man standing at the bow of the lead pirogue leapt, grabbed the stern deck railing, and tied up with a rope made from woven vine. He was tall and agile, his muscles lean and powerful, his skin wet and glistening like oil. Given his physique and grace, Scarlett thought he likely could have made the NBA had he grown up in the US instead of Africa, making millions of dollars a year playing ball.

Suddenly booted footsteps thumped down the staircase.

Everyone stopped talking.

Scarlett stepped away from the window and sat down, her back to the door, her chin snug against her chest so her hair fell down over her raised blindfold. She listened as words in Arabic and some falsetto tonal language shot back and forth. When the bartering or whatever they were doing finished, the door to the cabin opened and something heavy was tossed inside, landing with a thud on the floor. The door closed. The lock clicked.

Scarlett waited several minutes to make certain the men outside had returned to their pirogues and the top deck respectively before brushing the hair from her eyes and turning. A canvas sack lay on the floor, the top open, spilling out overripe fruit.

"Lunch time," she announced.

All at once Sal and Thunder and the embassy women crawled purposely toward the food. Sal—who owned a walk-in closet full of thousand dollar suits and who cut his toast and egg into bite-sized pieces—bumped a mango with a knee, found it with his mouth, and tore into it, juice dribbling down his chin. Miranda, unable to peel the skin from a banana with her teeth, squished it with her elbow and licked the meat of the fruit off the floor. Thunder and Joanna chomped back yellow-skinned grapefruit. It was, Scarlett thought, an incredibly depressing sight. Nevertheless, unlike the day before, she knew she could no longer hold out. If she did, she would die. It was as simple as that.

She swallowed her pride—her dignity—and got on her knees. She ate.

# CHAPTER 23

*Friday, December 27, 9:55 a.m.*

*Kalemie, the Congo*

T HE AIRSTRIP FITZGERALD touched down at was offi-
cially called a UN military installation, but it was nothing more than an open, unfenced area overgrown with
weeds and low brush. MONUC had set up several prefabricated,
air-conditioned housing units to serve as an arrivals gate. Inside
one, a woman in a blue-and-gray uniform with a Greek flag on
her nametag checked his name off the manifest, then he got on
a shuttle bus out front with the six other passengers from the
flight. An infantryman wearing a powder-blue helmet and flak
jacket drove them along a sandy road into Kalemie. Fitzgerald
got off in the center of town while the bus continued on to the
UN headquarters, which was located in some abandoned cotton
factory.

Kalemie had been one of Belgium's first colonial settlements
in the Congo. In honor of the Belgian king at the time, Albert I,
it had originally been called Albertville. It had also been called
the Pearl of the Tanganyika because it was the Congo's most important inland port, shipping all of the country's vast natural
resources—cobalt, gold, diamonds—across Lake Tanganyika to

what was currently Tanzania, and from there, to the rest of the world.

Today Kalemie resembled a ghost town populated by sad souls who had no better place to go. The buildings were broken, the corrugated iron roofs rusted, the brick walls crumbling. The people were subdued and quiet. Many were drunk. As Fitzgerald walked down the high street, ragtag peddlers tried to hawk him bottles of soda and knock-off batteries and other junk made in China. Women offered him salted fish wrapped in banana leaves. He told them all to piss off.

No one could afford cars or motorbikes, so the only wheeled traffic was kids on aged bicycles. Sometimes the kids rode close to him and yelled shit, likely trying to spook him into doling out some money. He ignored them but remained vigilant. Desperate people did desperate things, and a public tussle was the last thing he wanted. He didn't think the locals would react kindly to seeing a white bloke beat the snot out of several black kids. It could start a lynching, and he would be the lynched man.

Eventually he came upon a bar named Circle des Cheminots, which was French for "Railwaymen's Club." He stopped out front and tried to imagine the sagging, ramshackle building as it might have been sixty years before, filled with sophisticated people and sophisticated laughter, a Mercedes Benz 220S parked out front, chrome fenders gleaming. But he couldn't do it. The reality was too far removed from the ideal. It was like looking at pictures of Hiroshima or Nagasaki hours after the bombs were dropped and trying to imagine what the cities looked like days before.

He pushed through the front door. The interior was roughly the same size as the pubs back home in Ireland, the major difference being in an Irish pub you could hardly hear the bloke next to you, whereas here you could hear a pin drop.

The customers were all men. Most were sitting alone, a drink in front of them, a hand-rolled fag hanging from their lips, blue smoke drifting up their despondent faces. They all stared at Fitzgerald with dead eyes. He held each of those stares for several seconds until he was satisfied he had won each pissing contest, or at least managed a draw.

He went to the bar and ordered a beer. The barwoman set a mug filled with dark warm stout in front of him and told him it cost five hundred Congolese francs, which was the country's highest banknote, worth about ninety US cents. He took his money clip from his pocket, letting the woman see the fold of bills. "I need to rent a boat," he said.

"No boats here."

He peeled an American twenty from the wad and set it on the counter. President Jackson stared up at them, somehow managing to appear intelligent and confused at the same time, as if wondering what the fuck he was doing in the Congo.

"I have no change for that," the woman said. It came off her tongue like an insult.

"It's yours if you can find me a boat."

She stared hard at the money.

"So?" he said.

"Maybe I know someone who has a boat." She disappeared into a room behind the bar. Kalemie didn't have working landlines, and he didn't think she had a Blackberry or iPhone back there, so she'd probably left the establishment to find her boat friend on foot.

Leaving the beer on the counter, Fitzgerald sat down at an empty table. He took his MacBook out of the small rucksack he'd brought and set it on the table. He took the Glock out and set it next to the laptop, so no one got any funny ideas. He plugged in the Wi-Fi thumb drive and logged into his security-encrypted software. What he saw on the screen pleased him. The tracker was only twenty kilometers away, moving at less than ten clicks an hour down the Lukuga River, a tributary that connected Lake Tanganyika with the headwaters of the Congo River.

He leaned back in his chair and lit a Kent, his hand unconsciously rubbing the scar along his throat. He'd received the scar while he was still a kid, serving as part of the SAS's 22nd Regiment. The Sin Féin had been holding a meeting in Crossmaglen, a small village in Northern Ireland that bordered County Monaghan in the Republic of Ireland. Special Branch suspected the meeting was cover to smuggle a Provisional IRA bloke responsible for murders in Belfast back into the North. They wanted Fitzgerald's unit to photograph the man and his car. It should have been simple reconnaissance work.

It wasn't. The meeting had been a trap, a distraction to stage an ambush. Fitzgerald, who'd been hanging back as emergency cover fire, got a garrote around the throat. He bled a whole hell of a lot—enough that oxygen and glucose stopped reaching his brain and he passed out. Which was lucky for him, because the guy who'd jumped him thought he was dead and didn't put a bullet in the back of his head. He woke up back at base with twenty-seven stitches across his throat. No one else from his unit survived.

Fitzgerald chain-smoked a couple more fags until some twenty minutes later the someone the barwoman knew showed up at the Railwaymen's Club, pissed out of his gourd. He was wearing a pair of plaid shorts and an unbuttoned shirt, revealing his hairless chest and belly.

Fitzgerald met him at the door.

"My name is Michael," the man said. His eyes were bloodshot, his words slurred. "Like Michael Jordan, you know?"

"You have a boat?" Fitzgerald asked.

"I have a boat. Where do you need to go?"

"Up the river."

"The Lukuga?" The man shook his head. "There is nothing that way but trouble."

"That's the way I'm going."

"You don't understand. There are Mai-Mai rebels. They will kill a white man if they see one."

"Guess I won't let them see me."

"Hey, your life, my man. I warned you. I am not your mother, yes? What are you offering?"

"Show me the boat first."

The man named Michael shrugged and led Fitzgerald along the dusty high street. He turned down several side roads until they came to one sad house. The clapboard siding hadn't seen a fresh coat of paint in decades, and what remained of the peach color was blistered and peeling. Every window was broken. To top it off, the façade was pockmarked with shrapnel from mortar bursts.

"Pretty," Fitzgerald remarked.

"I have a generator inside," Michael said proudly. "It is one of the few houses in town that has power."

They followed a side passageway overgrown with weeds to a small backyard. In the middle of it, amidst waist-high grass and an assortment of junk, was a sixteen-foot wooden skiff resting upside down on its gunwales. Fitzgerald inspected the hull and found no holes or cracks. She would float. "There's no motor," he said.

"You never said you needed a motor."

"I'm not going on a fecking joy paddle."

"I can get you a motor, but it will be expensive."

"I also want two jerry cans of fuel."

"Good petrol is difficult to find."

"You have a generator. I'm sure you know where to find some."

"It will also be expensive."

"I'll give you one hundred American now, one hundred when I return the boat."

"Two hundred now, two hundred when you return the boat."

Fitzgerald knew that was more cash than this guy saw in a year. Still, he said, "Two hundred now. Another hundred when I return."

"You have a deal, my white friend," Michael said immediately. "Meet me under the bridge where the Boulevard Lumumba crosses the Lukuga River in two hours."

"One hour."

"Yes, fine, one hour."

THE DRUNK NAMED Michael was twenty minutes late. He arrived with two young, muscular men. The three of them carried the skiff between them, two at the stern, one at the bow. As they lugged it down the bank to the shoreline, Fitzgerald saw two rusty jerry cans sitting on the floor between the front and middle bench seats. A green 1950s-looking motor was mounted on the transom. "Johnson" was written in yellow letters across the power head. Below that: "Sea Horse 25." He flicked his Kent away and walked over.

Michael smiled at him. "There's your boat, your motor, and your petrol," he announced triumphantly.

"Does the motor run?"

"It runs."

Fitzgerald handed over two crisp one hundred dollar notes. Michael accepted the money, then seemed to consider something. "Thank you," he said. "But unfortunately this is not going to be enough. That is a good motor. I had to cash in several favors to get it. The petrol was more expensive than I thought. Also very good, very clean."

Fitzgerald said nothing.

"I want more money. It is only fair."

"How much more money?"

"Another two hundred up front."

"Four hundred dollars?"

"You will not find another boat in Kalemie. I can guarantee that."

"We had a deal."

"This is business." He shrugged. "I have to survive too, yes?"

Fitzgerald had expected something like this. He slipped the silenced Glock from the holster under his jacket and fired two rounds into the thief's chest.

Michael collapsed, an expression of surprise on his face.

"You don't have to worry about surviving anymore," Fitzgerald said as he bent over and plucked the two notes from the dead man's fingers. He folded them into fours and tossed them at the other two young men, who had ducked into defensive crouches, like they were either going to run or attack. "For the boat and the motor and the gas," he told them. "That was the deal."

With big smiles on their faces, the men each grabbed a bill for themselves and hurried back up the bank together.

Life in the Congo was cheap.

Friends were even cheaper.

FITZGERALD WAS SITTING in the jump seat of the skiff, his hand on the tiller, speeding down the eerily quiet Lukuga River. He eased up on the throttle and came to a full stop. He flipped open his MacBook and took another reading of the tracker's location. It had stopped moving fifteen minutes ago, less than seven kilometers away. Given that it was still bright out, still another two or three hours of sunlight left, he wondered why AQ had stopped so soon. Had they reached their final destination? Because if that was the case, he would be on them by nightfall—

The skiff's stern bucked suddenly and powerfully from beneath, launching him into the air. He crashed into the muddy-brown water, breaking back through the surface with a gasp. He glanced quickly around, and something inside him shifted, something queasy. Not more than a dozen meters away, two tiny ears and two bulging frog-like eyes were visible above the rippled water.

A hippo.

Fitzgerald had seen several herds of the mammoth suckers bathing together, usually just beyond a bend in the river, where the water had pooled and was still. In each case he had heard the deep grunting-snorts before seeing the animals, and he had given them a safe berth. Bulls were fiercely territorial and would run off other males, crocs, and even small boats that passed too close.

But this one had come from nowhere.

The hippo jointed open its cavernous pink mouth and roared, revealing four tusks protruding from the lower jaw, each more than a foot in length.

Fitzgerald knew his life depended on what he did within the next few seconds. The fight or flight hormone kicked in, and for the first time he could remember, he was going to flight. He splashed toward the skiff. The water and sucking mud beneath his feet made it feel as if he were dragging a train of cinderblocks behind him.

The hippo charged, half swimming, half running along the bottom.

*Bloody thing was fast.*

Fitzgerald hiked himself over the gunwale just as the hippo struck, coming from beneath again. The impact shot the stern into the air almost vertically. He gripped the transom with both hands, his feet dangling in the air. The hull crashed back to the water with jarring force, slamming the breath from his chest and throwing up curtains of spray along each side of the boat.

Wheezing, he lunged for the motor, pulled the selector into start—

The hippo heaved its massive bulk over the stern, roaring again, as loud as a lion, so close Fitzgerald could smell its foul, rotten breath. He stared into the beast's black, piggy eyes. Then he yanked the start cord. The engine kicked over. The growling propeller made a heavy, chainsaw-like buzz, as if it were sinking into a tub filled with lard. Bits and pieces of bloody flesh burst from the water like confetti. There was a loud, jarring noise as the propeller blades hit bone. The motor wanted to shoot back up, but Fitzgerald kept it pressed down, like the lid on a blender, the blades chewing, shredding.

The hippo made a bass-like bellow before vomiting a liter of blood. Fitzgerald snatched the Glock from its holster, pressed the barrel into the hippo's left eye, and fired four point-blank shots. The hippo's head jerked upward, the snout slamming Fitzgerald's hand and batting the pistol away into the water.

It made a final attack, trying to bite off Fitzgerald's head and shoulders. He moved back just in time and its gaping maw closed on air. Finally, it slipped back into the water, which had turned a diffused pink all around the boat. If the animal wasn't dead, it would be soon enough.

"Bleeding right!" Fitzgerald barked.

He shoved the gear selector into forward, cranked the throttle, and got the hell out of there. Despite what felt like one or two bruised ribs, he let out a whooping, raspy laugh. Then he straightened to see over the hydroplaning bow, the wind blowing in his face, feeling free, alive.

Seven kilometers to go

# CHAPTER 24

A T ROUGHLY THE same time as the hippopotamus was attacking Damien Fitzgerald upriver, Scarlett and the others were taken from the ship's cabin to the stern deck, where their blindfolds and restraints were removed (Scarlett had Thunder tug her blindfold back down over her eyes when the riverboat stopped earlier that afternoon). They all rubbed their wrists and looked around, suspicious at being allowed to see.

What did Jahja have planned for them now?

The riverboat was moored snugly against a steep, marshy bank. Jahja was on deck with them, along with the three gunmen dressed in jungle camouflage. One was the effeminate guy who'd given her the creepy rape-stare the day before. The other two were short and squat, one sporting a mustache, the other a full beard. They all carried large rucksacks.

Creep, Mustache, and Beard. Good enough names as any, she thought.

Creep set off down the gangplank first.

"You're next," Jahja told Scarlett.

"Where are we going?" she demanded.

"You'll find out soon enough."

"I'm not going anywhere until you explain to us what's happening."

Something on the good side of Jahja's face, the smooth side, twitched. "Do not test me, Miss Cox," he said, his voice dangerously quiet. "I will make you regret it one hundred times over. You do not know what I am capable of. You do not want to find out."

Scarlett stood her ground for another two or three seconds, but she knew she had lost that standoff. She might be able to see now, which made her feel more in control, but Jahja still held all the cards. She went down the gangplank. The tide was high, and she had to wade through knee-deep water before reaching the bank. She struggled up it, digging her hands into the mud and grabbing at plants. An African fish eagle watched her pathetic progress from its perch on the low branch of a riverside tree, probably thinking she was one hell of an uncoordinated monkey.

Once everyone made it to high ground, they set off in single file: Creep, Scarlett, Thunder, Sal, Miranda, Joanna, Jahja, Mustache, and Beard. The forest was a snarl of secondary jungle. Creep whacked at the vegetation with a machete every now and then, but the action seemed to be more for show or boredom rather than any real purpose. They were following some sort of path made either by wildlife or humans, and the passage was relatively easygoing.

The entire time questions burned in the back of Scarlett's mind. Where were they going? What could possibly be out here in the middle of the jungle? Some kind of terrorist paradise? Something along the lines of the hidden civilization in *King Solomon's Mines*? Only in place of Kaukauna warriors were suicide bombers, and in place of stone statues of pagan gods were statues carved into the likeness of bin Laden?

Sure, why not? she thought, teetering on mental and physical exhaustion. Why the hell not?

About ten minutes in they came across a python skin. It was dry and tubular and bunched at a crevice between two rocks, which the snake had apparently used to catch the skin on so it could slither out of its old coat. Next to the husk was a pile of brown and chalky-white feces, laced with bits of bone and fur.

Scarlett shivered at the sight and turned away. She hated snakes.

Sal and Miranda and Joanna had gone pale. Only Thunder seemed at ease. This wasn't so surprising since he was likely used to seeing such things back home in Australia. Jahja and the gunmen, for their part, looked indifferent, probably because they carried automatic weapons, which were more than a match for any size snake, anywhere.

"Would have made a good feed," Thunder mumbled under his breath.

"I heard it tastes like chicken," Scarlett whispered back.

"More like pheasant—with a lot of bones."

"So you see," Jahja said with a smug smile, "we may be your captors, but this land is your prison. It is very dangerous. You would not survive one day on your own."

Scarlett knew he was right. She pictured herself waking up in the middle of the night to find the python that had left that skin behind curled around her, squeezing ever so tighter each time she took a breath until the pressure became so intense she could no longer draw any more air into her lungs. But perhaps even before that happened, her head would already be inside its unhinged jaws...

They pressed forward again, for which Scarlett was grateful. The farther they put between them and the snakeskin, the better. She concentrated on her footsteps. One-two, one-two, on and on. Jesus, she was hot and thirsty. She glanced every now and then at the military canteen hanging over Creep's shoulder. She guessed he had a few bottles of water in his rucksack too. She was thinking about asking him for some, knowing he would likely ignore her request, but thinking about asking anyway, when they came upon a quick-moving river.

"Thank God," she said. She turned to Thunder—not Sal, she realized, but Thunder—and asked him if it would be safe to drink from.

"It's flowing, so it should be right," he told her. "Unless there's a rotting animal carcass in it upstream."

"I'll take my chances."

Jahja overheard them and said, "Yes, everyone, drink if you are thirsty. But do not over drink. You may become sick. This is not a place where you want to be sick."

"Reckon he was a personal trainer before he hung up the whistle for the machine gun?" Thunder said to Scarlett softly.

She surprised herself by laughing out loud.

Jahja frowned. "Do I amuse you, Miss Cox?"

Ignoring him, Scarlett forded the river behind Creep, who was gripping his rifle in both hands above his head. Halfway across, she stopped and scooped water into her mouth with her hands. After she'd quenched her thirst, she dunked herself under to cool off—and lost her footing. The swift current immediately took advantage of her weightlessness and whisked her downriver. She opened her mouth to cry out and water filled her lungs. She thrashed and clawed at the mossy stones on the riverbed, trying to get a handhold, but her efforts were in vain—

Someone grabbed her wrist and yanked her back above the surface. She coughed out a huge mouthful of water and kept coughing until her throat stung and her stomach cramped up. She blinked the water and tears from her eyes and looked around. Thunder was next to her, his arm around her shoulder. He was dripping wet and panting hard, apparently having dived in to swim after her. She looked upriver. Jahja and Sal and the others were still on the left bank. Mustache and Beard had their AK-47s trained on her and Thunder. Creep, she noticed, was on the far bank, his gun aimed as well. Small black monkeys were screeching and thrashing the branches overhead, as if amused by the show she'd put on.

"Going for a swim?" Thunder said with a grin.

"Thank...you," she stammered.

He winked. "Anything for a damsel in distress."

It was the same line he'd used when he'd picked her up on the highway outside Arusha, and she felt a sudden flush of guilt. If she hadn't waved him down, he'd be back in Brisbane right now. His being here, held captive by Al Qaeda, was all her fault. But he had not once blamed her or shown bitterness toward her.

In fact, he had been the exact opposite: solid, supportive, and amazingly good-natured. She had a wild urge to kiss him right then, which she might just have followed through with had Jahja not been shouting at them to come back.

"I hope *he* slips and drowns," she said.

"I hear ya," Thunder said. He took her hand and led her in a diagonal line toward the far bank. While climbing out of the water, she glanced back over her shoulder and saw Sal, halfway across the river, glowering at her. She released Thunder's hand.

"You must be more careful, Miss Cox," Jahja said when they had all regrouped. "As I told you, the jungle is a very dangerous place."

"I'm all for turning back," Scarlett said. "Just say the word."

"Very amusing. I'm glad you're keeping up your spirit."

Creep said something in Arabic. The four terrorists laughed.

"What did he say?" she demanded.

"Nothing meant for a lady's ears, Miss Cox," Jahja told her. "I can assure you of that."

She glared at Creep. He smiled at her, his teeth standing out in contrast to his dusty complexion. She turned away, more creeped out than ever by him.

They sorted themselves into single file again, and Creep led the way onward. Gradually the secondary jungle gave way to equatorial rainforest. The trees were impossibly tall and ancient and made Scarlett feel tiny and insignificant. Some soared two hundred feet in the air and had trunks wide enough to build roads through. The canopy formed a shadowy ceiling so dense it blocked out all but the occasional shaft of sunlight. Bromeliads, orchids, and lichen coated the untamed mesh of understory, adding small spots of vivid color to an otherwise murky backdrop. Lianas and vines and creepers looped and snaked through the branches and around the tree trunks like a tangle of woody intestines. Everywhere strangler figs ensnared their hosts in a centuries-long process of asphyxiation, a process so slow and aged it appeared static to the human eye, a freeze-frame in the reel of time.

Nevertheless, the leaf-carpeted forest floor was surprisingly open and airy, and Creep had little trouble pioneering a path through the saplings, ferns, palms, and other herbaceous plants. Even so, moss and fungi covered the rocks and felled trees and other decaying plant life, making the obstacles slippery and deceptively dangerous. Scarlett trod carefully. The last thing she wanted was a twisted or broken ankle. What would Jahja do then? Make another crack about how dangerous the jungle was? Or shoot her the way you shoot a lame horse? Leave her behind for that monster python—or something worse?

The deeper into the rainforest they went, the more Scarlett's wonder diminished and the more she found herself wanting to get through it as quickly as possible. A suffocating claustrophobia hung over everything like a heavy blanket, seeming to block out all sound. There were no more birdcalls, no chattering of monkeys. Nothing, in fact, but the omnipresent drip of water. It was, she thought, a dark and primitive world. Alien. No place for humans—at least modern-day humans for whom air conditioning, refrigerators, and paved roads were more necessity than luxury.

Abruptly Jahja called a five-minute break, his voice echoing eerily in the deathly stillness. Scarlett flopped down on the ground.

"I'd keep on my feet if I were you," Thunder told her. "Don't know what's crawling around down there."

"I haven't seen anything in ages."

"Most of it's too well hidden to spot. That, or it heard or smelled us a kilometer away and rocked off."

Scarlett stood and brushed her bottom. Then brushed it again, just to be safe. "I need to use the toilet," she said. "Tell Scarface and his goons that's where I went, if they come asking."

She wandered off behind the trunk of a tree large enough to conceal a minivan. She lifted her zebra-print dress, pushed down her panties, and squatted. She was alarmed to discover her urine was dark. Was that because she was dehydrated? Or was it a sign of something worse? Exhaustion or heatstroke?

God, either could cause organ failure, brain damage, even death. Not that the great, civilized Jahja would care. She and the others were just props to him in an elaborate play. And when the curtain closed? She was trying not to think about that.

She reemerged from behind the tree, fiddling with the thin leather belt on the dress, and noticed Creep sitting on a nearby rock, unloading and loading his pistol, watching her. She glared at him, then promptly returned to the others. They had been given a bottle of water to share, which she eyed longingly. Despite having her fill back at the river, she was parched. The bottle came around to her, and she drank as much as she thought fair before passing it on again.

"Has anyone been noting the direction?" Joanna asked quietly.

"We went due north from the riverbank," Thunder said. "But after we entered the rainforest..." He shook his head. "It's impossible to see the sun or any other marker."

"Everything looks the same," Miranda said. Her hair was knotted and greasy, her lips blistered. "I can't see more than fifty feet ahead of me."

It was true, Scarlett thought. Plants and brush and low branches no longer hampered their movement, but the forest of towering trees was dense. Visibility was limited and disorientating. It was like one of those optical illusion pictures. If you stared long and hard enough, the green-gray vegetation would start moving, or you'd see breaks and passages in it that weren't really there.

She was reminded of a choose-your-own-adventure game book she'd read as a child called the *Jungle of Peril*, where you had to choose the right path through puzzling, deadly jungle terrain. If you made the wrong choice, you'd meet a grisly fate or be banished back to the beginning; if you chose correctly, you'd be one step closer to the pyramid of Oraz and the lost treasure. Likewise, Scarlett had the antsy feeling she was going to have to start making some big, perhaps life-or-death decisions sooner than later if she wanted to reach her elusive treasure of freedom.

Sal nodded toward Jahja. "Even those jokers got tripped up. And it looks like they have some sort of map."

*Map*, Scarlett thought. "I have a compass!" she whispered, pulling the pendant out from the neckline of her dress and cracking it open.

"Why the hell haven't you been using it?" Sal said.

"Oi, take it easy," Thunder said.

"Don't tell me how to speak to my wife."

"I know tempers are a little short—"

"Get out of my face, you dumb shit."

"Mate. Look. We're on the same side here—"

Sal shoved Thunder backward. Jahja noticed the commotion and yelled at them to form a line. Sal and Thunder stared one another down for a tense moment before Thunder shook his head and turned away.

Soon they were trekking forward again, and Scarlett was surprised to find a warm tingling inside her chest. Thunder had stood up for her. And to Sal. She had not seen many men do that. In fact, she didn't think she'd ever seen someone openly oppose her husband like that.

What was Sal's problem anyway? It seemed as if he was getting more snappish by the hour. Was he cracking under the pressure of captivity? If so, she was surprised. She would have thought he'd be the last to break.

As they trudged on, it became a little cooler. Scarlett was no longer sweating. The sunlight that had managed to penetrate the canopy softened a little, changing from a brilliant white-yellow to a burning, muddy orange. Dusk was settling. It would be dark soon. And here they were still in the middle of the rainforest. Was Jahja planning on camping out here? She hoped not. She thought of that python skin again, of bird-eating spiders and foot-long centipedes and...and leopards. Yes, there were leopards in the jungle, weren't there? What if one grabbed her by the scruff of the neck while she slept and dragged her off?

Gradually the trees began to thin. The charcoal-gray air

lightened a few pencil shades, and they emerged from the murky rainforest into a clearing bathed red by the setting sun.

No, not just a clearing, Scarlett realized. The ruins of a long forgotten town. It looked as if there had once been fifty or so buildings in total. Most of them had since been reduced to skeletal timber frames or big piles of charred rubble. Only four Victorian-style structures remained intact. A church was the largest. It rose against the bloodying sky, creepers covering the redbrick façade and bell tower like a green disease. No terrorist paradise, that was for sure. A European colony perhaps? But why out here in the middle of nowhere?

Jahja consulted with Creep before leading the way down a lonely dirt road that had once served as the main street. Everyone followed. He stopped in front of one of the old yet intact buildings. Bushy plants surrounded the base while other tropical vegetation overhung the roofline. Carved into the weatherworn stone above the door was a blue-painted circle that sported an unrecognizable symbol. Below that were two words. Some of the letters had eroded away, and all that remained were: "NEEMA" and "O.N.G.O."

Scarlett had no idea what the first word was, but she had a good guess at the second one.

Congo.

So was that right? Were they in the Congo, the least explored landmass on the planet except for Antarctica? Great. Fan-tiddly-tastic. But it didn't surprise her or scare her. Not really. Because it didn't matter what country they were in. They were still in the middle of nowhere.

Jahja poked around inside the building, then returned and announced, "This is where you will be spending the next little while."

"For how long?" Sal asked.

"For however long it takes."

"What takes?"

"That doesn't concern you, Mr. Brazza."

"Of course it does," Sal snapped. "It's my life we're talking about here, you arrogant shit."

The three gunmen raised their rifles. Three safeties clicked.

"Some respect, please," Jahja said, unfazed by the outburst. "Now, as I was saying, this is where you will be staying. I don't encourage you to think about escape. As I've said, the jungle—"

"Is dangerous," Scarlett cut in.

"Very dangerous, Miss Cox," he said, eyeing her, apparently unsure whether she was mocking him or not. "It's pure wilderness in every direction. The only way out is the river, and even if you made it that far, which is highly unlikely, two of my men would be there to greet you. Also," he added, nodding at Creep, "he will be posted out front of your accommodations. Test him at your own peril."

Jahja smiled at them, smugly again. The waxy scar tissue twisted the smile into something unnatural and sinister, and Scarlett had the image of a monster trying to play a gentleman —or a gentleman made to play a monster. She wondered for the first time how he'd been burned, and whether it had anything to do with his hatred of Westerners.

Sal went inside the rickety building first, followed by Thunder, Scarlett, and the embassy women. It was a single room about the size of a large bedroom, furnished with a table, six chairs, and one plain wooden bench. There were no windows. Thin strips of light slipped through the cracks in the roof thirty feet up, painting rosy prison bars on the floor. It was better than the van and riverboat cabin certainly, but Scarlett wouldn't be recommending it to any of her friends any time soon. She slumped down in one of the chairs to rest her sore and blistered feet. Her legs and arms were covered with nicks and scrapes and insect bites. She began to worry about infection.

"No cable TV?" Thunder said, scratching a red welt on his arm.

"Are you all right?" she asked him.

"Just a bite."

She thought she saw something resembling fear cloud his eyes, but then it was gone.

He's just worried, she thought. Like all of us. He might be big and strong and an eternal optimist, but he's human as well. He's not immune to the hell we're going through.

"Yuck!" Miranda screeched suddenly. "Yuck!" She pulled a face and flapped a finger at her calf, where a black leech was attached, fattened with blood.

"Stay still," Joanna told her. "I'll pull it off."

"I wouldn't do that," Thunder said. "You'll leave part of the jaw in the wound. Could cause an infection."

"Well, we don't exactly have matches or salt, do we?"

"Not a good idea either. They cause the little buggers to regurgitate what's in their stomachs and can also cause an infection. It's best to let it get its fill and fall off."

"No!" Miranda said.

"You'll be right," Thunder told her.

"No!" She looked as though she were about to pass a kidney stone. "Get rid of it! Please?"

"Okay, okay. Take it easy, hey." Thunder glanced around. "Who has long fingernails? Lettie? You're going to have to break the seal of the oral sucker."

Scarlett came over. "How?"

"Slide your finger under the anterior end."

"Which end is that?"

"The thinner one."

Grimacing, Scarlett shoved her fingernail along Miranda's skin and under the plump, slimy leech. The leech came loose, thrashing violently. She flicked it away in disgust. It hung on. She tried again. The damn thing was like sticky glue. She went to a wall and rubbed it off.

"So much for the entertainment for the night," Sal said, sitting down at the end of the bench.

Thunder said to Scarlett, "Did you keep a compass reading?"

She nodded. "Checked every ten minutes or so. Each time we were heading northeast."

"So all we have to do is head southwest through the rainforest, then south along that path we followed through the jungle."

"Is that all?" Sal remarked caustically.

Joanna said, "That would take us right back to the boat, and the two gunmen."

Thunder shook his head. "We don't have to go to the boat. When we reach the river, we follow the bank out the way we came in."

"To where?" Scarlett asked.

"To somewhere away from here."

"Suicide," Sal said.

"Why?"

"Say we go through the rainforest. Southwest, like you said. The chance of ever finding the original path is slim at best. Without a machete we won't get through that jungle."

Thunder began pacing.

"What about the second river?" Scarlett suggested. "Even if we don't find the path, we'll still come across the second river. We can make a raft or something and float out, can't we?"

"That river was flowing in the same direction as the big river," Sal said. "The wrong way. Who knows where it would lead us?"

"We make paddles," Thunder said.

"The current is too strong. You saw how it almost flushed Scarlett away. We wouldn't get a dozen feet upstream."

"We can't just sit around here and do nothing."

"We don't have a choice," Joanna said.

"No. We get to the river. Follow the bank," Thunder said stubbornly. "We might see another boat. If we could get to one of those villages Lettie saw, we might be able to get the tribal people to lead us out of here."

"It would take days to get that far on foot," Joanna said. "I don't know about you, but I can't spend the night in the jungle. Where would we sleep? You saw the python skin."

"There're also scorpions and other bugs," Miranda said.

"If someone got sick or injured," Joanna went on, "they'd be finished."

"Not to mention food and water," Sal said.

Scarlett hated seeing Thunder get teamed up on. He was only thinking of a way to get them all out of this. But the others were right. They weren't going anywhere.

"Not to mention," Joanna said, beating the dead horse, "we would still need to get out of this building first."

"We don't know if someone is really out there." Thunder waved to the door in frustration.

"Why don't you go check it out?" Sal said.

"Right-o. I will."

Scarlett stopped him. "You don't know what he'll do."

"I reckon he's not even there."

Thunder stepped past her. He pressed his back against the wall and cracked open the door. He stuck his head out.

A burst of rapid-fire bullets zinged and pinged off the brick exterior.

Thunder ducked back inside, his face white.

A warning shot.

"I guess that settles that," Sal said, and he had the gall to smile.

Somewhere in the rainforest, a parrot screeched. The warm colors of dusk faded. Shadows pooled in the room, nibbling at the light until there was nothing left to devour but darkness itself.

# CHAPTER 25

I N THE SILVERY light of the full moon, Fitzgerald could make out the boxy shape of the riverboat moored against the north bank of the river. The design resembled a small Mississippi side-paddle steamer, something out of Mark Twain's time—only this one was equipped with twin outboard diesel engines. A lantern burned in the pilot house on the top deck. Nobody was visible inside. More light burned through the port-hole windows in the small aft cabin, which was about the size of a garden shed, maybe big enough for two men, maybe three if they were sleeping in bunks, or huddled around a table, playing cards. A much larger cabin dominated the main deck. The door was closed. The windows were dark. He didn't see any guards on patrol.

Fitzgerald had cut the skiff's engine several kilometers back and switched to the oars. Now he rowed to shore, kissed up against the north bank, and climbed out, sinking into the shin-deep mud. He wrapped the painter line around a tree trunk and secured it with a bowline knot. Then he waded into the water and used a silent breaststroke, careful not to open his mouth and swallow any water. The Ebola virus came from somewhere around here, not to mention a lot of other diseases he could do without.

While he swam he scanned the glassy surface of the water ahead and to the sides of him. It wasn't another hippo that worried him. Hippos went to shore at dusk to feed, when it was cool enough so they wouldn't risk sunburn or dehydration. It was the crocs he was now thinking about. He had seen countless of them during the day, lying on the banks of the river, unmoving, some with their jaws cracked wide to regulate their body temperature. They were cold-blooded and usually spent the day heating themselves up, leaving the hunting for the mornings and the evenings.

Or right about now.

Twenty meters from the riverboat Fitzgerald tread water, watching for movement on either of the two decks. He didn't see any and continued on. He reached the boat's hull, grabbed hold of a rubber bumper, and pulled himself up quietly onto the stern deck. He unlaced his boots and slipped them off. Waterlogged boots squished and squawked.

Because the Glock was now resting seven kilometers back on the riverbed, likely next to the carcass of One-eyed Bertha, he slid free his old SAS knife from his canvas ankle sheath. The handle was wood with solid brass rivets. The blade was eleven inches long and as sharp today as when the quartermaster issued it back in 1966. It was responsible for more deaths than his ageing memory could recall.

Many years ago he'd nicknamed it Carnwennan, after Arthur's dagger in the Welsh legends, which was known to shroud its wielder in shadows. He never called the dagger this out loud, of course; that would be silly. But that's how he thought of it. Carnwennan. It was a way to personalize it, to make it his own, the same way some men would give a name to their yacht, or residence.

He crossed the stern deck to the main cabin and peered through the window beside the door. He had expected to see Brazza and Cox and however many other hostages tied up inside, probably blindfolded. The room was empty. He frowned. Had AQ shed some of the hostages along the way, only keeping their golden eggs? And if so, were Brazza and Cox up in the aft cabin? No. Because if that was the case, where were the terrorists? He couldn't see them cozying up next to their hostages in a five-meter-square room. That left only one alternative. They had all gone ashore.

Words in Arabic floated down from the top deck.

Fitzgerald flattened himself against the shadowed wall of the cabin. He listened, but heard nothing more. He contemplated this and decided that a couple sentries must have remained behind to watch over the boat. That made sense, and it left him with two options. Go back to the skiff and spend the night there, wet and cold and hungry. Or clear out the lads upstairs, get a good meal, a good night's sleep, and set out warm and chipper in the morning. It was not a hard decision to make. Besides, from a tactical standpoint, it only made sense to take out the sentries. If he had to make a quick escape from the jungle tomorrow, he didn't want to worry about getting sandwiched between the bad guys.

Fitzgerald padded up the spiral iron staircase and stuck his head through the well-hole in the top deck. All clear. He dashed over to the aft cabin and pressed his back against the wall perpendicular to the cabin's door. He heard the occasional grumble from within the small room. Sometimes there was a response, sometimes there wasn't. After several minutes of this, he concluded there were only two men inside.

Wood scraped wood—the sound of a chair being pushed backward. The door creaked open. Footsteps crossed the deck.

Fitzgerald peered around the corner of the cabin.

A man dressed in plain clothing stood at the starboard railing, relieving himself. A Kalashnikov dangled from a strap looped over his shoulder.

Fitzgerald snuck up behind him, taking half strides for better balance, stepping down on the outer balls of his bare feet, as silent as the moonlight. The only noise was the continuous patter of urine striking water far below.

Fitzgerald stopped when he was within touching distance. He'd once seen a Polish thug put up a fight for well over a minute with a blade sticking out of his heart, and he knew there was no such thing as a quick and sure kill with an edged weapon. There was decapitation, of course, but without a sword that wasn't an option. Still, there were a couple close seconds: stabbing upward into the base of the skull, or downward into the soft spot behind the collarbone, severing the subclavian vein and artery, and, if you got lucky, maybe puncturing a lung.

Fitzgerald chose the simplest of all approaches. He grabbed the man by the hair and plunged Carnwennan into the side of the exposed neck, ripping outward toward the throat. The man jerked and flailed. Fitzgerald held him secure. Blood fountained everywhere, coating them both. The man was likely screaming, but he made no noise: he had no vocal cords left. He went limp.

Fitzgerald set the body down, wiped the dagger and his hands clean on the dead man's shirt, and collected the Kalashnikov. The safety, he noted, was in place. He left it that way. Moving the spring-loaded safety-cum-selector made a loud and distinctive click, which wasn't very productive if you wanted to keep the element of surprise.

He faced the aft cabin. He thought about simply kicking open the door and cutting down whoever was inside. But he didn't know how far away the land party was and didn't want to advertise his presence. Instead he returned to his original spot around the corner of the cabin and waited.

Two minutes later the man inside called out to his mate. When the dead man didn't call back, the door opened.

"Qasim?"

He made it about three paces before seeing his buddy lying in a pool of blood. He went immediately for his rifle. Fitzgerald was already moving, slipping around the corner of the cabin, stabbing the man twice in rapid succession. First in the right side, under his armpit, hilt-deep. Then through the underside of the bearded jaw, through the roof of the mouth, into the brain. Before the body hit the deck Fitzgerald had spun to face a possible third attacker.

No one came forth.

He eased open the door with the barrel of the Kalashnikov

and peeked inside. Empty. And lo and behold, there was a stock-pile of food and water. The food wasn't anything special—fruit and cassava, mostly—but Fitzgerald was ravenous, and it would make a feast. He unceremoniously dumped the two corpses into the river, then washed up and set out a large dinner on the deck table. Just as he was about to sit down to eat, he heard a splash in the water off the bow. He snatched the rifle and went to the railing.

A little ways downriver a croc was working on one of the dead men. Another croc was swimming toward the second body, silver ripples trailing from the nostrils. It reached the body, peeled its jaws wide, revealing rows of pointed fangs, then snapped down. Unable to tear meat like a lion, it shook its gnarled, saurian head, boiling up a whirlpool with its combed tail. Sinew tore loudly. Joints grinded and popped. Then the commotion died down, the black water calmed. In the after-math both the croc and body were gone.

Fitzgerald waited where he was, hoping for an encore. He wasn't to be disappointed. Moments later the croc broke through the surface of the water, its snout pointed skyward with a human leg poking out from between the jaws, the boot still on the foot. The croc gulped the leg down, its pale throat bulging like a pelican's. It sank back into the inky depth once more.

"Jaysus," he muttered. "Now there's something you don't see every day."

Whistling "Finnegan's Wake," he went back to finish his own dinner, albeit in a much less dramatic fashion.

# CHAPTER 26

I T WAS WELL into the night. Through the cracks in the roof Scarlett could see a sampling of stars, impossibly distant. They distracted her from her current predicament, made her think bigger, more philosophical thoughts than being kidnapped, made her feel as if the Congo wasn't so enormous after all, just a forest on a tiny planet. In fact, her plight was really an incredibly insignificant matter in the big picture of things, the picture of the fifteen-billion-year-old universe.

She shifted on the cold stone floor as she tried unsuccessfully to get comfortable. She'd fallen asleep for a little, but had woken a while ago. A migraine was digging in behind her left eye. It felt like someone was scraping around in there with a spoon. Yet there wasn't anything she could do about it. No aspirin here. No prescription meds. She'd just have to grin and bear it. It wasn't so hard though. She had a lot more serious things on her mind—maybe-I'm-going-to-die-tomorrow kind of things that the stars could distract her from but not make her forget.

She wished she knew the time or knew when morning would come. But the jackass terrorists had confiscated the gold wristwatch of hers—something she'd bought for herself after her first attempt at a romantic comedy had flopped at the box office. She'd thought buying an expensive gift would make her feel better. She had it engraved at the Tiffany's on Rodeo Drive, and it read: "To You, From Me." Sal had pestered her for months about who "me" was. She never told him; it had been her little joke. Now, it seemed, the joke was on her. "To Terrorist, From Scarlett."

Someone cried out. It sounded more like a word than a grunt, though she couldn't be sure what word it was. She sat up, grimacing against the pain in her head. She was just able to make out the shapes of the others in the feeble light. Sal was lying on the bench. Miranda and Joanna were in a far corner, curled against each other like spoons. Thunder was up front, near the door, away from everyone else.

The person cried out again, more of a moan this time. It was coming from where Thunder was sleeping. A bad nightmare? Or was he in some sort of pain? She got up and crept across the room toward him.

"Thunder?" she said softly, touching his shoulder. "Hey, are you okay?"

He came awake with a start.

"Shhh. It's me. Scarlett. You were making noises."

He tried to sit up but didn't seem to have the strength. She became more worried.

"Thunder, what's wrong?"

She felt his forehead. It was hot and drenched with sweat. God, what could he have? Dengue fever? Sleeping sickness? It couldn't be malaria, thankfully. Malaria symptoms, she believed, took about a week to show themselves.

She remembered the welt on his arm. It was difficult to find in the dark, but she made out a hard, swollen bump just above his left wrist.

"How old are you?" he asked groggily.

The question surprised her. "Thirty," she said, and for a moment she thought about the birthday party that never was. "Thunder, look at your arm. What happened?"

"It's just a bite."

"From what?"

"I'm thirty-six."

"Thunder, you need—" She was going to say "a doctor," but realized how ridiculous that would sound.

"I'm not married," he said.

Scarlett brushed his hair gently back from his forehead, wondering if he was speaking through a fever. She decided the least she could do was keep him company.

"Why not?" she asked. "Why aren't you married?"

"Was in a relationship for ten years. No rush to get serious again. Thought I had all the time in the world." He licked his lips and swallowed. "How long have you been married?"

"Four years now."

"He's a lucky bloke."

"Thank you, Thunder."

"He's also a complete arse."

Scarlett was so surprised by the comment she laughed out loud. She quickly caught herself and glanced in Sal's direction. Was he sleeping? Or awake, listening to them?

"Any ankle biters?" Thunder said.

"Huh?"

"Kids?"

"No."

"Have you ever been to Oz?"

"Sydney a couple times, to promote my films. Some strange animals you got there. Why do they all hop?"

"It's a big land. Hopping's faster than walking, I reckon."

"Have you always lived in Brisbane?"

"Grew up in Canberra, the capital. It's where my parents met. Mum's tops. You'd get along with her. She teaches kindy—kindergarten."

"What about your father? Is he a teacher as well?"

"Foreign diplomat. He was invited to the school where Mum taught, to get the kids stoked about politics or something like that. She was his chaperone. They got married a few months later. His post in Canberra was only for three years. When the State Department called him back, we were both supposed to go. But then Mum's sister got sick, so we stayed behind."

He squeezed his eyes, as if he was in pain.

"You need to rest," she told him.

"No, this is good. Talking." He opened his eyes again. Even in the darkness they seemed to sparkle blue. "The next year my dad was elected to the House of Reps. He was busy a lot. LA to Canberra was a long flight with a big time difference. Bottom line, it didn't work."

"They divorced?"

"That's life sometimes. Anyway, Mum's all apples. She remarried. She's happy."

"What about your father? Did he remarry?"

"Twice. He was engaged to his third wife when he was murdered."

"Murdered? God, why?"

"I don't know. No reason, pointless." He shivered. "I'm cold."

"I don't have anything to give you." She made a spontaneous decision. "Roll onto your side."

Thunder did as she'd instructed, grunting with the effort. She stretched out beside him, pressing herself against his back, how Joanna and Miranda were sleeping to keep warm. It felt as though she were doing something wrong, but it felt right too. Thunder didn't say anything.

"Do you think about your father much?" she said quietly. Her mouth was right next to his ear now. She could feel his body heat. It was coming off him in waves.

"Every now and then. I didn't really see him much after the divorce. How about you? Your folks must be mad with worry."

"My dad was a police officer. He was killed trying to prevent a convenience store robbery when I was six. He died over fifty bucks and a couple bottles of booze. My mother became clinically depressed and hanged herself the following year."

"I'm sorry, Lettie."

"I lived with my uncle and aunt for about two years before they handed me over to child welfare. Then I shuffled between three different foster families. They were all doing it for the money, I think. The upside? I don't think I ever would have gotten into acting if I'd had a normal childhood. Being an orphan gives you a good imagination. I had a make-believe family in my head until I was sixteen or seventeen. If that's not method acting, I don't know what is."

"Every cloud has a silver lining, hey?"

"Even this safari," she said softly. "You know that? I'm glad I met you, Thunder."

He was silent for a long moment. "It's been nice meeting you too, Lettie."

They were quiet after that. Eventually Thunder's breathing became deep and regular. Scarlett didn't want to move. She felt safe and content right where she was. Not so alone. Not so scared. The migraine had even softened a little.

She fell asleep next to Thunder.

# CHAPTER 27

FITZGERALD ROSE TO the murky half colors of predawn light. He scavenged an empty rucksack—his was still in the skiff, having not gone overboard in the hippo attack —and filled it with food and two large plastic bottles of water. He didn't need anything more, given he hoped to be back out of the jungle by nightfall.

He surveyed the riverbank, noting in particular a gnarled mangrove bent over the water, which he filed away in case the riverboat was gone for whatever reason when he returned. He disembarked and climbed the muddy bank. At the top he blotted his nose, forehead, and cheekbones with dark mud, using lighter dirt for the recesses under his eyes and along his throat. The camouflage not only masked his white pigmentation but also prevented the oil in his skin from forming a sheen, which would stand out in the dark jungle the same way a fish's scales would glint under sunny water. Next he decorated himself with leafy vegetation to break up his outline while providing him with a layer of earthy colors and textures.

Suitably prepared, he studied the ground and immediately spotted the trail Brazza & Co. had taken. It was well-beaten and easy enough to follow. He counted nine sets of footprints. Based on size and depression, he guessed three were female. Of the remaining six, one set obviously belonged to Brazza, leaving five potential bad guys.

Not ideal odds, five against one, he thought, but manageable.

He started along the trail, noting a number of animal tracks as well. A forest elephant, a gorilla moving with a knuckle-walking gait, a large leopard, and what he guessed was a red river hog and her piglets. He even came across the papery skin of a python. This one was only a baby, but he knew African rock pythons could grow to be eighteen feet long, large enough to swallow just about anything—including unsuspecting humans.

Once upon a time, years and years ago during the jungle warfare part of his SAS training in the jungles of Belize, Fitzgerald had been on patrol and came across a group of Mayan Indians searching for a little girl who'd been missing from the village for two days. He lent a hand with the search and shortly thereafter they discovered a large boa with an ominous bulge extending its middle section. They cut the snake open and found the missing girl inside, curled into a fetal position, partly digested.

Not exactly a nice way to go.

As the morning progressed, the rising sun burned away the damp mist, and Fitzgerald began sweating profusely. He drank a full liter of water, then refilled the bottle from a quick-moving river. Soon he entered old-growth rainforest. The trail he'd been following disappeared.

However, AQ had not been concerned with anti-tracking, and their spoor of upturned leaves was as clear as Hansel's breadcrumbs. An hour later, Fitzgerald slowed his pace. He would be closing in on his quarry and needed to reduce any unnecessary noise. The night before he'd used the southern star to chart his location and determine the tracks up the riverbank led due north. To confirm he was still heading in the same direction, he examined the stump of a felled tree. Growth rings were always closer together on the side of the stump facing the equator. Given what he saw, he concluded he was now heading northeast.

As he pressed on once more, he found himself thinking about the future. He was sixty-one, retirement age, even for an assassin—especially for an assassin. His body was not as strong as it had once been, his mind not as sharp. Most of all the fire had burned out of him. For so many years he had been addicted to the thrill and adventure and challenge of the job. But recently he found he was going through the motions more than anything else. Still, he kept at it for one simple reason. He was afraid to stop. Because what would he do with himself then? Sit around the flat all day? Read his books? If Eryn were still alive, he could have done that. In fact, he would have enjoyed nothing better. Hell, they might even have had grandkids by now—

He froze.

He had just broken through a wall of foliage into an open clearing. A man was chopping wood by a fire pit two hundred meters away. The man glanced in Fitzgerald's direction, as if he'd sensed another's presence. Fitzgerald dropped to his stomach, scrambled back through the underbrush, and flattened himself against the trunk of a tree. He counted to twenty, slowly, then looked around the trunk.

The man was gone.

Cursing himself, wondering if he'd been spotted, he moved through the forest until he found a good spot to lie up. He studied the clearing again. It was filled mostly with stone and timber ruins, and he guessed it had once been a colonial mining town that had been razed by a fire. The door to one of the intact buildings, a church, opened, and the woodchopper emerged. He gathered up some grass and headed off to the forest.

Going to the loo.

Fitzgerald relaxed. He hadn't been spotted after all. As he waited and watched, the African rainforest came slowly awake all around him. Red-chested cuckoos and Tambourine doves hooted and squawked. Old world monkeys howled. The sun inched higher into the rich blue sky, warming the air and lighting the seemingly infinite canopy like a match to green fire. He breathed the earthy, lush scents of the surrounding vegetation, and he felt extremely at peace right then, at one with nature, just as man had existed in his natural state for hundreds of thousands of years. He took out a bottle of water and drank a third.

Two more AQ came out of the church. One started a cooking fire while the other collected sticks to burn. Fitzgerald shifted his weight and settled in for the wait until Brazza needed to move his bowels himself. When Brazza did, and wandered off into the trees, he would be there waiting for him...

Fitzgerald frowned, suddenly uneasy.

Brazza?

The loo?

*The gunman hadn't returned from the bush yet—*

"Hands up!" a voice behind him barked. "No gun!"

The Kalashnikov was resting directly in front of Fitzgerald, within easy reach. But his chance of grabbing it, spinning around, and getting off an accurate round before being filled with holes was slim at best.

Smiling acidly, he raised his hands.

# CHAPTER 28

S CARLETT AWOKE STIFF and tired and depressed. She had only been in captivity for three nights, but it felt more like three months, like she was aging in dog years. Her head was on her arm, her nose against someone's neck, just below the hairline. For a moment she thought she was lying beside Sal before realizing with a start that it was Thunder. She sat up quickly and looked around. Miranda and Joanna were still asleep in the corner. Sal was sitting up on the bench, watching her.

"Good sleep?" he said, and it was almost a snarl.

"He was shivering last night. I was sharing my body heat."

"Bullshit."

"I don't need to explain myself to you."

Thunder stirred and sat up. A sheen of sweat covered his face.

"How do you feel?" Scarlett asked him.

He blinked a few times. "Pretty crook, to be honest."

"Stand up," Sal told him, standing himself.

Thunder frowned. "Huh?"

"Get to your goddamn feet."

"He saw me lying next to you," Scarlett explained. She addressed Sal. "He's sick. Can't you see that? Leave him alone."

"I don't care how sick he is. I'm going to make him a whole lot sicker."

"Stop this right now, Sal. You're acting like a child."

Thunder put a hand on her shoulder and lumbered to his feet, looking terribly weak. "Listen, mate—"

Sal swung a right hook. It connected squarely with Thunder's face, knocking him backward into the wall. Blood dribbled from his nose, tracing the groove of his upper lip.

"Stop it!" Scarlett shouted.

Miranda and Joanna came awake, confused and alarmed.

Thunder lowered his shoulder and bowled into Sal's gut, lifting him off his feet and dive-bombing him to the floor. Both men spat out breathless "oomphs" upon impact. They rolled back and forth, their arms and legs intertwined, each struggling to gain the advantage.

A frantic shout came from outside.

Everyone in the room—including Sal and Thunder—turned to stare at the door. More cries of alarm followed the first.

"What does that mean?" Miranda asked.

Before anyone could hazard a guess, the door flung open and Jahja appeared. His eyes were wild and wide. He looked at each of them in turn. He paused on Joanna.

"You!" he said. "Come outside! Now."

"Why?" Joanna asked, clearly frightened.

Jahja aimed a black pistol at her. "Obey me! Or I will shoot you right here."

Joanna kissed Miranda on the forehead, then went to the front of the room. Her face was white, her jaw set. She looked like a woman walking to her execution. Jahja grabbed her by the wrist and yanked her outside. The door banged shut behind them.

Scarlett glanced at Sal and Thunder, who both appeared as clueless as she felt.

She hurried to the door and inched it open and peered out between the crack.

Jahja was dragging Joanna toward the three other gunmen—all of whom had their guns trained on a tall man dressed head to toe in black and covered in camouflage.

Scarlett's knees went weak.

Who was he? Army? Marines?

*Could it be true? Were they about to be rescued?*

"There's someone out there," she said, her voice husky.

Sal was immediately behind her, looking over her head. "What the bloody hell is *he* doing here?"

Scarlett's mind spun. "You know him?"

"That's Benjamin Hill."

"Who? Jesus—you're right!" *Benjamin Hill.* Nothing made sense right then. But she didn't have the chance to work it out because Jahja pulled Joanna against his chest and shoved the barrel of the pistol against her temple.

"Tell them to come out!" he shouted. "Tell the rest of your men to come out of the forest or I will blow her brains out!"

The Irishman didn't reply.

"Call them out!"

No reply.

Jahja turned in a tight circle, glaring at the trees, as if they were sentient beings staring back. "Come out. Come out now! Or I will shoot her. On the count of three. One!"

He danced in a circle.

Joanna started to cry.

"Two!"

"No!" Scarlett shouted.

Jahja and the other gunmen whirled toward her.

Creep fired a round into the air.

Scarlett stumbled backward into the room. The door swung shut.

"Three!"

An electric silence followed. It seemed to stretch on forever. With each passing second, relief crept over Scarlett. Jahja wasn't going to do it. He was only bluffing—

A gunshot rang out.

AFTER SHOOTING THE middle-aged woman in the back of the head, execution style, the leader with the burned face com-

manded the three gunmen with the AKs—two AK-47s, one AKM
—to secure Fitzgerald to a chair in the left-wing transept of the
church. That's where he was sitting now. Across from him, the
arching stained-glass windows cast washed-out colors across
the bare walls and stone tiles, highlighting dust motes drifting
lazily in the air.

The leader held up Carnwennan. "This is military issue, yes?"

Fitzgerald said nothing.

"It's old. You're old. What is your rank?"

Fitzgerald said nothing.

"Green Beret? You are Green Beret? Or Navy SEAL?"

He said nothing.

"How did you find us?"

He said nothing.

"I don't have the patience for such games." The ugly sod
pointed a nine-millimeter Ruger P38 at his head. "Maybe I'll
shoot you right now."

Fitzgerald stared past the pistol. He'd interrogated more
people over the years than he could count, and he knew the
procedure inside out, knew the best course of action was to
keep quiet for as long as possible. The reasoning was simple.
The longer you could get by without saying anything, the better
your chances were the situation on the ground might change,
and with that, the possibility of escape. Not to mention if he
told his compatriot here that he was alone, the man would
likely kill him on the spot.

The leader lowered the pistol and sighed. "My name is Jahja
al-Ahmad," he said genially, suddenly the good guy. "What is
your name?" He was doing it all textbook style, as predictable
as a sunrise. Fitzgerald would have applauded had he been able.
"Would you like food? Water?"

Fitzgerald didn't answer.

"Are there others like you around?"

He didn't answer.

"Are they behind? Are they coming?"

He didn't answer.

"How did you get here?"

Fitzgerald cracked his neck.

"Where are the men on my boat? I can't reach them? What did you do to them?"

He didn't answer.

Jahja glowered at him for a long moment, then crossed the room to a table and returned with a pen. He slipped the pen between Fitzgerald's knuckles and squeezed Fitzgerald's fingers together, slowly, applying more and more pressure. It was an old trick and much more painful than it sounded. It felt as if the bones in his fingers were about to break.

Jahja asked more questions; Fitzgerald gritted his teeth and didn't answer them. Jahja finally gave up and barked something in Arabic to one of his men, who went outside and returned with a three-foot-long two-by-four.

"Okay," Jahja said, smiling hideously. "Let's try this one more time."

SCARLETT WAS IN some kind of shock. She could think of only one thing.

Joanna.

Dead.

After hearing the report of the gunshot, she had stuck her head out the door and saw Joanna lying facedown, blood encircling her head, coloring the brown dirt black. Sal had put his arm around her shoulder and said something, words of comfort likely. She couldn't remember what they were. They were just words. Words wouldn't change anything.

Joanna was dead. And she or Sal or Thunder or Miranda was going to be next.

Distantly, from what seemed nauseatingly far away, she became aware of Sal and Thunder talking about the Irishman, their animosity between one another at least temporarily suspended. It took her an immense effort, but she managed to pull herself out of the stupor. The room came back into focus, colors, shapes, sounds.

"He's an assassin," Sal was saying as he paced back and forth.

"Who's he here to kill?" Thunder asked.

Whatever burst of adrenaline he'd had earlier was gone. He was slumped against the opposite wall, his arms folded against his chest, shivering. The tan had drained from his face, leaving it a sickly pale white. Caked blood covered the gash in his forehead from the car crash, while more blood, still fresh and bright, smeared his mouth and jaw.

"Me," Sal replied. "He was trying to kill me."

"I don't follow."

"Good. I'd rather not get into it."

"Sal made enemies...with a man he used to work with," Scarlett told Thunder, her voice sounding oddly robotic to her ears. "A man with a lot of shady connections." She looked at Sal. "You really think Benjamin Hill is the person after you?"

"What else is he doing here? Besides, Danny told me the second assassin was an Irishman."

She frowned. "You never told me that."

"Why would I?"

"Why *wouldn't* you?"

"I never made the connection before now."

The fuzz cleared, and Scarlett became more incredulous by the second. Her voice was no longer robotic; it was fiery. "How could you not, Sal? Danny tells you an Irishman is after you. One shows up at the resort where we're staying. I even mentioned he likely wasn't a guest."

"I know all of that," Sal snapped. "You think I didn't connect the dots? But it made no sense. If he had wanted to kill me, he could have done it anytime. He didn't."

"How did he...?" Thunder swallowed. "How did he find you?"

"Thunder's right, Sal. How did he find you—us? How did one man accomplish what the entire US armed forces failed to do?"

"He followed us. It's the only explanation."

Scarlett ran the logistics through her head. "He couldn't have known we would be robbed. Couldn't have known we'd be making a detour to the embassy. Which means he must have either followed Thunder and me, or you. Did you see him on the plane?"

"Yes, cara mia. I offered him the window seat."

She ignored that. "It was one of those small turboprops, right?"

"When you're out shopping, do you check to see if you're being followed?"

"Let's assume he was on the plane, for argument's sake. Then what? How did you get from the airport to the embassy?"

"They sent a car for me."

"So he followed you to the embassy—and what? Watched us get thrown in the van? Then he followed us again for maybe ten, fifteen hours?" She shook her head. "We stopped in the middle of nowhere at one point. You might not have been looking for a tail, but the terrorists certainly would have been."

"Who the hell cares how he did it? Danny said the man was good. And Danny doesn't award compliments liberally."

"Whacking vice."

Scarlett looked at Thunder. His condition seemed to be deteriorating by the minute. She scooted over next to him and felt his temperature. It was even hotter than it had been the night before. "What did you say, Thunder?"

"Tracking device."

Sal snorted. "Let's not get carried away here."

"Jeepy..." He shivered. "GPS."

Sal laughed bitterly.

"Would you leave him alone?" Scarlett said. "Can't you see he's—"

"Dying?"

"Sick. He's sick, you, you—" She trailed off, unable to think of a suitable insult. "And what's so far-fetched about a tracking device?"

"When would he have had a chance to attach a transmitter to the van? Or the boat, for that matter?"

"Maybe it's smaller than you think. What about your

clothes? Maybe he slipped it on you during the drive up the crater. Or maybe he was in our room when we were out."

Sal stopped pacing.

"Check your clothes," she said.

While he took off his blazer and searched the pockets, she examined her sandals, dress, everywhere, but didn't find—

"Found something." Sal was kneading the crimson lining at the hem fold of the blazer's back vent. He tore the fabric and shook the garment until a small metallic something fell to the floor. He picked it up. "Bloody hell," he said. "I should have known it. His name. Benny Hill. He was mocking us the entire time."

Scarlett was stunned and numbed. Benjamin Hill was the assassin. Lightheaded, she recalled their meeting on the deck overlooking Ngorongoro Crater.

*Have you been down there, Mr ... ?*

*Hill, Benjamin Hill. And no, not yet. I'll be going tomorrow as well.*

*Perhaps we'll see each other?*

*Perhaps we will, Miss Cox.*

She remembered the strange smile he'd given her when she and Sal had transferred from his truck to the ranger's Land Rover. Had he had something planned for them, something that didn't work out? Had they narrowly escaped death? The skin on her scalp seemed to shrink a size.

"What's his real name?" she asked.

"Damien Fitzgerald," Sal said. "At least, that's what Danny thinks. He's not certain."

"What else did Danny tell you about him?"

"Nothing. Nobody knows anything about the man. He's a damn ghost."

"Nothing?"

Sal shrugged. "His wife and kid were murdered. He goes by the name Redstone. What a chump."

The door suddenly opened. Mustache and Beard poked the barrels of their automatic weapons into the room. "You," Mustache said to Sal. "You come."

"No!" Scarlett cried, thinking of Joanna.

Sal slipped the tracking device in his pocket. "It's okay. They likely only want to question me about Ben—Fitzgerald."

Sal left with the gunmen. Scarlett waited in agony to hear another gunshot. It never came.

"Thunder," she said urgently. "You were right. We need to get out of here as soon as possible."

He nodded, but his eyes were closed, his chin resting on his chest, and she didn't know if he heard her or not. How would he make it? He didn't look like he could stand. Regardless, she wasn't leaving him behind. No way. Either everyone got out or no one did. *All for one and one for all,* she thought, feeling like a damned Musketeer, and she didn't know if she wanted to laugh or cry.

"When Sal comes back," she went on, "we'll wait until dark. Maybe the gunman won't be outside tonight. Or if he is, we'll wait until he falls asleep. Then we'll make a break for it. Okay?"

The door opened again. This time Creep stood at the threshold. He looked directly at her and said, "You, your turn."

She gave Thunder's hand an affectionate squeeze, then glanced over at Miranda. The girl was sitting on a chair, staring at the ground. She hadn't moved or said a word since Joanna was shot. "Sit tight, Miranda," she said, then followed Creep outside.

It was an absurdly bright and sunny day, the kind of day you go for a picnic in the park or a stroll along the beach. Not one in which you had some lunatic sticking his gun in your back and marching you toward an uncertain future.

Before they reached the church—which Scarlett assumed the terrorists were using as a makeshift HQ given the limited alternatives—Creep ordered her to turn down an overgrown path that ran the length of one of the smaller buildings. She continued to the end, then stopped. There was nothing ahead of her except grass and, beyond that, the base of a hill prickled with trees.

"Move," Creep said. "Straight."

"Where to?"

"You go. Okay? Go."

Scarlett continued forward. With each step the sinking sensation in her gut deepened. This wasn't right. Why was he taking her to the forest, away from everyone else—?

She came to an abrupt halt, turned, and looked Creep in the eyes. They were swimming with lust. Just like on the riverboat. Just like in the forest.

Scarlett went cold all over.

Seeing that she understood his intentions, Creep's single eyebrow dipped in the middle, forming the letter M. Scarlett made to run, but he grabbed her hair and yanked her backward. He clamped a hand over her mouth and tugged her body against his. He pulled up her dress. His fingers dug beneath the elastic waistband of her panties, tearing them away. To her disgust, she felt that he was already aroused.

She twisted wildly, but couldn't shake free. She bit into the hand over her mouth with all the ferocity she could muster. She tasted a gush of hot blood and a chunk of flesh. Creep howled in pain. His grip slackened. She managed to push away, but before she could make it two steps, he had her again, spinning her around and slapping her so hard she fell to her back.

Then he was on her.

Scarlett screamed.

He slapped her a second time. When she blinked away the stars, her dress was up around her waist; his pants were down around his knees. She thrashed from side to side, but he was too heavy. She couldn't buck him off her. He flicked aside her necklaces, yanked at the neckline of her dress. Buttons popped. Desperate, she grabbed the three-inch lion claw that Cooper had given her and raked it across Creep's face, drawing a long gash down his left cheek. She swung it again, this time jabbing it into his forehead and tugging down, through his eye.

Clear fluid erupted, like juice squeezed from a grape. Roaring now, Creep rolled off her, allowing her to crab-crawl away. He looked up at her, one hand cupped under the dead eye in a losing effort to catch the pooling, overflowing blood. His seeing eye radiated pure hatred.

Scarlett shot to her feet and ran as fast as she could toward the forest, propelled by sheer terror. Above her labored breathing she could hear Creep giving chase right behind her. The forest drew closer, thick and impenetrable. Her screaming mind told her it would stop her dead in her tracks, but she didn't know where else to go. *If he catches you he's going to rape and kill you—rape and kill you after he cuts out your eyes to get even...*

She spotted a gaping crevice in the hill. It was about the size of a door and framed by slabs of stone and timber and so overgrown with vegetation she hadn't seen it from farther away.

A mine entrance?

She didn't care. It didn't matter. All that mattered was getting away.

She made a beeline toward it.

The waist-high grass flapped past her legs. The ground was hard and uneven, and she kept expecting herself to trip and fall. She never did. If she did, she would die. Then, before she knew it, she was rushing straight into the mouth of the mine, raising her arms for protection against the vines and branches that snapped past her face. Darkness engulfed her. She charged deeper, one hand surfing the stone wall. She was running too fast, too reckless. She was going to hit something. Still, she barely slowed.

She could hear Creep right on her heels. All he had to do was reach out and—

The ground lurched. Scarlett stumbled and smacked wooden boards, which swung wildly beneath her weight. Creep tripped over her, going down as well. She scrambled on all fours past him. One of her arms plunged between the planks into nothingness.

*How far up was she? What was below?*

Just as she freed her arm, Creep reached her, his hands tearing at her clothes, his body writhing against hers, his putrid breath wafting over her.

Suddenly her dress was up around her waist again. The

boards scraped and chafed her bare legs and rear. She felt *it* on top of her. Small. Hard. Poking. She was revolted.

He was trying to pry her legs apart. She squeezed them more tightly together.

Then there was a sharp, whip-like crack, followed immediately by another.

Scarlett felt herself falling.

# CHAPTER 29

"**I**F YOU DON'T get him to talk," Jahja told Sal, "I will kill you. Do you understand that?"

Sal stared at Damien Fitzgerald. The assassin was strapped to a wooden chair, his legs extended straight out in front of him, his pants rolled up to reveal ripped and bleeding shins. Skin hung away in flaps that exposed the flesh beneath. Next to the chair was the two-by-four which he assumed the terrorists had scraped up and down the man's shins, like a cheese grater.

Good.

"What do you want to know?" Sal asked.

"Who he is. What he is doing here."

"His name is Damien Fitzgerald. He's a halfwit assassin."

Sal went on to explain everything he knew, from the Prince Tower fire to what Danny had learned from Don Xi in Macau. The entire time he kept his eyes fixed on the Irishman, who didn't seem to notice or care. It was as if he'd withdrawn into himself.

"Here's some proof," he finished, taking the tracking device from his pocket.

Jahja examined it. "This is true? What you tell me?"

"Why would I lie?"

Jahja nodded. "Yes, maybe I do believe you. And if this is the case, it would be only prudent to get rid of the assassin. I see no further need of him."

Fitzgerald finally looked at Sal. His eyes were daggers.

Abruptly a woman screamed. It was distant and shrill. A man cried out in what sounded like excruciating pain moments later.

Jahja and the two gunmen exchanged a few quick words in Arabic. Then Jahja and the goon with the beard ran outside, while the one with the mustache went to the church entrance but didn't leave. Sal remained where he was, wondering what the hell was happening. His helplessness, his inability to act, enraged him.

"You're a fecking pillock," Fitzgerald said.

Sal looked at him. "That's the best you got?"

"Do you want to live?"

"You're asking me that?" he said, amazed. "You're about to be executed, my friend."

"And you soon after."

"I'll take my chances."

But in truth Sal was concerned. He wasn't dealing with rational people. They'd shot Joanna in cold blood, and they'd said nothing so far about ransom negotiations. So what if he'd been wrong all along? What if they didn't want money? If that was true, then the Irishman was right. He was living on borrowed time.

"I can help get you out of this," Fitzgerald told him. "First give me your word you'll release me afterward."

"Fine." Sal shrugged. "You have it. My word."

"Is it worth anything?"

"It's worth your life. Do you have any other choice?"

Fitzgerald straightened in the chair and pulled his legs in, grimacing with the effort. "I'm going to make a distraction," he explained. "When the wanker by the door comes to investigate, you grab the two-by-four and take him out."

"That's it?"

"What the feck else do you want? A sodding airstrike? Take him out. Take his weapon. Get rid of the other two when they return. Do you have a better idea?"

Sal ran the plan through his head. It could work.

"Time's running out," Fitzgerald said. "Make an executive decision."

Sal let the jibe pass. "Fine."

"Step back, closer to the two-by-four."

Sal stepped back.

Fitzgerald rolled his eyes up in his head and started convulsing.

"Hey!" Sal shouted. "Help him!"

The gunman returned from the entrance, cautious, likely expecting a trick. The AK-47 was gripped tightly in both hands. Sal took another step back, giving him room, while positioning himself closer to the two-by-four. The gunman didn't try to help Fitzgerald. He just stood there, watching him convulse. The distraction wasn't going to work, Sal thought in frustration. There would be no chance to grab the piece of wood. He glanced at the entrance. The other two would be back soon. He had to do something—

Fitzgerald's legs shot out and locked around the gunman's left knee. He jerked his body sideways, sending himself and the chair and the gunman all crashing to the floor. The gunman's cocked elbows struck the stone, hard, causing him to release the assault rifle, which clattered harmlessly away.

Sal took two quick steps and snatched up the two-by-four. He swung it with all his strength at the back of the gunman's head. It struck with a satisfying crack, like a home run. The man's skull caved in, and he went limp.

"Quickly now, move the body," Fitzgerald barked from his position on his side. "They can see it from the entrance. Then take his rifle and get to one side of the door, out of sight, out of their line of fire. As soon as they enter, spray them from behind. They won't be expecting it."

Sal didn't like taking orders, but what the Irishman said made sense. He dragged the corpse between two front rows of pews and picked up the assault rifle.

"Is it on semi- or full-automatic?" Fitzgerald asked.

"Hell if I know."

"See the selector? If it's in the lowest position, it's on single fire."

Sal moved it up. "It's in the middle now."

"Good. Pull back and release the charging handle."

Sal followed the instructions, then went to the narthex, which was nothing more than a barren stone rectangle. He pressed himself into the corner adjacent to the tall doors as he heard voices approaching, chattering urgently in Arabic.

When the two terrorists stepped into view, Sal squeezed the trigger. The roar of gunfire was deafening in the small enclosure, punctuated by the fragile sound of expended casings striking the stone floor. The terrorist with the beard dropped. But his body acted as a shield, protecting Jahja, who immediately leapt back through the church doors.

Sal charged after him, itching to let loose another burst of bullets. As soon as he stepped outside, however, two gunshots boomed. He pivoted back inside. "Christ!" he swore, peering out the doors right as Jahja ducked into the building-cum-prison.

*Go after him or wait?*

Before Sal could answer that question, Jahja burst back out-side, holding Miranda against his chest, the pistol to her head. "Don't shoot!" he shouted. "I'll kill her!"

Sal aimed the rifle. They were two hundred fifty feet away.

Jahja backed up, keeping Miranda between himself and the church.

He was going to make a break for it.

Sal considered letting Jahja go, but quickly changed his mind. He might regroup with the remaining gunman, wherever he was, making it two against one. Or he might double back to the riverboat and return with the two gunmen they had left be-hind. Which left only one option.

Sal peered through the iron sight, said a silent apology to the embassy girl, and squeezed the trigger. Bullets chewed the ground ten feet in front of Miranda and Jahja.

He aimed higher, fired again.

Miranda's body jerked and flapped like a shirt caught in a strong wind. Jahja's face stretched wide in surprise. He shoved aside the dead girl, let off two shots, and ran. But a bullet must have hit him, or gone through Miranda and into him, because after a few steps he dropped the pistol and sank to his knees. He started to crawl.

Sal left the cover of the church and approached cautiously, the rifle's laminated wood butt stock pressed tightly against his shoulder, his left hand on the forend grip, his right on the pistol grip, his index finger taking up the slack in the trigger. He reached the discarded pistol, picked it up, and crossed the final few feet to Jahja, who was still trying to crawl away. Pathetic. He put his foot solidly on the man's back and shoved him to the ground.

Jahja rolled over. His eyes burned with black hatred.

"*Allahu Akbar!*" he shouted, blood spurting from his mouth.

Sal raised the handgun and squeezed the trigger.

Jahja flopped to his side. His legs twitched. Then he lay still.

Resisting the urge to empty the entire magazine into the fanatic, knowing he needed to save ammunition, Sal returned to the church to finish the Irishman off. He didn't care if he had given his word or not, the man was too dangerous to set free.

As soon as Sal entered the nave, however, he froze. The overturned chair in the transept was empty.

Damien Fitzgerald was gone.

# CHAPTER 30

BLACKNESS AND PAIN. Christ, the pain! Was she hung over? That's what it felt like. The worst damn hangover in the existence of alcohol. Everything throbbed—her head, her arms, her shoulders, her butt.

The fall.

Scarlett opened her eyes. More blackness, more pain. She sat up and cried out. Her back felt broken. She knew that couldn't be true though; if it were, she wouldn't be sitting up. She blinked, but there wasn't anything to see except darkness. Her head was muzzy—mashed potatoes—but she pulled herself together and knew she must be somewhere in the bowels of the mine. She remembered falling for what seemed an incredibly long time...and then nothing.

She tried to stand. Every muscle in her body cried out in protest, as if she were doing something unnatural. She instinctively looked up, but couldn't make out anything.

How far had she fallen? Twenty feet? Twenty-five? More? Did it matter? Well, yes, because she had to somehow get the hell back out. She thought it could have been twenty-five feet or more. That was not cheerful news.

She shuffled around, trying to get a feel for her surroundings. Her foot brushed something warm and hairy. She yelped, jumping away.

It was Creep. Had to be. She must have landed on him. He

broke her fall. That's why she only felt like an animated corpse and wasn't actually one.

Steeling her nerve, she checked his pulse.

None. He was dead.

"Thank God," she said softly. Reassured by the sound of her voice, she added, "You deserved it, you sick bastard."

Scarlett patted around for his assault rifle, touched cool metal, worked the strap loose from around his neck, and hooked it over her shoulder. Right. Now what? A gun wasn't going to do much good against darkness. She probed blindly with outstretched arms. It took her a few minutes because she was moving slow, not wanting to knock her head on something, but she eventually determined she was in a tunnel approximately five feet wide.

Given that she could only go one way or the other, she went right, hoping it didn't lead her deeper underground. She walked cautiously, one hand against the rocky wall. With each step, her head cleared and she became more frightened as the reality of her new predicament settled over her like a lead cloak, wanting to crush her strength, her spirit.

The mine could be like an ant farm, with hundreds of tunnels zigzagging every which way. How would she ever navigate her way out? There were likely animals around as well. Certainly bats and insects. Maybe something worse. Maybe something huge and reptilian and ancient that hadn't been discovered yet because it lived in the middle of the Congo at the bottom of an abandoned mine.

Fresh panic fluttered in Scarlett's gut. What if she never reached the surface? How long would she last? Even if she was lucky enough to find water—flowing water, not a dirty, stagnant pool—she would never find food. She would be doomed to die the slow and painful death of starvation, not much more than skin and a skull on an emancipated body, her final moments spent curled up in a fetal position, as if rigor knew what was coming and decided to prematurely settle in.

Then again, she thought, she might slip and crack her head

long before that.

Abruptly her hand brushed a vertical strip of wood.

*A ladder.*

A tremor of relief rocked her body. She gripped the worn and roughly hewn parallel stringers and tried to rattle them. They were solid, affixed somehow to the stone wall.

Scarlett climbed.

Ten feet up the rock closed in around her so she was ascending through a tight tunnel drilled through the earth. Twenty feet. Thirty. Thirty-five. Had she really fallen this far? When was the shaft going to end?

A rung snapped under her weight.

Scarlett cried out, her feet dangling in the air. Holding on only by her hands, she kicked frantically until she found purchase. She clung fiercely to the left upright, her breath coming in deep and ragged gasps in the dark.

Once she got herself under control, she continued upward, now stepping on the outermost edges of each rung, which she thought would be stronger. It turned out she'd been almost at the top because several steps later the ladder came to an end, the top poking a couple feet above the floor of a new lateral shaft. Carefully, very carefully, she shifted onto the dirt ground, where she flipped onto her back, grateful to have something beneath her again. She stared into the blackness, listening to her breathing. Then she frowned—in a good way. Was the air less stuffy, less dank? Was this the original level she'd been on before crashing through the rope bridge?

Scarlett pushed herself to her feet and started in the opposite direction she'd gone earlier, believing it would take her back the way she'd come. She went slowly, knowing her next step could send her plummeting down a different ladder hole. After about twenty paces the blackness started to lighten, or at least she thought it did. Another twenty paces confirmed it. The blackness was now a deep gray. The air had changed as well. It smelled cleaner.

Hope welled in her chest. She'd never felt such euphoria; she felt as if she were floating. A little farther on spears of sunlight pierced the dark. Scarlett ran the remaining distance, not caring about ladder holes or rocks in her path or anything. Maybe she was a little crazy right then. Maybe something had ticked over inside her head from sane to insane. Maybe—but she didn't care. All that mattered was getting out of the god-awful mine.

She kept running and before she knew it she burst through the mesh of vegetation overgrowing the exit, crashing into a bramble of bush and small shrubs. She fell to her chest and laughed and sobbed. The smell of dirt and grass was divine. Emerging from the darkness to the light felt like some miraculous rebirth. She was free!

*Not just from the mine,* she realized, still high on ecstasy, *but from the terrorists as well.*

Scarlett didn't know how long she laid there for, reveling in her freedom, but eventually she pushed herself to her feet and turned around in a circle.

Some of her elation dripped away. There was no field ahead of her, no scattering of ruined buildings. All she could see in every direction were masses of verdant green trees and bush. It took her a moment to realize what had happened. She'd exited a different mineshaft than the one she'd entered. That worried her. If she went the wrong way now, she would be utterly lost.

Her temporary high plummeted to a new low and she felt defeated. She slumped down on a large rock and ran her hands through her oily hair. Her tan sandals were mud black. The frosty-pink nail polish on each of her toenails had been scraped away. Her legs wept with sores. Her dress was filthy and spotted with blood. The top three buttons were missing so it hung open around her neck, exposing her white bra and the necklaces.

*The necklaces.*

Sitting straighter, Scarlett yanked the steel pendant over her head and cracked it open to reveal the compass. *Thank you, old woman!* Knowing she would only have one chance to get this right, Scarlett cleared her mind of everything but the matter at hand. The compass had said they'd gone northwest from the riverboat. The original mine entrance was directly opposite where they'd emerged into the clearing, which meant it was in the same direction, northwest—which meant if she headed south, she should find her way back to the clearing.

Right?

Right.

She hoped. She turned the compass housing until the direction of the travel arrow was facing the south marker. She adjusted her feet until the red part of the needle—the part that faced south, because she was in the southern hemisphere—was aligned with the orienting arrow.

Holding the compass flat, she set off in a southward direction.

The vegetation was dense. Several times she was forced to circumvent impassable obstacles such as thickets of razor-sharp thorns or gigantic spider webs dotted with thousands of tiny spiders. At one point she heard a primal, ghoulish screech echo through the towering canopy. She looked up and saw shadowy shapes swinging through the branches. They were agile and stealthy and most likely chimpanzees—ruthless and organized hunters that fed on smaller monkeys. She might not be a small monkey herself, but she didn't want to wait around to see if they knew that. She began to run, tripping and falling several times in her haste, only slowing again when the otherworldly cries faded behind her.

Nevertheless, the farther Scarlett went with no sign of the clearing, the more disillusioned she became with her orienteering skills. What if she was going the wrong way? What if she'd gone too far east or west and had walked straight past the clearing? Or what if the compass was in fact made for the northern hemisphere, not the south. Did that make a difference? All she knew was that magnetic compasses were fitted with weights, because the needle not only pointed either north or south but also down, since both poles were buried deep within the earth. If the counterbalancing weights were indeed mixed up, would that affect the reading? Did her compass even have weights?

After all, she'd bought the damn thing from a third-world market.

Scarlett wanted to scream. She was no freer than when she was under the thumb of Jahja and his henchmen. Regardless, stopping wasn't an option, nor was turning back. So she trudged on, the rifle strap digging ever deeper into her shoulder, the barrel smacking the back of her legs. She focused on the pain, welcomed it even, because it kept her moving and alert.

Then, like stepping through a magic curtain, the forest vanished and the field appeared, golden-green in the sunshine. It was beautiful, picture-perfect. If Scarlett had the energy, she might have whooped with joy. But all she did was sag, exhausted, against a tree and try to catch her labored breath. Her dress, she noticed, was now ripped in several places and was so saturated with sweat she could have just stepped out of a swimming pool. Her throat was on fire, as if she'd just run a marathon.

Minute by minute, however, she began to regain her strength and pull her thoughts together. And she became increasingly glad she hadn't celebrated after all. It would have been premature and foolish, because what was she going to do now? Run in bullets flying à la Chuck Norris, cutting down all the bad guys?

She straightened and surveyed the backside of the cluster of brick-and-stone buildings. Creep had been the one guarding the door to the prison the day before, but now that he was dead, she hoped no one would be watching it. If that turned out to be the case, and she could slip inside the prison unnoticed, she'd rally Thunder and Sal and Miranda and make a break for the river.

*Was that the plan then?*

Apparently so. Simple and sweet and likely suicidal, but it was the best she could come up with.

Scarlett crept along the edge of the forest until she had a clear view of the street—and what she saw confused and terrified her.

There were three bodies lying in the dirt.

One belonged to Joanna. But who did the other two belong to?

Before Scarlett allowed herself to begin on wild speculation, she dashed across the open grassland to a lone silk cotton tree that was halfway between the edge of the forest and the ruins. The diameter of the trunk was at least six feet, providing her ample cover. She peered over a buttress root and gasped. One of the bodies was Miranda. She recognized the girl's long hair and lanky limbs. The other was pudgy and dressed in olive green.

Jahja?

Scarlett experienced a sudden disassociation of sense. *Why did they kill Miranda? And who the hell killed Jahja? Where were Thunder and Sal? Were they dead or alive? And where were the other two gunmen?* She closed her eyes briefly against the dizziness that threatened to drop her.

There was only one way to find out.

Scarlett hefted the AK-47 in front of her. It was heavy, maybe seven or eight pounds, and smelled of oil. She said a silent prayer, apologizing to whoever was listening for being an atheist for so many years, then darted out from behind the tree. She covered the last fifty yards to the back of the prison, slunk along the side of the building, and peeked around the front corner.

The street was empty except for the three bodies.

She followed the façade of the building to the front door and slipped inside. Coolness, darkness—and Thunder, curled into a ball, exactly where she'd left him.

*He was alive!*

She knelt beside him. "Thunder," she said urgently. "What happened?"

He opened his eyes. They were rheumy and unfocused. "Shooting," he mumbled.

"But why?"

"Don't know."

"Where's Sal?"

"Took him."

"I know. I was here for that. He never returned?"

"Don't think."

"Okay, hold on. I'm going to go look for him. Then we're getting out of here."

Outside, holding the assault rifle in both hands, diagonal across her chest like a soldier, Scarlett felt like a pretender, considering she didn't even know how to use the stupid thing. But she felt more confident gripping it that way than letting it dangle uselessly at her side. She looked left, then right, like she'd been taught by the police officer who'd visited her elementary school twenty years ago. No drunk drivers. No terrorists pumped to rape or kill her. She dashed across the road without incident and before she could think better of it rushed through the church's front entrance, pointing the rifle ahead of her, ready to fire at anybody in camouflage.

She slipped in a slick of blood and went down hard, stinging her hands and jarring her knees. She whirled and spotted one of the gunmen—Beard—lying on the floor a few feet away. His body was riddled with bullet holes. She looked at her apple-red palms and thought she might be sick.

"Scarlett?"

She bumbled for the rifle that was still hanging on the strap around her neck and swung it toward whoever had called to her.

It was Sal!

He was behind the high altar, pointing his own rifle at her. A rush of euphoria coursed through her body.

"Sal!" she exclaimed. She ran over and threw her arms around him, almost knocking him over in the process.

"Where were you?" he demanded. His voice was firm yet gentle at the same time.

"He took me to the woods," she blurted into his shoulder. "He wanted to rape me. I got away. He chased me into a mine. The bridge broke. We fell. I landed on him. He's dead."

"Who?"

"Creep—one of the gunmen."

"Good lord!" Sal broke apart. His eyes were feverish with satisfaction. "That's all of them then."

Scarlett did the math. Creep. Jahja. Beard. That was three— three out of four. They were missing Mustache. "No," she said.

"There's one more."

Sal gave her his own count, which included a terrorist lying between the pews. She couldn't see the floor between the pews from the chancel where she stood, but she did see a bloody smear leading from the transept into the rows of wooden benches.

"They're really dead?" she said, dumbstruck. "All of them? They're all dead?" It seemed too good to be true.

"Except for the Irishman." Sal nodded to an open door in the outer wall of the ambulatory. "Bastard escaped."

She felt a shot of fear. "He's around here somewhere?"

Sal shook his head. "He heard my story about Don Xi. Knows the man paying his bill is dead. And he was in pretty bad shape. I'm guessing he would have been eager to simply get the hell out of here."

"Don Xi's dead? I thought—"

"I'll explain later."

Scarlett was about to protest, but didn't. She didn't give a rat's ass about Don Xi right then. "Where would the Irishman go?" she asked instead.

"He got here somehow. I'm sure he had a way to get back out again."

"What about Miranda? I saw her body. What happened to her?"

"She tried to run away. The guy by the door shot her."

"What else happened? How did you kill them all?"

"It's complicated," he said shortly. "I'll explain later."

Scarlett nodded understandingly. She didn't want to talk about what Creep had done to her either. Not now, at least. There'd be time in the future to sit down and sift through it all. God, she thought, she had a future again. "So what should we do?"

"Wait for Danny."

"What?"

"Danny's coming," Sal said nonchalantly, as if Danny's arrival had always been a foregone conclusion. "He'll be here in a few hours."

"But how?"

"I called him on that."

Sal indicated a hard orange case about the size of a laptop sitting on the center of the altar. It was open, revealing something slightly larger than a regular cell phone cushioned in blow-molded gray foam.

"How does he even know where we are? *We* don't even know where we are."

Sal pulled a square from his pocket and unfolded it.

"The map!" she said.

He nodded. "Complete with latitude and longitude markers. We're just inside the Democratic Republic of the Congo, about halfway between the eastern border and the Congo River."

So I was right, she thought inconsequentially. It's the Congo.

"Danny's really coming?" she said.

"I gave him our grid reference. He should be here in a couple hours."

"How can he possibly get here so quickly?"

"You have to give the man more respect, cara mia. He's been in Tanzania for days now. He chartered a helicopter, which he's kept on standby, ready to fly as soon as he got wind of our location."

Scarlett's years of pent-up hostility toward Danny Zamir instantly went up in smoke. She felt as though the best player in sport, her competition for so many years, had suddenly been traded to her team. She decided she owed him a big apology when she saw him, maybe even a hug.

"What about the police?" she said. "Did you call them?"

"No need. The jet's fully fueled and waiting in Dar es Salaam. We can be back in the States by tomorrow morning.

"Can we do that? Just leave? Don't we—"

"I'm not sitting around here while the locals try to sort this bloody mess out. It could take weeks, and I don't know about you, but I'm sick of Africa. We're not criminals. We didn't do anything illegal. Everything that happened was in self-defense.

If they have questions for us, they can contact us in LA."

"I don't think it works like that, Sal."

"They can talk to my lawyers then."

"What about Thunder?"

"We'll drop him off at the airport. They can take him to a hospital from there."

"He's in bad shape. I wish there was something we could do for him now."

Sal nodded to the three rucksacks the terrorists had carried in on their backs. They were resting in a heap against the apse. "Maybe there's some medicine in one of those?"

Scarlett rifled through the top one and found a first-aid kit. She messed through adhesive and gauze pads and bandages until she found several packages of aspirin. She stuck two in her pocket for Thunder, thinking they might help his fever, then tore open another two and dry-swallowed the tablets.

Sal was watching her. "Migraine?"

"It's been on and off since we were thrown in the van."

"Guess this really wasn't the R&R you were expecting?"

"We should have gone to the Caribbean," she told him dryly.

Back outside, Scarlett noticed the sky had darkened to an ominous gray. Her eyes fell on Miranda and Joanna's bodies. Her relief at finding Sal okay and her excitement upon learning Danny was on his way to rescue them were immediately doused. The embassy women were dead. Emptiness swept through her.

"We should bring them inside the church," she said. "It's going to rain."

Sal nodded. As they walked over to the bodies, Scarlett tried to avert her gaze, but her eyes were drawn to the corpses the same way a motorist's eyes were drawn to a gruesome roadside accident. Death might be horrible but, like it or not, it was fascinating. In this case it had made parodies of the embassy women's former selves—schlock-horror B-movie zombies.

Joanna, dignified in life, was facedown in the mud, a big piece of her skull missing. Her arms were at her side, her legs slightly apart, the left one bent at the knee. Miranda was on her back, staring up into the gray sky with sightless eyes. Her skin was ghostly white, her mouth open in a silent scream, her blouse shredded from shrapnel. Through the holes in the silk her skin and bra were visible, both painted a dark crimson.

"We'll move Miranda first," Sal said. "She's lighter."

Scarlett took hold of Miranda's wrists, which were cool and clammy, while Sal grabbed her by the ankles. Rigor hadn't set in yet so she was still flexible and easy enough to lift. As they carried the girl to the church, Scarlett could smell urine and sweat. They returned for Joanna and brought her inside as well. The two bodies now rested side by side in front of the altar.

"We should cover them with something," Scarlett said.

She went to the recessed apse, where a five-by-ten-foot tapestry hung on the wall. The woven picture displayed a large cross hovering in the blue sky with golden beams of sunlight slanting away from it over a small village surrounded by trees. It took her a moment to realize the village was probably a depiction of the one she was in now, before it had been burned to the ground.

She gave the tapestry a solid tug. There was a brief rip-tearing noise, then the entire thing was lying in a heap at her feet. And she was left staring at a wooden door in the stone wall.

# CHAPTER 31

"LOOK AT THAT," Sal said, coming to stand beside her. He gripped the black doorknob and pulled the door open. The hinges groaned like something out of a haunted house. A stone passageway curved away into darkness.

"Where do you think it leads?" Scarlett asked.

"An undercroft, I presume."

She could feel cool air coming up from the passage. "Maybe we should take Joanna and Miranda down there? It would preserve their bodies better until help arrives for them."

"It's too dark. If you tripped on those stairs, you might break your neck."

"Hold on." She went to the rucksacks and dug through them, retrieving the two flashlights she'd noticed while searching for the first-aid kit. She flicked them both on to make sure they worked. They did. She returned to Sal, handed him one, and started down.

"You forgot the bodies," he said from behind her.

"I'm checking it out first."

The stairs were narrow and steep and curving. The yellow beams of the two flashlights cut circular swaths in the darkness, revealing grimy, crumbling stone walls. The stairs seemed to go on and on before they emerged in a large open space. Scarlett felt dwarfed, like a spelunker who'd just stumbled upon a vast cavern.

She directed the flashlight around. The undercroft was brick-lined with high vaulted ceilings. It seemed to extend not only below the chancel but the nave and transepts as well. Corridors stretched away from the main section at right angles. Except for the slow plink-plink of dripping water, it was tomb quiet, the air dank and smelling of mildew and age.

"Spooky," Sal said from beside her.

Scarlett said, "Let's go get Miranda."

"Not so fast. You wanted to check it out, so let's check it out."

"I've seen enough."

"Just a few minutes."

Before she could reply, Sal walked away from her to the nearest corridor, leaving her alone. She hurried to catch up. The arched alcove was about twenty feet deep. At the end of it was a rectangular box.

"Don't tell me that's a coffin," she said. She was whispering, though she didn't know why. Nobody was around to hear her. But it seemed appropriate considering this place wasn't an undercroft as they'd previously assumed; it was a crypt—a place for the dead.

"Give me a hand with the lid," Sal said.

"Are you nuts?"

"What's the problem?"

"Why do you want to open it?"

"To see what's inside."

"I think I have a pretty good idea, Sal."

"It'll give us a clue as to who ran this village before it burned down. Now are you going to help me or not?"

Scarlett wanted to say no, but she knew Sal would do it himself anyway. That would take longer, which meant they would be down here longer.

They each took an end of the wooden lid and lifted. The lid came free with a small puff of escaping air. Scarlett leaned forward to look inside the coffin. The smell of mold and human dust and dried meat hit the back of her throat like a physical presence. She gagged and stumbled away, dropping her end of the lid. It crashed to the floor, the rotten wood splintering on contact.

Sal, left with the entire weight, cursed and dropped his end as well. Learning from her mistake, he covered his nose with his arm and looked inside the coffin. Scarlett did the same. Although she had seen several corpses in the last few hours, none of them had been dead for very long, and all had looked human.

What she saw now didn't look human one bit. The face of the skull stared at her in broken horror. The jaw hung open in a silent yowl, slightly lopsided, showing peg-like teeth. The eye sockets were gaping black holes filled with dust and other decomposed organic matter. The skeletal body was dressed in a royal-blue jacket with a line of bronze buttons down the front, wide knickerbockers, puttees, and leather ankle boots.

"Some sort of colonial soldier," Sal said. "French or Belgium maybe."

Scarlett stared, transfixed by the clothed skeleton, the ghastly thing that had once been a man—a man who likely at one time had a wife and a house and a family, a man who had felt fear and happiness and love, who had seen beauty in a sunrise and put value to money and obeyed the rules of right and wrong. A man who was now bones in a box.

Scarlett felt like she was being let in on some age-old secret. This was what death looked like, she thought. How Miranda and Joanna would soon look. What she herself would one day be.

She blinked and turned away. She was freaking herself out, and this was not the place where she wanted to be freaked out.

With a jolt of panic, she realized Sal was gone.

Frowning, she swept the flashlight beam across the mouth of the alcove. Shadows danced and leapt. "Sal?" she called.

"Come here!" His voice echoed slightly from somewhere to the right.

"I want to leave."

"Come here."

Scarlett found him in the next corridor over, examining another coffin.

"Opening one coffin, fine, Sal," she said, reprimanding. "But two? That's perverse."

"Look."

He aimed the light at the floor, revealing several sets of footprints in the dust, which weren't hers or his. They all led from the stairs directly to the coffin and nowhere else.

Scarlett's first thought: *vampire.* Some undead thing sleeping its days away down here, waking at dusk to feed on blood during the night. But then the rational side of her brain kicked in, reminding her that there were no such thing as vampires and witches and other monsters.

There was a much more logical explanation for the footprints.

"Jahja?" she said.

"Who else?"

"Why would he be interested in that coffin?"

"That's what I want to find out. Give me a hand with the lid again. And try not to drop it this time."

She joined him at the coffin. On the count of three they heaved the lid off and set it on the floor so it leaned at a forty-five degree angle against the wall. They covered their noses and peered in. The coffin was filled with a smorgasbord of automatic weapons, boxes of ammunition, magazines, grenades, and other miscellaneous military gear.

"Jackpot," Sal said.

Scarlett uncovered her nose. This time the only smell was that of oil and metal and cardboard. "Why would Jahja be stashing all these weapons out here?"

"I have no idea."

"Well, whatever. Can we leave now? I want to get Joanna and Miranda down here so I can attend to Thunder."

Sal nodded, but not before he selected a grenade and stashed it in his pocket.

Scarlett frowned. "Why do you want that?"

"We're still in the jungle, cara mia. Still vulnerable. Until Danny arrives, it's better to remain safe than sorry."

"Safe from what?"

Sal didn't have an answer to that—or if he did, he wasn't telling.

# CHAPTER 32

SCARLETT AND SAL sat shoulder to shoulder against the stone wall of what had only recently been their prison. Thunder lay along the floor in front of them, Sal's torn blazer bunched beneath his head as a pillow. Scarlett had given him the two aspirin and made him drink some water she'd brought from the church. That had been almost two hours before. He seemed to be doing better now. At least his fever was in remission.

The rain, a steady drizzle, hadn't let up yet, but it hadn't gotten any worse either. It was still thundering and lightning, each white blaze visible through the cracks in the ceiling. Scarlett was deep in thought, going over everything she wanted to do when she returned home to LA, which included eating a mammoth cheeseburger from Dukes on the Sunset Strip, ordered in, taking a long hot bubble bath in her Jacuzzi, and maybe calling up her masseuse, Rose, for a three-hour-long pampering.

Thunder's eyes fluttered open.

"Thunder!" she said, cheeseburgers and massages instantly forgotten. "How are you feeling?"

He grimaced. "Like I just woke up on the bottom of the scrimmage."

"Is there anything I can do for you?"

"Got any food?"

"There's some in the church. We ate some earlier. I'll go get you something."

He looked confused. "What about...you know...the bad guys?"

"They're all dead."

Hearing herself speak those words gave her a thrill. It shouldn't. Death was still death, regardless of who it had ferried across the Styx, and she wasn't sadistic, but she couldn't help the feeling. Jahja and his cronies were dead; she and Sal and Thunder were alive. All was as it should be in the world.

Except for Joanna and Miranda, she thought dourly. Don't forget about them.

Apparently her words gave Thunder a thrill too. His eyes widened and his mouth opened, as if to ask what she was talking about.

"I'll explain when I get back," she told him.

"I'm coming too," Sal said.

"I can get it—"

"Yes, I know," he said, cutting her off. "Still, we should stick together."

Scarlett nodded. She understood. They didn't know for sure whether the Irishman was truly gone or not. They collected their assault rifles—Sal had shown her how to use hers—and went outside.

Halfway across the road, Scarlett froze. She grabbed Sal's forearm and pointed to the west side of the clearing, where a short column of people had emerged from the forest and were now walking toward the town.

"Who are they?" she said.

Thunder grumbled loudly. The line of men grew more distinct. She counted at least two dozen. One of the half-naked tribes she'd seen living along the riverbank? A rat-pack of bushman-like Congolese villagers? Yes, it must—

A zigzag of lightning crackled overhead, momentarily illuminating the clearing. Not villagers, she realized. They wore backward or sideways baseball caps, bandanas, and baggy T-shirts and shorts. A few even had on mismatched military uniforms and too-large combat helmets. They walked with a swagger, like the Mexican street gangs in LA. They all carried automatic weapons.

"Rebels," Sal said, stating what she was thinking. "I think that was their stash of weapons we discovered earlier."

Scarlett wondered if Sal had suspected this back in the crypt, and if that was the reason he'd taken the grenade. But there was no time to press the matter. The rebels had spotted them in the flash of lightning as well. They let out a collective cry and broke into a run toward them.

Sal raised his assault rifle.

"Don't," Scarlett said, yanking his arm back down. "There're too many of them. If they see you pointing that thing, they'll shoot us down." She was aware of the quiver in her voice.

"What the hell do you want me to do?"

"Nothing. There's nothing we can do."

When the large group of men came to within fifty feet, they stopped and shouted incomprehensible words and waved their guns in the air.

Scarlett and Sal raised their hands.

Bolstered by the show of peace, the rebels advanced slowly. It turned out they weren't men; they were boys, most no older than teenagers. It was like a scene out of *Lord of the Flies*. Or, more precisely, *Lord of the Flies* meets *Boyz n the Hood*. Even so, she was trembling. Their expressions were murder, their eyes bloodshot. A few were holding bottles of a murky white drink that she was pretty sure wasn't milk.

A long, thin, tubular object was strapped to the back of one of them.

*A rocket launcher?*

"Hello," Sal said, and the confidence he displayed amazed her. "Do you speak English?"

The oldest kid, who was maybe in his early twenties, stepped forward. He was wearing wraparound sunglasses and an extra-large Eminem T-shirt. A red beret sat atop his thick, tightly curled black hair. He looked simultaneously ridiculous and terrifying.

"I am Killer," he announced.

Scarlett and Sal exchanged a look. A burst of lightning sparked the sky, chased by heavy thunder. The rain fell harder.

"Killer is your name?" Sal said. A little less confident?

"Sergeant Major Killer. I want money."

"We don't have any money."

"You give me drugs then."

"Do I look like I carry drugs, chief?"

Scarlett rested a warning hand on Sal's forearm. What was he thinking? These might be kids, but this was their world—a world without rules or repercussions. If they decided Sal was patronizing them, they'd likely shoot him for his insolence.

Undeterred by the rain, the kid with the red beret took out a rolled cigarette and lit up. Not tobacco, Scarlett realized when the waft of smoke drifted in her face. Cannabis.

They were drunk and high.

Killer took off the shades, hooked them on the neck of his shirt, and said, "Give me your guns."

"No," Sal said.

"Yes, Sal," Scarlett said harshly. She lifted the rifle strap over her shoulder and handed the weapon to Killer stock first. He examined it for a moment, then fired a burst of bullets into the air.

Scarlett ducked, covering her ears. Sal stepped backward.

Killer tossed the AK-47 to one of the other kids and said, "I want that one also."

This time Sal gave it to him without protest.

"Why are you here?" he asked, handing the joint to a guy with a Leonardo DiCaprio T-shirt.

Scarlett knew full well that her face could just as easily have been on that shirt, and she wondered if she should tell these kids who she was. Would they suddenly treat her to a big feast with music and dancing like something out of *Romancing the Stone*? Or would they rape her and kill her for the bragging rights? She looked in Killer's blood-crazed eyes. She kept quiet.

"We're Americans," Sal said. "We were taken here by terror-ists."

"You lie. You are FDLR."

"Do we look like FDLR?"

Scarlett wiped rain from her eyes. "What's that?"

"A Rwandan rebel group," Sal told her.

"See, I am right," Killer said. "You are FDLR."

"Why would we be down here, this far south?"

"You are running from the Rwanda Army or the Congolese government."

"Look at me, kid," Sal said curtly. "Am I black?"

"You are undercover." Killer laughed. "No, I know who you are for real. You are UN. You are MONUC. You are working with the armed forces to get rid of us."

"And who are you?"

"I am Rambo. Major General Rambo."

"That's not what I meant."

"So you are MONUC?"

"No."

"I think you are."

"Listen, Killer—"

"Rambo."

"Okay, Rambo—"

"Major General Rambo."

Sal took a frustrated breath and said, "Look, Major General Rambo. There's a helicopter coming for us very soon. When it gets here, I can get you some money, if that's what you want. Just relax for now and be patient."

"We will kill them."

Sal's eyebrows shot up in surprise. "Yeah?" he said. "Good luck."

"We will eat them."

Scarlett couldn't help but feel as if she'd fallen down the rab-bit hole. The conversation sounded comical, absurd even, but there was an underlying menace that made the hair on the back of her neck stand tall.

A burst of forked lightning turned the sky dark blue. The kid with the DiCaprio shirt shouted and pointed to Jahja's body lying twenty-five feet away in the middle of the road.

"You killed him?" Rambo said to Sal.

"Yes."

"Why?"

"I told you. We were kidnapped. He was one of the kidnappers."

"He is a soldier?"

"He's a terrorist."

"How many more soldiers are here?"

"None."

Rambo barked something to his gang. Two of the kids jogged off to search the buildings. They emerged from the prison dragging Thunder by the arms and tossed him onto the muddy road. Thunder, still semi-unconscious, raised his head and started to say something. One of the kids kicked him in the face with his boot. He collapsed and lay still.

Scarlett cringed but held her tongue.

"You lied to me," Rambo said, then fired a slug into Sal's leg. Sal gasped, collapsing to the ground.

"Don't!" Scarlett screamed, flabbergasted by how quickly they'd gone from talking to gunshots. "Don't!"

Rambo barked more orders. His child soldiers dragged Sal and Thunder and prodded her around the side of the church to a fire pit, where they pulled back a blue plastic tarp to reveal separate piles of dry tinder, kindling, and larger sticks. They started tossing leaves, grass, and bark into the ring of stones.

Scarlett, however, was focused solely on Sal. He was lying beside her, his eyes closed, his face wet. She took his hand in hers and squeezed, thinking briefly about how he'd done the same to her last week in the hospital. He squeezed back weakly. His jaw muscles were bunched, as if he was in severe pain, and she had no doubt he was. The bullet had gone into his thigh, just above the knee. Given the amount of blood soaking his pant leg, it looked as if it might have hit a deep artery or vein—and if that was the case, she knew he wouldn't make it until Danny arrived.

She was losing him, and there was nothing she could do about it. She felt as if she'd been caught up in a powerful mudslide, and all she could do was hang on to something and pray for the best.

She gripped the hemline of her dress with shaking hands and tore upward, creating a slit. She pulled horizontally, parallel with the lower edge, until she'd ripped free a long piece of fabric. She folded the cloth in half, corner to corner, then folded it again and again until she had a makeshift bandage that was roughly three inches wide and several layers thick. "Can you hear me, Sal?" she said softly.

He nodded.

"You're bleeding a lot. I have a tourniquet. I'm going to tie it around your leg. It's going to hurt—"

"No."

"I have to, Sal."

"It's too late."

"Don't say that."

His eyes opened. They were filled with rage.

"Help me up," he said.

"What? Why?"

"Help me get to my feet."

"You can't stand. Not with your leg—"

"I'm not going to die lying down."

"Sal—"

"*Help me.*"

Fighting back tears, Scarlett moved beside him so he could loop an arm around her neck. She stood, pulling him upright with her, taking half his weight. Her mind was numb; she was just going through the motions. But a part of her, a part she didn't want to recognize, thought maybe she knew what she was doing—knew she was helping Sal kill himself.

Rambo, who had been overseeing the fire, saw them and laughed. "Where do you think you are going?"

Scarlett could feel Sal shaking—the stress of trying to stand on one leg.

"I love you, cara mia," he said in a gruff voice. "I'm sorry. I should have been a better husband."

"I love you too, Sal," she told him, and now the tears were flowing freely. "Always."

Rambo barked something to two of his men. They set down the firewood stacked in their arms and started toward them. Sal abruptly shoved Scarlett aside, hard enough she fell to the ground. She stared up at him through the rain and tears and watched as he reached behind his back and took out a pistol that was stuck in the waistband of his pants, against the small of his back.

"Sal! Don't!"

He swung the gun around and fired two shots at the two manboys coming toward him. He took the grenade from his pocket, tugged free the pull-ring of the safety pin with his teeth, and lobbed it twenty feet away into the fire pit, where five-foot-tall flames were now tangoing in the storm.

Mayhem immediately broke out. The rebels darted for cover —only there was no cover to be found. Seconds later the grenade went off with a deafening explosion that out-boomed the thunder overhead. Scarlett turned her face away, flattening herself against the ground as a wave of heat blew over her. It scorched her neck and arms and calves. She turned back. Smoke was rising from where the fire had been. Burning sticks and tinder lay scattered everywhere in a twenty-foot radius. Several rebels were writhing in the mud, screaming, limbs missing, stumps spraying blood. Others were doubled over, clutching shrapnel wounds.

Sal, who had either dropped to his chest moments before the blast went off, or had been blown down involuntarily, now pushed himself to his feet once more. He fired off several rounds into the confusion. One kid went down, blood arcing from his throat. The rest who hadn't been injured or killed—which was still a good dozen or so—took aim and let loose a phalanx of bullets.

Sal stiffened and spasmed. The pistol fell from his hand. He collapsed to his side. His face lolled toward Scarlett, and she watched in abject misery as the last of his life drained from his eyes until they stared at her like marbles, glassy and dead.

"No..." she said, the word trailing off into a sob.

Rambo, who had apparently survived the chaos unscathed, stomped over to her. He pinched her cheeks between his fingers painfully, pulling her face to within inches of his own. His skin was rain-streaked and black as polished onyx, his lips curled back in menace, showing bone-white teeth.

"I was going to give you a quick death," he hissed furiously, spittle flying from his mouth. "Not anymore. Now you are going to watch me eat your friend. Then I am going to eat you! Alive."

He released her face and snapped his fingers. Two rebels pulled Sal's body across the grass toward what remained of the fire.

"Stop it," Scarlett said, her voice flat, mechanical.

A third rebel pulled a machete from his belt.

*Jesus Mary, don't do that!*

With the first two kids holding Sal's arms from his body at a ninety-degree angle, the third swung the machete down in a deadly arc. The blade made a wet sound as it disappeared into Sal's shoulder. Scarlett lurched forward and vomited. Through stinging, tearful eyes she saw one of the kids toss the dismembered limb onto the fire.

"Please," she said. "Please stop..."

They cut off Sal's other arm.

Scarlett fainted.

# CHAPTER 33

THE STORM WAS at its apex, fully unleashed. Fists of thunder and claws of lightning pounded and tore at the belly of the sky, ripping fresh wounds that bled more rain.

Fitzgerald watched from his vantage point high atop the church bell tower as the Mai-Mai rebels hacked off Salvador Brazza's arms and legs. He shook his head. No man deserved a death like that. But he was more concerned about what the arrival of the rebels meant for his escape.

After Brazza had left the church to chase Jahja, Fitzgerald had worked his way across the floor until his bound hands could reach Carnwennan, which was lodged in the belt of Mr. AQ with the caved-in skull.

Just as he'd finished sawing through the restraints, a gunshot had gone off, and he'd known that either Brazza or Jahja would be coming back at any moment. Jahja would kill him, and trusting Brazza was about as foolhardy as trusting a hungry shark not to eat you.

So he had shoved open a door that led outside, to serve as a diversion, then limped stiff-legged to the stairwell behind the chancel, climbed several stairs until he was out of sight, and readied himself to spring on whoever came looking for him. No one did.

Brazza returned, swore up a storm when he believed Fitzgerald had vamoosed, then made a call on the sat phone, arranging for transport to pick him up. Cox returned next and spun a story about a struggle in a mine.

After fussing around with the bodies of their fellow hostages for a while, they left the church to help another apparent hostage. Fitzgerald lumbered to the narthex and retrieved the AKM from Mr. AQ #2. He was in no condition to finish off Brazza, let alone make an escape, so he slowly and painfully crawled to the top of the bell tower, where he could watch the cavalry arrive and hold off an attack if it came to that.

He had never planned on Mai-Mai rebels.

There was only one explanation for their unexpected arrival: they used the town as some sort of base, holing up in the church from time to time whenever they were in the neighborhood.

It seemed Al Qaeda wasn't as smart as he'd given them credit for.

Down on the ground the rebels had finished quartering Brazza, placing each limb on the fire to cook. Now they turned their attention to Scarlett Cox. They spread her arms and legs wide, like da Vinci's *Vitruvian Man*. They were going to butcher her as well.

Fitzgerald closed his eyes. She was none of his business. He had to watch out for himself. Keep a low profile. Get out in the morning when his strength had improved. But in his mind's eye one scene played itself over and over again. His wife, Eryn, and daughter, Biddy. Eryn and Biddy chopped up into pieces, their mutilated trunks preserved in the subzero Northern Ireland winter weather, frozen in an ice rink of blood on the floor of the living room where he had opened presents with them on Christmas day one month before. Steel railway spikes nailing their limbs unceremoniously to the wall above the sofa. Waterfalls of dried blood staining the wallpaper. Their heads sitting on the fireplace mantel like game trophies. Framed family photographs—purposely untouched by the mobsters—mocking and contrasting their smiling faces with their hideous death grimaces.

Fitzgerald's eyes flashed open. He could feel them burning with hatred, burning red. His jaw was clenched so tightly it hurt. He wanted it to hurt. His hands squeezed the grips of the AKM hard enough to turn his knuckles white. A deep, primitive growl escaped his throat.

*Hell if he was going to sit by and watch an innocent slaughtered when he could do something about it this time.*

He shoved the barrel of the Kalashnikov through the carved stone pillars of the balustrade, flipped the selector to semi, tugged back the reloading handle, and took aim through the open iron sight.

A rebel kneeling beside Cox's limp body raised a machete in the air.

Fitzgerald squeezed the trigger. The full-metal-jacketed bullet ripped a hole through the center of the man's chest. Inside the heated bore of the rifle expanding gas set off a domino effect that ultimately drove the bolt carrier back, ejected the spent round, and chambered a new one from the magazine, all in a matter of milliseconds. Fitzgerald zeroed in on a second rebel staring dumbly at his dead mate and squeezed the trigger again. The bastard dropped like a rag doll. The rifle spat out another spent casing from the ejection port.

Pop, pop, pop. Three more down and out.

The rebels finally figured out what was happening and returned fire. Bullets chewed into the stone around Fitzgerald's face. He flattened himself against the floor. The shit-for-brains continued firing, wasting ammunition.

Five down so far.

He no longer had the leisure to take proper aim, so he flicked the selector up to full automatic, shoved the barrel between the pillars once more, and squeezed off a firestorm of bullets.

The rebels scattered like billiard balls, but they had few places to take shelter.

Six, seven, eight.

Four remaining—

Fitzgerald saw the rebel with the RPG-7 too late. There was a great boom. A puff of gray-blue smoke.

The grenade screamed toward him.

# CHAPTER 34

**W**HEN SCARLETT OPENED her eyes, she felt as though she were in the middle of a warzone. Rain gushed from the purple-black sky in driving sheets while gunfire rattled and burst all around her. The stench of burnt gunpowder and death filled her nostrils and mouth. She had no idea who was firing at whom until she saw the muzzle blasts from high atop the church bell tower.

From behind her came a startling boom. A line of smoke streaked through the sky. The upper part of the church tower exploded in a burst of stone confetti. The tat-tat-tat of gunshots continued for a few more seconds before trickling to a stop.

Scarlett looked numbly around. Bodies lay everywhere. And Sal...

Oh God, Sal.

She turned away.

Rambo shouted at his three remaining soldiers, who took off toward the church, apparently to finish off whoever had been up there attacking them. Then he marched over to where she lay. "Who was that?" he demanded.

She shook her head.

Rambo fired his gun so close to her face she felt the displacement of air as the bullet whistled past and plowed into the earth. Her already ringing ears rang louder than ever. He continued shouting at her, but she couldn't hear anything. He spat out a final curse, then turned his attention to the three man-boys who had reemerged from the church. They were carrying the Irishman by the arms and legs, just as they'd carried Thunder. They tossed him in the mud.

*So he never took off after all.*

Rambo slapped Fitzgerald back and forth across the face until he came to. For a split second his eyes met Scarlett's, and something passed between the two of them, though she had no idea what.

A peal of thunder crashed overhead, and she realized she could hear once more.

"You killed my men!" Rambo was yelling.

"A jolly good time," Fitzgerald hissed in that gravelly voice of his.

Rambo said something to the kid with the DiCaprio T-shirt, who quickly scavenged the machete and handed it to Rambo. He pointed the blade at the Irishman and grinned wickedly.

"What should I take first?" he snarled. "Your balls or your heart? I like the taste of both."

# CHAPTER 35

THE BELL 206L LongRanger was flying low and fast over the treetops. Danny was seated beside the pilot in the cockpit. Both men were wearing night vision goggles, which made the sky and ground appear a bright pea green. Danny's M249 SAW was propped between his legs, the same belt-fed light machine gun every branch of the US armed forces used. Two members of his team were in the rear cabin. He'd been forced to leave four behind in Dar es Salaam because the helicopter only seated seven, and Sal had told him there were three survivors in total, including himself and Scarlett.

"There," Danny said through the microphone in the Kevlar helmet. "A clearing."

"I see it," the pilot confirmed. "What's that? A fire?"

"Do a flyby."

The pilot banked left and flew over the fire. "Jesus, are those bodies?"

Danny frowned. Sal had told him he'd taken out four terrorists, but it looked like at least a dozen bodies down there. And he counted five, not three, people standing erect. Something was wrong. "Land," he said. "Quickly."

The pilot swung back around, braked, and flared as he prepared to touch down. Danny was still watching the ground when one of the grainy-green people started waving. He or she apparently didn't think the pilot could see them. Then Danny realized the person wasn't waving but pointing. He followed the direction of the signal and identified the very recognizable shape of a man with an RPG on his shoulder. "Bank!" he shouted.

"What?" the pilot said.

Danny lunged across the cockpit and yanked the cyclic to the right. The helicopter rolled, but not fast enough. An explosion rocked the tail rotor. The pilot tried a desperate autorotation, but the helicopter continued to oscillate wildly, drifting sideways toward a building. There was a loud beep-beep-beeping, like a truck backing up, as the stone wall rushed up to meet them.

Danny guessed he had about three seconds to live.

# CHAPTER 36

WHEN SCARLETT HEARD a throbbing noise, she looked up into the raging sky and saw a helicopter beat past fifty feet overhead. The downwash of the rotors caused her torn dress and the knee-high grass to blow wildly.

*Danny!*

Rambo tossed the machete aside and ran. Not fleeing, she realized. He was going for the rocket launcher. The helicopter came back and hovered. She screamed and waved, pointing frantically at Rambo. It was no use. Rambo reloaded the rocket launcher and fired, scoring a direct hit. The helicopter's tail rotor burst into a ball of flames. The entire thing spun out of control and careened inexorably toward the church. The main rotor scraped stone, threw up a flare of sparks, and snapped free. It whirled through the air and slammed into the ground like a giant shuriken, shooting a fan of mud into the air. Half the church wall collapsed inward while the crumpled helicopter fuselage crashed to the ground like a big, broken toy.

The rescue/extraction was doomed. Scarlett understood that in an epiphany of despair. Knowing she had no choice left but to make a run for it, she glanced around madly for Thunder, unwilling to leave him behind. She saw the Irishman instead. He stood tall, a bloody knife in his hand. The two teenagers who had been holding him were lying at his feet, dead. He must have taken them out while everybody had been focused on the helicopter above.

He looked at her, cocked his arm at the elbow, launched the knife.

She yelped.

The blade flashed past her head. She spun to follow its trajectory and saw it splat into the chest of Rambo. He released the assault rifle he'd picked up, scowled as if life was suddenly unfair, and collapsed to the ground. Scarlett turned back to the Irishman and was about to say something—maybe even thank him —when, beyond him, the door to the ruined helicopter cockpit shoved open. A dark shape stumbled out, dragging a large gun. The words that had been on the tip of her tongue faltered, and she rushed toward the bedlam scene to help whoever had survived.

The man pulled off his helmet, and Scarlett immediately recognized the dark good looks of Danny Zamir. He heaved over in a fit of coughs.

"Is anyone else in there?" she demanded. The fuselage hadn't exploded, but it was on fire, engulfed in billowing black smoke.

Danny shook his head, and something inside her shriveled.

"Sal?" he said.

"No."

Danny didn't react. Or at least she didn't think he did. Not until she noticed the cords of muscle standing out in his neck. "How?" he asked very quietly.

She told him.

"*Harah*," he mumbled. Then he hefted the machine gun across his chest decisively. "Who's left?"

"Just me and Thunder and—"

"Hey! You!" Danny shouted. "Where do you think you're going?"

The Irishman, who had been limping away toward the forest, stopped. "Where there are some rebels," he said, "there are likely more. I for one am going to be gone when they arrive."

Danny stiffened. He'd obviously had no idea the man was the

assassin sent for Sal until he'd heard the accent.

"Let him be," Scarlett said. "He saved my life."

Danny ignored her. "I was told you were here," he said to the Irishman, walking forward. "I thought you would have scurried off by now."

"Do I know you?" Fitzgerald asked.

"No. But I know who you are."

"Congratulations. You're in a rare club." He started to turn.

Danny raised the deadly looking gun. "You're not going anywhere, *koos*."

"Excuse me?"

"Drop the knife," he said, referring to the machete the Irishman had retrieved from Rambo's corpse.

"What are you going to do? Shoot me?"

"Drop it."

Fitzgerald tossed the knife into the mud.

"Good," Danny said, setting the machine gun down as well. "Now it's fair."

"You want to fight me?"

"Yes."

Fitzgerald seemed amused. "But why?"

"Because," Danny said, "it's what capo would have wanted."

# CHAPTER 37

FITZGERALD DIDN'T KNOW who the man was, but if he wanted to fight, then fine, they would fight. The man was well built and carried himself like a professional soldier. The Israeli accent meant IDF, probably Mossad. Brazza wouldn't have hired anything less. Fitzgerald wasn't going to underestimate him.

"Redstone, is it?" the man said.

"You've done your homework."

"I'm Danny Zamir."

"Should I be impressed?"

"It's only right you know the name of the person who's going to kill you."

Fitzgerald figured the boisterous talk on Zamir's part was to psyche himself up. In a fight to the death, you needed to be in the frame of mind that you would be the one left standing, or else it was over before it started. Fitzgerald was in that frame of mind. Always was.

They had been circling each other like boxers, each waiting for an opening to attack. Now Zamir lunged, swinging a low right fist.

Fitzgerald stepped back, dodging the blow. "You're right-handed," he said.

"You figured me out."

"That's too bad."

"Yeah? Why's that?"

"Left-handers have an edge in close combat."

Zamir swung again. Fitzgerald parried and countered, knife-chopping the top of Zamir's forearm just below the elbow, striking the radial nerve and numbing the arm. Almost simultaneously he followed up with a left-handed thumb jab to Zamir's left shoulder, numbing the man's other arm as well. But Zamir proved resilient, pivoting with a roundhouse kick to Fitzgerald's ribs. Fitzgerald threw up his arms and blocked the powerful attack at the last moment.

They broke apart.

"Not bad for an old man," Zamir said, rolling his shoulders to get the feeling back in his arms.

"Not bad for a Jew," Fitzgerald shot back.

Zamir rushed, obviously thinking he could wear his much older opponent down with a brute-force, concerted onslaught. Fitzgerald countered by spinning away to the left and landing a hammer fist to Zamir's temple. He yanked the man's head down while bringing his knee up.

Teeth shattered.

Zamir wobbled backward, dazed, blood gushing from his mouth. Fitzgerald finally took the counteroffensive. He struck the side of Zamir's neck with another closed fist, knocking him backward. But he was too confident. As he moved in for the kill, Zamir—somehow still with it—sprung a short hook punch to his solar plexus, blasting the breath from him.

They stumbled apart, both breathing heavily.

Zamir faked left, lunged right, getting close enough to grapple, bringing an elbow up under Fitzgerald's jaw, stunning him. He tried another elbow strike, this one to Fitzgerald's face, but Fitzgerald moved with it, twisting around and ending up behind Zamir. He grabbed the man's collar and tugged him back off balance while jabbing him in the left kidney. He kicked the back of Zamir's knee, collapsing him to the ground.

Before Fitzgerald could swoop down, however, Zamir executed a low sweep kick, striking Fitzgerald's injured shins. He cried out and dropped.

Zamir was on him immediately, raining fists into his face, over and over and over.

Fitzgerald heard cartilage crunch, started to see black. He tapped into a last reserve of strength, grabbed Zamir's hair, yanked down, and brought up his own forehead to land a Glasgow Kiss right between the man's eyes.

Zamir grunted and went limp. Fitzgerald rolled over so he was now on top. He raised his left fist, intent on finally ending the fight—

Someone slammed into his side, sending him sprawling into the mud.

# CHAPTER 38

WHILE DANNY AND the Irishman went at it, Scarlett sat on the sidelines, torn between who she wanted to win. Danny, of course, was on her side. He would help them leave this godforsaken place. But then again, the Irishman had saved her life, and that was something she could not ignore.

Thunder, finally lucid, or at least partly so, appeared beside her. He was wide-eyed and confused. "Who are they?" he said, nodding at the fight.

"The Irishman and Sal's security chief."

"The Irishman? Which one?"

"The older man, in the black—"

Thunder charged recklessly forward. Scarlett saw he was gripping the machete the Irishman had discarded.

"Thunder!" she shouted. "No!"

Fitzgerald had just rolled on top of Danny and appeared ready to finish him off when Thunder crashed into him in some sort of kamikaze rugby tackle, sending them both tumbling six feet through the mud before coming to a rest. Thunder straddled the Irishman. He raised the machete above his head.

"No!" Scarlett shouted again.

This time Thunder hesitated.

Fitzgerald's mangled legs shot upward, scissoring around Thunder's neck from behind, ankles locking under his chin. He twisted his torso sideways, flipping Thunder off him. The machete flew from his hand, landing some distance away.

Thunder's face turned red. He was struggling to breathe.

Scarlett scrambled for the nearby rifle, pointed it in the air, and pulled the trigger. It was on full automatic and spit half a dozen rounds into the sky, rattling her entire upper body so hard she thought she might drop the weapon. She recovered and aimed the barrel at the Irishman.

"Let him go!" she ordered.

Fitzgerald only stared at her. Thunder continued to flop and twist, trapped in the death pinch.

Scarlett fired another, albeit more controlled, burst into the air.

After a dreadfully long wait, Fitzgerald unlocked his legs and rolled away into a crouch. One hand was pressed against the left side of his torso where Thunder had crashed into him. The rain had washed away the mud that had covered his face, and now she could see that his nose looked broken while ugly purple circles had begun to form around his eyes. A white scar tattooed the length of his throat.

Thunder, rubbing his own throat, got to his knees. To the right of him Danny stirred, shaking the cobwebs from his head. Rise and shine everyone, Scarlett thought stupidly. When Danny noticed Fitzgerald crouched a short distance away, he immediately spun to face the Irishman, as if to continue the interrupted fight.

Scarlett swung the rifle at him. "Don't move, Danny," she said.

"He's an assassin," Danny told her, never taking his eyes from the Irishman. "He followed you here to kill Sal."

"I know."

"Then why are you pointing that damned thing at me? Let me kill the bastard."

"He saved my life."

"Didn't you hear what I said?"

"Didn't you hear what *I* said?" She swung the rifle back at the Irishman again. "Why did you do it?" she said, blinking rain from her eyes. "Why help me?"

He didn't say anything.

Thunder got to his feet, wobbling a little before steadying himself. He looked at Danny, then at Fitzgerald. "Well, this is a bit of a pickle, isn't it?"

"There's a satellite phone in the church, Thunder," Scarlett said. "It's on the altar. Can you get it? Also, there's some rope in one of the wings. Get that too."

Thunder nodded and jogged off.

"Give me the rifle, Scarlett," Danny said, taking a step toward her.

She swung the barrel back at him. He stopped.

"You'll shoot him," she said, glancing at the Irishman, who remained in a crouch, watching everything that was happening with dark, calculating eyes.

"What alternative is there?" Danny said.

"We tie him up. Take him prisoner."

"He's too dangerous. It's not worth the risk. Give me the rifle. You don't have to watch."

"No," she said, shaking her head. "Nobody else is dying. Nobody."

Lightning flashed, flooding the black sky with white light. Danny ran a hand through his soaked hair. "At least let me get my gun then."

"You won't shoot him?"

"If you don't want me to, no."

Scarlett knew she couldn't play mediator forever, and so she reluctantly conceded. Danny retrieved his monster machine gun from the mud and looped the strap over his shoulder so the weapon hung in a shoot-from-the-hip position. He swung the barrel at Fitzgerald. Scarlett held her breath, waiting for him to squeeze the trigger. He didn't. Thunder returned a minute later with the rope and secured the Irishman's hands behind his back. Scarlett finally lowered her rifle and relaxed, feeling as if the tiger had just been caged.

"Where's the sat phone?" she asked Thunder.

"Couldn't find it. The wall that collapsed buried the altar."

"Can we dig it out?"

"Not a chance. Even if we could, I reckon it would be crushed to pieces."

"Then we walk out," Danny said.

Scarlett shook her head. "There're terrorists on the boat."

"They're dead," Fitzgerald said, not looking at anyone in particular.

"I suppose you killed them?" Danny said.

"You suppose correctly. And I suggest we get moving. As I mentioned earlier, where there are some rebels, there are likely more. They might have heard the explosion. They'll be here soon."

The prospect chilled Scarlett. She'd cheated death enough times today to know better than to press her luck.

Danny picked up the machete and said, "We head due south and try to keep in as straight a line as possible until we reach the river."

"Actually," Fitzgerald said, "we should go southeast."

"He's right." Scarlett withdrew the pendant-compass from her shirt. "And I think this will help."

Danny nodded. "Okay. Keep a reading." He yanked the Irishman to his feet, shoved him forward. "You. Start moving. I'll follow. Scarlett, you come next and ... ?"

"Thunder, mate."

"Thunder, you take up the rear."

"Okay," Scarlett said. "But first, Thunder, can you take care of Sal's body? Put—" She was about to say "the rest of it" but stopped herself. "Put it on the fire. Cremate it."

She would have offered to help, but she didn't think she could stand to see what remained of her husband.

Thunder went to do what she'd asked. When he returned a few minutes later, he nodded solemnly, to say the deed was done. Danny, his face wooden, shoved the Irishman forward and started off toward the howling African wilderness.

Scarlett followed, resisting the nearly overwhelming urge to look back at the fire, silent tears spilling down her dirty cheeks.

PROGRESS WAS SLOW and wet. The dense canopy blocked out most of the rain from reaching the small party, but Scarlett was still soaked and shivering. She focused on putting one foot down in front of the other, trying not to think, although her thoughts were banging around inside her head, impossible to ignore.

The last time she'd felt this lost, this scared and miserable, had been the day the woman from Child Services had come to her school to tell her that her mother wasn't going to be picking her up that day—or any day ever again (she would learn years later that her mother had been hanging by an electrical cord from the backyard swing set that afternoon). Only then, all those years ago, Scarlett had had a child's resilience, a child's amazing ability to forget and move on. Now...well... now she didn't think she'd ever be able to forget what happened. How could she? Against her will images of Sal's mutilated body jumped to the forefront of her mind, cutting cruelly through the out-of-body unreality she'd been floating through since his death.

I'll never see you in one of your William Fioravanti suits again, she thought, knowing she shouldn't be going down this road but unable to stop herself. Never tease you about looking like a gangster. Never see the excitement and pride in your eyes when you spoke about your hotels.

How insignificant the brief affair seemed now in light of everything else.

When they eventually left the rainforest for the secondary jungle, they didn't find the path they'd come in on, and Danny was forced to use the machete to carve a new route through the tropical vegetation. Just as Scarlett was beginning to think they were hopelessly lost, they came upon the river in which she'd almost been swept away.

"Thank God!" she blurted. "This means we're only twenty, maybe thirty minutes away from the main river."

"Good," Danny said. "It gets dark fast at the equator. We don't have much light left."

Fitzgerald, who hadn't said a word since they'd left the ruins, forded the stream first. Danny went next. Thunder took Scarlett's hand and they followed together, wading through the chest-deep water. By the time they climbed out on the far bank, Thunder was huffing for breath.

"You okay?" she asked him. She knew he was still suffering from whatever ailment had afflicted him. "Do you need to rest?"

"I'm all right."

She glanced at the welt on his wrist.

"I've been bitten by a funnel-web back home," he explained. "Never a widow before."

She was shocked. A black widow? She'd found a few in her garden back in LA, and she'd always killed them on sight. Their venom might rarely be fatal, but the symptoms from a bite could become severe if untreated.

"Walked right into its web yesterday while, pardon the slang, hanging a piss."

"You're sure that's what it was? A black widow?"

"Nah. Brown widow. Venom's twice as poisonous."

"You said you didn't know what it was."

He shrugged, appearing both boyish and bashful. "Guess I didn't want to worry anybody."

They almost bumped into the back of Danny before they realized he'd stopped.

"What is it?" she asked.

"Ask him." Danny nodded at the Irishman.

"Well?" she demanded.

Fitzgerald looked at her. His face was pale and expressionless. "We're being followed," he said simply.

Scarlett's blood turned to ice. She glanced fearfully about. She couldn't see anything except gloomy shades of greens and grays.

"More rebels?" Thunder asked.

Fitzgerald shook his head. "A leopard—and a big one, at that. I saw its tracks coming in."

"Did you see it?" Scarlett asked Danny.

"No. I was watching him"—he tipped his head at the Irishman—"not the forest."

"I reckon it's just curious," Thunder said.

"Leopards are opportunistic hunters," Fitzgerald said. "They'll eat anything. Moths or crocs, it doesn't matter. If it thinks it can take us down, it'll try."

"We're not far from the river now," Scarlett said. "Let's just keep moving."

They agreed and pressed on. Scarlett found herself wishing she hadn't left the AK-47 behind. But it had seemed rather redundant considering Danny's machine gun looked like it could take down an elephant. Thunder, too, had brought no weapon, saying he'd felt too weak to carry one.

Danny stopped again. He pressed a finger to his lips and pointed silently. At first she didn't see anything, then she made out a black shape slightly darker than the background of shadowy foliage. It gradually resolved itself into the shoulder and long abdomen of a large animal.

Moments later it shifted and was gone.

"That wasn't a leopard," Scarlett said softly. "It was completely black."

"It's called a melanistic leopard, lass," Fitzgerald told her.

"What does that mean?"

"Melanism is a genetic mutation, the opposite of albinism, a selective advantage for survival in dark rainforests. It's also known as a black panther."

"Great," she said cynically. "But why is it following us?"

"Isn't it obvious?" he said without mirth. "It's hungry."

A branch snapped ahead of them. Danny shoved Fitzgerald to his knees so he couldn't make a break for it, then swung the machine gun toward the noise.

"Will that stop it?" Scarlett asked.

"It'll pulverize it," Danny said. "But I think all it needs is a little warning shot. Cover your ears, if you want." He pulled the trigger. Nothing happened. Frowning, he checked a plastic box attached to the underside of the weapon, which contained a linked belt of green-tipped brass cartridges. He swore. "Feed tray's mangled. Must have happened during the crash."

Fitzgerald laughed. Scarlett's jaw dropped.

"It doesn't work?" she said.

"No."

"Can you fix it?"

He never had time to answer. The leopard finally abandoned stealth and burst from the bush. It was a low dark blur, nothing but yellow eyes and white teeth and pink tongue. Scarlett grabbed Danny's arm to the left and Thunder's to the right. The Irishman remained on his knees in front of them.

"Don't run!" she shouted, thinking wildly of what Cooper had told her back in the Serengeti. "Whatever you do, don't run!"

The leopard didn't slow.

She felt both Danny and Thunder stiffen beneath her grip.

"Trust me! Don't—"

Danny broke away and ran. The leopard swerved from its course and plunged into the forest behind him.

# CHAPTER 39

DANNY KNEW HE shouldn't have run.

Nevertheless, some wild, primal urge had overwhelmed him, and his legs were moving before he could think better of it. Now he heard a crashing sound behind him: the leopard, following its hunting instincts to pursue the fleeing prey.

He had only gone about ten or fifteen meters when he felt two paws on his back, dragging him to the ground. He managed another few steps, but the leopard was too heavy, and his legs collapsed beneath him. He dropped the machete.

A fiery heat spread through his left leg. He flipped onto his back and saw that the leopard had seized his calf between its jaws. Its sharp claws mauled his upper legs. He shook and twisted, but the cat was too strong. His struggling did nothing to free himself. Crying out in pain as the claws continued to shred his flesh, he brought his free leg back so his knee was almost touching his chest, then he kicked forward, landing the rubber heel of his boot square to the leopard's sensitive snout. The leopard made a furious hiss and released his leg.

The victory, however, was short-lived. Even as he shoved himself backward and away, the cat lunged for his throat. He threw up his right arm in time, and instead of tearing out his larynx, the leopard now had his forearm in its vice-like jaws. It shook its head back and forth with such power Danny feared it was tearing his arm right out of his shoulder socket.

Desperate, he smashed the cat across the side of the head with his free hand. The leopard didn't let go. He smashed it again and again. It still didn't let go. Finally, with his strength failing, Danny formed a claw with his index and middle fingers and dug it into one of the leopard's eyes. The beast went ballistic, making a noise like ice cubes being crushed in a blender. It released his forearm.

Instead of scrambling backward again, he rolled onto his knees, shoved himself to his feet, and started limping away. His injured leg could barely support his weight, and he knew he wouldn't get far. His only hope was that the leopard had had enough—

Claws sank into his back, pulling him down once more. Stiletto-like fangs punctured the flesh surrounding his eyes. To his horror, he realized the leopard had his head in its mouth. He heard a low, hot growling next to his ear. A dreaminess washed over him, replacing the agonizing pain and terror and filling him with a sense of tranquility—and distantly Danny realized there was one positive to being eaten alive.

You didn't feel a thing.

# CHAPTER 40

FITZGERALD KNEW HE was dying.

For the past hour or so he'd been pressing ahead through the difficult terrain on sheer willpower alone. The fight with the Israeli had taken away most of whatever strength remained after his interrogation in the chair. His legs continued to bleed profusely and were now surely infected. On top of that, the Australian's tackle had broken at least two of his ribs, one of which had surely pierced a lung, for his breathing had become wheezy and bubbly and he continued to hawk up blood.

It seemed he now had two options. Remain where he was on the ground, close his eyes, and give up the good fight, drifting away quietly and peacefully. Or go out fighting.

He lumbered to his feet and started off in the direction the Israeli and leopard had gone.

"Stop!" Scarlett Cox yelled from behind him.

He ignored her and continued on, his eyes scanning the jungle floor to see whether the Israeli had dropped the machete in his panicked flight. With each step, more and more adrenaline flowed into his body, sweeping away his exhaustion and filling him with a much-needed reserve of strength.

He became acutely aware of every detail in the surrounding forest, every blade of grass brushing past his legs, every scent. He breathed in the peaty, mossy air, knowing it would be the last time he would experience the smell. That thought gave him a pang of regret. He had enjoyed his life immensely, and he didn't want to die. Nevertheless, some things you simply had no control over. He understood that. And because he understood that, he accepted it.

Through the dense tangle of branches and bracken he made out the black hide of the leopard. It was hunched over the prostrate form of Danny Zamir—at least what remained of Danny Zamir. The man's legs were bent at ugly angles. His stomach was torn open. The leopard had its snout in the soup of intestines. It tugged its head upward, pulling out a mouthful of stringy pink guts.

Six meters away the machete glinted silver on the dark scrub-covered forest floor. It was equal distance between Fitzgerald and the leopard.

Out on the African savannah, you could never sneak up on a leopard that had just made a recent kill. They remained extremely vigilant, knowing lions and hyenas would be close by, looking to steal the hard-earned meal. But here, in the jungle, the leopard was king. There was no other carnivore large enough to threaten it.

Fitzgerald crept forward, slowly and softly, making sure there were no sticks or twigs underfoot that might crack before stepping down with his full weight. The leopard remained unaware as it feasted on the Israeli. A dozen or so steps later he reached the machete. He squatted until his bound hands gripped the weapon. He rose again, sawing the rope that secured his wrists. The final twines parted with an audible snap.

The leopard glanced back over its shoulder and blinked at him with a very human-like twitch of surprise. For three long seconds it stared silently, snout and whiskers coated with blood. Then it curled back its lips and snarled, showing a flash of tongue and yellow fangs.

Fitzgerald planted his feet firmly in a fighting stance and turned his strongest side, his left side, forward, keeping his chest and hips at a ninety-degree angle to the leopard. He pressed his right elbow and arm against his side, to protect his ribcage, while bringing his left arm in front of his body, shielding his chest and abdomen. The blade of the machete hovered inches from his chin. He had never felt as alive as he did right then, facing down the formidable predator with nothing but an edged weapon. The knowledge of his inevitable death no longer caused him regret; it flooded him with an ecstasy that bordered on enlightenment. Every nerve ending buzzed with macabre excitement.

"Come on, kitty," he snarled. "Come and get me."

The black leopard charged, coming fast and hard at him on its short legs. He held his ground. The leopard leapt. At the very last second Fitzgerald ducked and spun, bringing the machete around in a semicircle. He swiped air. The leopard had been too quick, sailing past him, unharmed. He whirled to face the cat, which had landed on its feet. It was now padding back and forth, never taking its yellow eyes off him.

A grin split Fitzgerald's face. "Not your average monkey, am I?" he said, his voice barely more than a dangerous rasp.

Monkeys—baboons especially—were the leopards' main prey, and leopards knew exactly how to take down a primate. They lunged for the head or throat and, if finding purchase with their fangs, kicked down with their hind legs, tearing open the belly. Knowing this, Fitzgerald had anticipated the first attack and had been able to dodge it easily enough. But now the leopard knew he was aware of its MO, and it likely wouldn't try the same approach twice.

It didn't.

This time it came at him low, going for the legs. There was nothing he could do to block or avoid the attack. If he rolled left or right, the leopard would correct its course and pounce. It was much more agile than he was.

So he did the unexpected: he charged. The leopard, surprised, sprang off its feet, intent on coming down on top of its prey, the way a housecat does when toying with a mouse.

Fitzgerald shoved the machete as far as it would go into the leopard's exposed underside, somewhere near the heart, just as the cat knocked him over with its nearly two-hundred-pound frame. The leopard began swatting his head with its paws.

Everything went black. Fitzgerald wasn't sure if he passed out for seconds or minutes, but when his vision cleared, the leopard was collapsed on top of him, unmoving. The pungent, gamey smell of the beast filled his nostrils. He tried to shove the animal off him, but it was a halfhearted effort. He knew he wasn't going anywhere. His eyes fluttered, then closed.

It was time.

Fitzgerald's life did not pass before his eyes. History did. The history of warfare. What he'd dedicated the good part of the last decade to understanding. Wars and more wars and more wars, death and blood and suffering, the human condition. Something by Plato drifted through his dying thoughts: *Only the dead have seen the end of war.*

Darkness did not rise to greet him, only white light—white light that grew brighter and brighter, and in that brightness he saw the faces of Eryn and Biddy.

Damien Fitzgerald greeted death with a smile.

# CHAPTER 41

AFTER THE IRISHMAN took off into the jungle, Scarlett and Thunder had remained where they were, listening to the sounds of the subsequent fight. They hadn't heard the Irishman make any noise. Not a single scream or cry or curse. In contrast, the leopard had hissed and growled and roared until the forest went suddenly quiet. Either the Irishman had killed the leopard, or the leopard had killed the Irishman. Either way, it was high time to get the hell out of there.

Thunder seemed to read Scarlett's mind. Without a word, he took her hand in his and plowed south through the thicket. Light was fading fast, turning everything muted shades of gray. A seemingly endless prison of trees flashed past them. Branches slapped their heads and shoulders and arms. Scarlett didn't think she could keep going, but she did, somehow she kept running, until finally the trees thinned and the river appeared, winding and black and glorious. She stumbled the last few yards to the bank and collapsed to her knees in a patch of soft grass. Her throat stung from exertion and her legs felt like they were made from overcooked spaghetti. She was so weak and nauseous she thought she might pass out.

Thunder knelt beside her. "Hate to be a downer," he said, panting hard, "but we're not out of this yet. We still have to find the riverboat. And the sooner, the better."

She knew he was right. There would be time to rest later. She nodded.

"This is the plan," he went on. "We head upriver along the bank for an hour or so. Try to cover a couple of kilometers. If we don't find the boat, then we work out somewhere to sleep and backtrack the way we came in the morning. When we see that"—he pointed to a sixty-foot, single-stemmed marula with a spreading crown—"we know we're back where we started. We continue for another couple kilometers downriver. In total that gives us almost four Ks along the bank."

"And if we still don't find the boat?"

"We work out a new plan."

He held out his hand for her. She took it, pulling herself to her feet. Her legs were still mush, but she could stand on her own. The sun had dipped below the horizon, and it was now near dark. If they had still been in the jungle, they wouldn't have been able to see a thing. But since there was no canopy of branches spanning the river, the sky was visible, the moon and stars bright enough for them to navigate the river's vegetation.

They'd only been walking for a few minutes when Thunder stopped abruptly. She glanced up from the marshy ground, and what she saw turned her insides to gold. Because there it was, cast in the ethereal light of the moon and just visible through the overhanging branches of a mangrove tree.

*The riverboat.*

Scarlett turned to Thunder for confirmation she wasn't imagining it. He grinned broadly at her. She threw her arms around him and mumbled something, nonsense, into his shoulder.

THUNDER STEPPED APART. "I'm going to check it out. Make sure it's clear. I'll be back in a flash."

She frowned. "Clear?"

"I know the Irish bloke said he took out the other two terrorists, but he's not exactly the most reliable source, is he?"

Scarlett felt a fresh jab of fear. "I'm coming with you," she said immediately, and before he could reply, she added: "Think about it, Thunder. If anybody's there, and they kill you, then I'm dead anyway. What am I going to do out here by myself?"

He thought that over, then nodded reluctantly.

"Stay close," he told her. "And keep your eyes peeled."

They started forward side by side and came to the same muddy bank they'd climbed only the morning before. They slid down it, waded through the murky, smelly water, and pulled themselves up onto the stern deck. Thunder pointed to the main cabin. Scarlett nodded. They went to the window, looked inside. Empty. Thunder pointed to the top deck. Another nod.

They climbed the spiral staircase and poked their heads through the well-hole. The deck and pilothouse were deserted. Thunder held up his hand, palm forward, indicating he wanted her to wait where she was. He hurried over to the aft cabin and peered inside. He turned back to her and made the thumbs-up sign.

"Home free," he said, grinning.

SCARLETT SNAPPED OPEN her eyes. "Did you hear that?" she whispered.

She was lying in the hammock in the aft cabin. Thunder was on the floor next to her, using an old blanket he'd found as a pillow. Earlier, they'd known they couldn't navigate the river in the dark—it would be disastrous if they got beached on a sandbar or hit rocks—so they'd decided instead to get some rest and start out at first light.

Thunder, who must have been sleeping just as lightly as she, said, "Hear what?" His voice was quiet but alert.

"A splash."

They listened in silence. The only noise was the patter of rain and the continuous drone of insects.

"Maybe it was a frog?" he said.

"It sounded bigger."

"A croc?"

"Maybe."

"What else could it be?"

"We don't know for certain that Danny was killed. Or the Irishman, for that matter."

Thunder shook his head. "They're dead."

"How can you be so sure?"

"You heard Danny."

"Fine, yes," she agreed. "But what about the Irishman? We didn't hear him make a sound. Maybe he got away?"

"You saw him while we were walking through the jungle. He was on his last legs. I don't know how he even made it as far as he did. That's why he went off after the leopard, I reckon. He knew he was a goner. He wanted to die on his terms—"

Scarlett heard another splash.

"There!" she said, still whispering. "Did you hear that?"

This time Thunder nodded. He got silently to his feet and looked around the cabin. He picked up the sack of fruit from which they'd eaten earlier.

"What are you doing with that?" she said.

"I need a weapon."

"Fruit?"

"See anything else?"

The door was open a crack. He pushed it open farther. A gust of cool, swampy air swept inside. Thunder went out first, Scarlett on his heels. The rain had picked up again sometime during the night, and it drenched them within seconds. They went to the portside railing, which faced the north bank of the river, and scanned the water below. It was midnight black and pock-marked by the falling raindrops, but otherwise undisturbed.

"I don't see anything," Thunder said.

Scarlett went to the starboard railing and peered over. Nothing. She returned to Thunder. "Maybe it was just a frog or crocodile after all." She shook her head. "I'm sorry. Guess I overreacted. It's just that after everything—"

"No worries. I understand. Let's just get back inside. We stay out here any longer, we're going to catch pneumonia."

Scarlett nodded. At the cabin door, however, she glanced

back over her shoulder one last time—and her heart seemed to stop in her chest.

Sticking up through the well-hole in the deck was the silhouetted shape of a head. In a silent flash of lightning she saw the face clearly.

Scarred, disfigured, horrible, it was the face of a monster.

It was Jahja.

# CHAPTER 42

"DON'T MOVE," JAHJA said, coming up the rest of the stairs. He held an AK-47 in his hands, pointed at them.

"You're dead," Scarlett said, not believing what she was seeing.

Another flash of lightning went off, and she saw that he did indeed look as if he were dead. His face was deathly white, his lips and chest and stomach covered with blood.

*How could he be here? How? It's impossible!*

Her fear and confusion quickly gave way to anger. They should have checked to be sure he was dead, should have put a final bullet in him, like a stake through the heart of a vampire.

"Sal," she went on. "Sal said he shot you. I saw you lying there."

Jahja's deformed lips curled into a weak smile. "I guess you underestimate my will to live, Miss Cox. As I told you before, I have a beautiful wife and daughter I am very much looking forward to seeing again. Perhaps love is stronger than death? Hmmm?" He coughed, spitting up blood. He wiped his mouth with the back of his hand. "Or does a radical or extremist or whatever you choose to label me not feel love? I believe that is what you Americans would like to believe. What was it your greatest of writers said? 'If you prick us, do we not bleed? If you tickle us, do we not laugh?'" He paused meaningfully. "'And if you wrong us, shall we not revenge?'"

"And if we shoot you," Thunder said, "you're supposed to bloody well die."

Jahja leveled the gun at him. "Cute, Mr. Young. However, the time for talk is over. Set the sack in your hand down and open the door to the cabin. Wide."

Thunder looked at Scarlett. She didn't know what to tell him.

"She cannot help you, Mr. Young," Jahja said. "Do as I say. I do not have much patience right now."

Thunder dropped the fruit and pulled the door open.

"Very good. Now untie that rope supporting the hammock. Don't get any ideas. If I see you make any move for a weapon, I will shoot you both."

Thunder entered the cabin and untied the knot attached to the canvas hammock. The end closest to him dropped to the floor. He undid the anchor point secured to the rafters, then came back outside, carrying the six-foot-long piece of braided rope.

"Thank you," Jahja said. "Now throw it to me."

Thunder did what was asked of him. Jahja caught the rope with his free hand. He lowered the rifle, took a knife from his belt, and began to cut the rope into thirds. Scarlett saw the window of opportunity and thought about rushing him. But she was one hundred twenty pounds, maybe one twenty-three with her clothes on and wet as they were, and she couldn't see herself doing much damage. Not to mention he was still a good fifteen feet away—more than enough time for him to raise the rifle and blow her guts out across the deck. He finished up and lobbed one section to her.

"Now would you be so kind as to tie Mr. Young's wrists behind his back?" Jahja told her. "Tightly. I will be checking your handiwork."

Scarlett's mind raced for another option, but there weren't many when you had a gun trained on you. She reluctantly tied Thunder's wrists behind his back.

Jahja came over, gave the knot she'd made a solid tug, and smiled. "Very good, Miss Cox. Now turn around yourself."

She did as she was told and felt the rope loop around her wrists three times before biting painfully into her skin. "Why are you doing this?" she said. "Everybody is dead. It's over."

"It's far from over, Miss Cox. Do you think Al Qaeda's plans or resolve have changed just because we have lost a few men? We have thousands more lining up to die as true mujahedin on Allah's path."

"What are you going to do with us?"

"I think you know the answer to that…" He trailed off, breaking into his worst fit of coughing yet. He wiped his bloody lips with the back of his hand, wiped his hand on his tunic. He marched them down the stairs to the main deck, where he opened the door to the cabin and ordered them inside.

"Listen, mate," Thunder said. "Take the boat, but let us go. That helicopter that crashed into the church was our ride. When it doesn't report back tonight, more reinforcements are going to be sent out. They'll be here tomorrow. They'll find us."

Jahja shook his head. "You underestimate the size of the Congo, Mr. Young. There are literally hundreds of tributaries off this river alone. If we go farther downriver, we'll reach the Lualaba, the greatest headstream of the Congo River, which itself is the second longest river in Africa, after the Nile." He smiled humorlessly. "So you see, there are plenty of places to go. No one is going to find us. I can assure you of that."

He closed the door and locked it.

"Bloody hell," Thunder said. "We're right back where we started."

Scarlett went to the stern window. She didn't see Jahja, which meant he'd gone back to the top deck. "I'm not going through this again. No way. Not in a thousand years. I can't. I simply can't. We have to escape. Right now."

"I'm with you there, one hundred percent, but how?"

She wriggled her wrists. No give whatsoever. She shook her head, frustrated.

Thunder said, "We can always break the window, jump ship, and hope to swim away."

"And be sitting ducks. He would pick us off in the water." Her brow creased in thought. "Unless..."

"Unless what?"

She sketched out a plan for him. When she finished, he was frowning.

"It's dangerous," he said.

"What hasn't been dangerous so far?"

"It could go wrong."

"It could work."

Thunder studied her for a long moment, his blue eyes bright and intense. "All right," he said. "Let's do it."

THEY WENT TO the window.

"On the count of three," Thunder said.

"Okay."

"One," he said.

"Two," Scarlett said.

"Three," they said together.

They kicked the large square pane of glass in unison. Their feet smashed through it, leaving twin basketball-sized jagged holes. They watched as physics took over and the weight of the glass collapsed down upon itself, spilling out of the wooden frame, splintering on the teak deck into thousands of slivers.

"Go!" Thunder said. He gave Scarlett a half nudge, half lift with his shoulder, helping her up and over the low window ledge. Then she was running to the portside railing, straddling it, leaping to the river below. She hit the water with a splash and was immediately enveloped in darkness. For a moment she had no idea which way was which. Panic swelled inside her. She swung her head from side to side, her hair trailing in front of her eyes. A foot brushed the bottom, and she knew up from down. She looked up and saw what she thought was the dark hull of the riverboat. She kicked toward it.

The riverboat had a shallow draft, only a couple feet deep, which made it easy for her to swim beneath. The width, however, was much wider than she would have thought possible. She barely made it to the keel before her lungs were aching and her head pounding from oxygen deprivation.

She kept kicking until the darkness finally lightened and she knew she had cleared the hull. She fought the natural instinct to crash through the surface. That would likely earn her a bullet in the head. Instead she poked her head above the water as quietly as possible, sucking back a huge gulp of air, which for her overworked lungs was like sucking back gasoline fumes. She made a sound like a rusty door opening, but she didn't think it was loud enough for Jahja to hear. Her eyes watered and she thought she was going to sputter and cough. Nevertheless, she bit back the gagging impulse and got her breathing under control.

She started swimming away from the riverboat.

THUNDER REMAINED BY the window until he heard Scarlett jump over the portside railing, then he flattened himself into the crook next to the door. Seconds later Jahja stomped down the staircase, pausing when he reached the stern deck. Thunder imagined he was studying the broken glass. Then the lock clicked, the door swung inward. If Jahja had shoved it open all the way, it would have bounced against Thunder's chest, giving away his presence. Luckily, he only opened it enough to stick his head inside and give the room a quick perusal before hurrying over to the portside railing.

Thunder left the hiding spot and peered out the door. Jahja was bent over the railing, looking down at the river, the AK in one hand, a kerosene lantern held high in the other. The clear yellow flame was constant and bright, bathing him in a circle of light.

Thunder started across the deck, taking large steps to gain momentum, while trying to remain silent at the same time.

Glass crunched underfoot.

Jahja turned, his eyes widening in surprise.

Roaring, Thunder lowered his shoulder and barreled into the bastard, sending them both sprawling to the deck. The lantern smashed the floorboards a few meters away, the glass globe exploding on impact. Kerosene spilled and caught fire. Two-foot-tall flames whooshed into existence.

Jahja, however, managed to hold onto the AK. Before he could swing it around, Thunder kicked him in the neck. This time Jahja released the rifle. It clattered across the deck, slipped beneath the iron railing, and splashed into the water below.

Shouting something in Arabic, Jahja leapt at Thunder. Thunder planted his feet firmly in Jahja's chest, catching him in midair, and using the terrorist's own momentum to toss him over his head. He landed with a thump and an unearthly howl. Thunder twisted around and saw Jahja flopping from side to side in the pool of flames, which were now nearly a meter high and spreading quickly. Jahja sprang to his feet, a human torch. Screaming, he ran blindly around in circles until he collided with the starboard railing, cart-wheeled over, and plunged into the river seconds later. The night smelled like burnt flesh and hair and clothes.

"Thunder!" It was Scarlett, faint, somewhere far away. "Get off the boat! It's going to blow!"

Thunder looked left, to the fire. The flames were licking the twin diesel engines. He scrambled to the railing, scissor-hopped over it, and was just about to jump when there was a deafening explosion. The pressure wave from the hot, expanding gas caught him from behind and launched him like a rag doll through the night.

"THUNDER!" SCARLETT CRIED, swimming back toward the riverboat, kicking with her feet. She stopped a few yards away from the now burning wreckage and tread water, her eyes darting from each piece of fiery floating debris. She didn't see him anywhere.

A hand grabbed her shoulder from behind.

"Thunder?"

Even as Scarlett turned, she knew the hand couldn't belong to Thunder because his were bound behind his back, as were hers. Instead she found herself staring in horror at Jahja—or at what had once been Jahja—because what stared back at her was no man but something from a nightmarish world, a Halloween mask come to life.

Every inch of his face was bright red and purple and mushy, except for his nose and lips, which were black and charred. The skin along his left brow had clumped and now drooped in front of his eye, almost completely covering it, while that around his right eye had melted away, leaving the eyeball unnaturally wide and round. His mouth was open in a soundless scream.

Scarlett tried desperately to shake the hand off her shoulder, but it held her firm. His other hand grabbed her around the throat and squeezed. She brought her legs up to try to kick away from him. But to do that, she had to stop treading water, and her head immediately sank beneath the surface. In her panic she swallowed mouthfuls of water. She coughed, swallowing more water.

She was going to drown.

Then she remembered what the Irishman had done to Thunder. She stopped kicking and shot her legs straight up, out of the water, locking them around Jahja's neck. She corkscrewed her body, the maneuver working like a teeter-totter, dunking Jahja beneath the water while buoying her up. Her head broke through the surface again.

Jahja's hands clawed at her legs. She squeezed her thighs and ankles tighter. The clawing became less persistent. Five long seconds later it stopped altogether. She held firm for another five seconds, just to be sure. Finally she released Jahja's neck and, with the last of her strength, kicked to shore. When she felt mud beneath her knees, she stopped kicking and began waddling. She got halfway up the bank before she could go no farther.

She collapsed beneath the great black African sky.

# CHAPTER 43

I T WAS MIDMORNING when Scarlett noticed Thunder stir.

"Wakey, wakey," she said.

His eyes fluttered open and he squinted against the bright, golden sunlight.

"Lettie?" He blinked several times. "What…? Where…?"

"Take it easy," she said. "You had a rough night."

He sat up, groaning. He rubbed his head, stopped, and looked in amazement at his hands.

"I sawed through my rope on a rock during the night," she explained. "Then I untied yours."

He arched an eyebrow at the small fire in the crudely erected fire pit a few feet away. "You've been busy," he said.

"I borrowed a few flames from the burning boat."

He looked toward the river. "Christ!"

"Yeah."

The scattered flotsam from the explosion the night before had burned out quickly, but the actual riverboat, or what remained of it, had continued to burn throughout the early hours of the morning. Just as the sun was rising, it began to sink until only the tapered bow remained visible, protruding at an angle five feet from the water.

"I remember a flash of light, heat…" He shook his head. "That's it. What happened?"

"First things first," she told him. "Jahja's dead."

"I saw him catch fire. He jumped into the water. Maybe—"

"He's dead." Scarlett explained everything that had happened. "I managed to get to shore okay," she finished. "After I caught my breath, I went back in the water to look for you. But I didn't find you—at least, not until I was back on shore again, looking for a rock to free my hands."

"Where was I?"

"Right here."

Thunder looked at the riverboat, twenty yards away, then back at her. "Are you having a go?"

She shook her head.

"Blimey."

"Do you think you can stand? I want to show you something."

He tried pushing himself off the ground, but collapsed back to his rear. She helped him the second time, then led him along the bank. With each step he grew more surefooted until he was walking on his own. A little farther on she stopped and pointed. Instead of looking where he was looking, following her finger, she watched his face. His eyes widened and he broke into a grin that lit up his entire face. Then she, too, turned toward the small skiff tied up against a tree stump. She smiled the first real smile in days.

"There's even an extra tank of fuel between the seats," she said.

"The Irishman's?"

"Has to be."

Thunder didn't say anything more, and Scarlett realized he was choked up with emotion. She took his hand and they continued the rest of the way to the boat. They untied the painter line and pushed away from shore. She tugged the starter cord. The 25hp Johnson motor fired up on the first go. It was one of the most beautiful sounds she had ever heard.

She opened the throttle and pointed the skiff upriver.

They were going home.

# AFTERWORD

Thank you for taking the time to read the book! If you enjoyed it, a brief review would be hugely appreciated. You can click straight to the review page here:

The Taste of Fear - Amazon Review Page

Best,
Jeremy

# ABOUT THE AUTHOR

## Jeremy Bates

 USA TODAY and #1 AMAZON bestselling author Jeremy Bates has published more than twenty novels and novellas, which have been translated into several languages, optioned for film and TV, and downloaded more than one million times. Midwest Book Review compares his work to "Stephen King, Joe Lansdale, and other masters of the art." He has won both an Australian Shadows Award and a Canadian Arthur Ellis Award. He was also a finalist in the Goodreads Choice Awards, the only major book awards decided by readers. The novels in the "World's Scariest Places" series are set in real locations and include Suicide Forest in Japan, The Catacombs in Paris, Helltown in Ohio, Island of the Dolls in Mexico, and Mountain of the Dead in Russia. The novels in the "World's Scariest Legends" series are based on real legends and include Mosquito Man and The Sleep Experiment. You can check out any of these places or legends on the web. Also, visit JEREMYBATES-BOOKS.COM to receive Black Canyon, WINNER of The Lou Allin Memorial Award.